MERCENARY

" Do whatever for the paper it ain't on my conscious "

ICE MONEY

i

Mercenary

Printed in the United States of America

ISBN: 978-0-9992646-3-8

Cover design by: Steven J Catizone

Table of Contents

ABOUT THE AUTHOR

Ice Money is a native of Milwaukee, Wisconsin. He is a proud father of one, an entrepreneur, the Vice President of So Geeked Records, a man with a business mind, he's charismatic, versatile, a good basketball player, and he loves music and his family.

Growing up in poverty and a city of high crime, he would eventually find himself heading down that road. Trouble with the law sent his life spiraling out of control, but through incarceration, which he considers both a curse and a blessing, he has found another talent that he didn't even know he had: writing books.

He regrets none of his life experiences because they have made him who he is today. Instead, he uses his experiences as fuel to succeed and always strives to reach his full potential.

Ice Money is a writer of urban fiction and erotica at this point. However, his books are in no way meant to encourage people to adopt a criminal's path in life. They are lessons and entertainment, simply the reality of what takes place in many inner-city ghettos and hoods around America. Therefore, enjoy his work as he expresses his imagination on a level that will keep you turning pages and wanting more.

Ice Money is currently incarcerated, but like most things, that will soon come to an end. Until then, he will continue to put out real urban street literature for your entertainment.

Also, be on the lookout for some of So Geeked Records hottest artists: Party Boi, Amazin, Young Major, Cheddar Boy, King Los, and many more.

ACKNOWLEDGEMENTS

First and foremost, I would like to give praise and thanks to Allah the most gracious most merciful for giving me the creative ability to articulate these words. I pray that he continues to bless and guide me to keep me humble and mindful of my many blessings through my successes as well as my failures.

Next, I would like to give the biggest shout out to the following people. My mom and G-Mama (what can I say? You two are my biggest inspirations and I love you both), my little prince Tony (I do it for you son, and I love you boy!), grandma Ms. Day, granddad Jesse, uncle Willie, my sisters Enjanae, Yolanda, Erica, Netta and Dana. My brothers Telus (this is only the beginning bro), Nic'Querion (hold ya head), Denzel, Segal, Perry, and Deandre. Shout out to auntie Tracy (thanks for being you), auntie Luana, Rose, my nephew Kylan, my sister-in-law to be Raynea (LBVS), Dion (I appreciate you), Karen, Tiffany, Sheena, Darryl, Reece, D. P., J. P., Keyzia, Inez, Cnelle, my cousins Dusty, Devon, Landis, E, Meeko, Tyler, Terrell, Trinell, Dionca, Deja, Boo, Briana,

Malachi, Dez, Khadijah, Damion (it's going down when I touch in the 'A'), Jeris (boy I can't believe you), Sheena, Chris, aunty San, Shanay, Ciera, Ke, Patty, Kendrick, Jarvis, Justin, Missy, Michael, Erin, Mel, Chevy, Mike, Mandy, Marreon, Vanessa, Keefe, Vonny, cousin Bubba (I haven't forgot about you). Lexy, Karen, Tiffany and Sheena (what it do?), Fee, James, Dre, Alex, Mary, Amir, Misty, my cousin Bubba (I haven't forgot about you), Nakia, Alana, Vashawn, Man, Shorty, Quan, Chas (what it do?), Bretta, Nina, Cherry, B. M. B (what's good my dude?), Lisa, Marc, Millie, Angie, ReRe, Shay, Trina, Shea (what's good?), Fookie (I learned a lot from you; I'll never forget you), Umar (I won't ever forget about you AKH), Nafi (animal on the beats!). Also, shout out Jessica (you already know what it is!), Brittany, Suge, Moss, Tray 6 Wayne, Red, Myesha, Teresa, Precious, Peaches, J. Ferg, Eastside Quinn (time to turn up my dude!), Goldy Mack, Malik, Wakil and Corde (what it do?), Jirnmy P., Maleek, Jaido (hold ya head), Smooth, Chris Gezzy, Sidney, Lance, Snake, Marcus, Head, Omar, Marcus, Mike, Angel, Tricia, Jasmine, Sharice, Fat Daddy, Mike K (what it do pimpin?), Terrell (ice them knees for the season, LoL), Black,

Maniac, Cain, Juan, Blanco, Remy, Big Solid, Jack, Lil Solid (hold ya head), lil Shugg, My Mad Town guys Big Ryan (I see you fool), Quell, Tray Boi, Goon, Ouece, E-Reala, Ace, J. R. Schad, Short Snake, Snake Davis, Face, Tray Mack, Zack (with the dreads), and Black. My Racine guys: Old School Mack, Maceo, D. C., Big J, Tone Low, and Palong. Ray, Nuke, Buck, 7grams, B. E. (hold ya head), J. Mitch, Ibrahim (what's good with you my dude?), Muhammad, Halim, Tez off the East, Keem, Bump, Gee, Lil Tez, D. Mack, Mitch, J. R. Buck (what's good fool?), T. D (hold ya head up fool), Murda, Anwar, Eshawn, Smurf, PeeWee, Southside, Big Slim, LJ off HPT, Rocco Shay off the East (it's almost over my dude), Rachod, Talib, Luqman, El-Amin, Big Mix Money,Vell, Los, Baby G, J. Frost, Scotty, D. L o, Spook, Fat Dog, Tony Cash, Dave, Kirb, Dizzy, P, June, Von, K 'halif, Lil Ro, Ricco, Hard Head Rell, Mac, Pistol, Big Feezy, Dave, Drew, Corn, Dre, Mack, Lil Kenny, Tanya, Ms. Lovey Tracy, Von F., Nell, Meech, Keefe, Sandra, Boo, Terrell, Dennis, Mumeen, June, Blue, S. Dot, Tree, One Pac, Fab, Mustafa, Dip, Los, Aldrick, Daylight, Javi (off the east, Hold yo head up my dude), Hot Boy, Woo, June, Ike, Kenny D,

Moe, B.A. (Ant), JuJu, Scrap, Burt, Dan, Jose, Screw, Juice, Breed, Ceichai, Chub, Earl H (off the east), Suave, Troub, Armstead (Dirty), White Cloud, Face, Joel from Green Bay, Hitman, K.V., Gus, HB, my cousin Steve, and M.D. (my sports agent), Red, Rome, M. J., A.Z., Tanio, Pooh, Smack, Whistle, Melvin James and camera man Chris (I like what you're doing for the city, I see your vision, and I support that!). Shout out all my Milwaukee up and coming artists, we got talent in the city and if we come together we can be the next Atlanta, the only thing stopping us is you, let's get it! Shout out to the DJ's at 89. 9, Boss Lady, Big Juice, Sed The Jerk, Taz Raw, T. Low (I wrote a lot of my books while staying up listening to y'all all night on the weekends, so thanks for that). Last but certainly not least, Bagz of Money Content and Ace Boogie for the opportunity to put my work on display it' s greatly appreciated bro. Since day one, you've been one hunnid and I won't ever forget that.

To my loved ones who are no longer with us. Emannuel, Ethel Thompson, Albertine Gilmore, Grandfather J. T., Pops, Jesse, aunt Judy, uncle Sammy, uncle Willie, Robbie, Mary B. K.A Lilly, Boosie (TM), uncle Billy,

Quincy, Jimmy, Rell, uncle A. J., Donny, Mr. and Mrs. Patterson, uncle Winford, uncle Johnlee, Mr. May, Ms. Flow and lastly Butter. I love and miss you all.

To anyone I may have forgotten who I truly deal with, charge it to the mind and not the heart. Love!

Prologue

Legacy Duncan sat in the third row of the Milwaukee County courtroom dressed in a pair of black Chanel jeans, matching tight-fitting t-shirt, and a pair of black Chanel sunglasses over her teary eyes.

She lifted her head from her saddened state just as the door opened and in walked the love of her life wearing an orange jumpsuit shackled at the hands and feet while being escorted by two sheriffs' deputies. They briefly made eye contact and he instantly noticed the pain as she removed her glasses. He winked at her and she responded with a smile before he took his seat next to his lawyer and they began exchanging words.

The court rung with "all rise!" as the judge entered the courtroom from his chambers and took his seat at the bench.

Legacy sighed optimistically that the hardest thing she's ever had to deal with would soon come to an end.

"The state V.S Orlando Paul, case number 257-2011". The judge said going through the paperwork. "We are here for a motion to dismiss for lack of evidence on two charges. Accessory to commit murder and felon in possession of a firearm," the judge continued.

"Mr. Montana," the judge added

"Daniel W. Montana appearing on behalf of the state," District Attorney Montana said.

"Mr. Hastings," said the judge said

"Good morning your honor, Orlando Paul appears in person by Raymond Hastings," boss's attorney stated. Legacy seemed to drift off into another world while replaying the night the DA. was vividly describing. "On December 12th, 2011, the defendant met up with a few accomplices. They rode around talking while the defendant made drug transactions with various people. One of his accomplices stated they knew where Mr. Martin Combs' residence was and where he moved his drugs. The defendant called a buddy of his and they all met up at a discreet location and improvised a plan which was to rob

Mr. Combs' two drug houses which apparently had a few safes, drugs and weapons.

Mr. Combs was targeted because of the alleged rape of the defendant's cousin, a MS. Sharee Paul. However, no charges were ever filed on that claim your honor. Anyway, they proceeded with the plan, the victim in this case put up a fight and tried to flee. One of the defendant's accomplices chased him down, a scuffle began, and the victim reached for a crowbar and struck the guy with it, knocking him out cold. The other accomplice showed up and shot the victim three times; once in the shoulder and twice in the chest.

Waking up the victim, the second accomplice picked up the crowbar and beat the victim lifeless. He woke up his partner, they got what they came for and vacated the premises. They were later apprehended with a couple stolen guns that were in the victim's name.

During interrogation, both accomplices expressed that the defendant Mr. Paul, A.K.A Boss, was the alleged ring leader because of what Mr. Combs allegedly did to his cousin and I quote your honor they both stated that Mr.

Paul said. "That nigger is gonna pay for that shit, nobody fucks over my family and gets away with it,"

"Objection your honor! I demand that last statement be struck from the record, we have no way of knowing that my client made that remark, it is simply hearsay. This is just a further attempt by the DA. to slander my client with frivolous and ill-advised remarks," Mr. Hastings said after standing up and hitting his fist on the table. Mr. Hastings was privately attained by Boss for $40,000. He was among the top two lawyers in the state and very good at his craft.

"I'll grant that, please remove the last statement Mr. Montana said from the record," the judge told the clerk.

"Your honor this man is a criminal, I haven't even brought up the felon in possession of a firearm or the two previous drugs charges that he…" D. A Montana said but was cut off.

"Mr. Montana, can we please get back to why we are really here," the judge said irritated.

"Your honor, can I have a recess?" Mr. Montana asked, he was furious on the inside.

"I'll grant that, court resumes in ten minutes," the judge said before banging his gavel and getting up to leave.

Legacy went to the restroom and looked at her puffy eyes in the mirror from all the crying just as Chante busted in the bathroom door and put her arm around her.

"I know how you feel, it's tough to have a man behind bars," Chante said with sympathy. Legacy looked her in the eyes and stared blankly before saying "my man aint behind bars."

Chante chuckled before she began "it's cute that you still have faith, Boss is like family and I love him, but the reality of the situation is he might be going away for a while," she explained.

Legacy threw her hands up in an attempt to cut her off, but Chante grabbed her wrists and told her "I been there before, you gotta be strong or how can you hold him down? You already know what type of nigga he is."

Legacy sighed because she knew Chante was telling her the truth. As Chante left the bathroom, Legacy got herself together and returned slowly to her seat in the courtroom as if she was afraid of what was about to be said.

The prosecutor continued "we wanted to question Mr. Paul, but the record shows that he was out of town, apparently on a trip for his anniversary, so we had detectives sitting outside of his residence for two days. Upon his arrival, he and a young lady were taken into custody. The young lady was released, but Mr. Paul was questioned and said that he doesn't know a Mr. Henton or a Mr. Lemon, but ironically, we have several texts and voicemails between all three parties. However, Mr. Paul denies any wrong doing or any knowledge of this case, he's been very uncooperative during questioning. He is hiding something your honor and he should be prosecuted to the fullest extent of the law," the D. A. stated firmly.

Mr. Hastings countered and even tried to get Boss out on bail, but he was unsuccessful in his attempts.

"The defendant will be held over for trial, starting July 25th, 2012, bail is denied at this time due to the defendant being a flight risk," the judge stated before he slammed the gavel down and got up to leave.

Chante looked over to Legacy and was surprised to see her chuck up the tears, blow Boss a kiss, put

her shades back on and leave the courtroom.

At that moment, Legacy realized she had to finish what Boss started. She was a 'Mercenary' - a soldier of fortune - and she had to be as strong as ever and support him. She was positive that she could do that and hold the fort down in his absence.

CHAPTER ONE

The next day, Legacy woke up to the sun peeking through her blinds. She rolled over to the vacant spot in her bed where Boss usually slept and whispered, "until you get here baby, I'mma hold it down." Pulling the covers back, she revealed her naked body. After two bottles of Berry Cîroc, she was a little bothered that her baby wasn't there to take care of her needs last night, so she handled her business herself. Putting her foot on the floor, she stepped on 'Henry', her dildo. As she got out of bed, she bent down to pick it up. On her way up, she stopped on a picture of her and Boss at the hotel lobby in Montego Bay which made her smile. Grabbing her phone, she put the toy away and noticed she had 21 missed calls and 17 voicemails. 'Damn, I was out of it' she thought while scrolling through her call log. It was calls from Train, the workers, her sister Chante, and a few other people.

1

Pressing the voicemail button on her phone, she put it to her ear while she ran the bath water. Walking past the

full-length mirror, she admired her 5'6, 14Olb, 36DD-28-41 frame, flaws and all. She was a 'Bad Bitch'. After listening to her messages, she sent a few texts and immersed herself in the hot bath water while contemplating her next move.

Twenty minutes after soaking her body, Legacy got out of the tub, dried off, went to her bedroom to oil her body down before putting on a lace Dolce&Gabbana panties and bra set. Grabbing her phone, she called Train to see where they should meet up. After deciding on a place, she hung up, and went into her walk-in closet. Putting on a pair of indigo blue-back pocket less stretch denim Capri pants, which hugged her ass snugly, she threw on her navy blue 'STOP SNITCHIN' T-shirt, and her suede navy blue and baby blue Air Max 95's.

Going in the home office, she swung the picture of her and Boss from one side to the other and put her finger on the Biometric finger scanning safe that only recognized her and Boss's right index fingers. Opening the safe, she grabbed a couple hundred dollars, her .380 and she put Boss's gold Cuban link chain on her neck with the letter 'B' charm in crushed VVS diamonds. Picking up the phone, she made the call.

"Hello," Chante answered.

"I'm on my way to get chu, I need to holla at chu for a minute," Legacy stated while closing the safe.

"I'll see you when you get here," Chante responded, she knew her sister was going through a lot and she was going to be the big sister she needed her to be.

Legacy grabbed her keys and decided to drive Boss's car. Going into the garage, she hit the button to let the big door up and deactivated the car alarm. She pulled the cover from the car, raised the lambo door, and got behind the wheel of the 1987 Chevy Monte Carlo SS. The car was candy painted navy blue with the gold flakes. The Pirelli tires held the 28" gold Asanti rims in place. The navy-blue Ostrich leather seats, fiber glass dash and door panels put this car in a league of its own. Boss had well over a 100K invested in the car.

Legacy put the key in the ignition and the 383 stroker dual exhaust engine came roaring to life. The digital dash and touch screen gave off an incredible glow along with the 6-TV's. Finding some music, she put on "Focused" by Kaylee Crossfire and backed out of the garage. Hitting the garage opener, the door lowered, and she pulled off, heading to pick up Chante.

∞

Turning the music down, Legacy made a right turn on 37th and Townsend and spotted Chante on the porch engaged in a conversation with some dude. Upon seeing her sister, Chante abruptly ended the conversation, walked towards the car, raised the door up, and got in.

"Who is that nigga?" Legacy asked curiously about the dude who didn't seem to be her sister's type.

"Jay, he getting a little money around here and thinks that's enough to fuck every little bitch around here, so he been sweating me tough but I ain,t goin at gunpoint. I guess he don't know it's levels to this shit," Chante launched. "Besides, he fucked Meka and I ain't wit a nigga running through the clique shit, and she told me he couldn't perform anyway," she added, being her usual blunt self.

"Perform?" What, he a minute man?" Legacy asked while laughing hysterically.

"Naw, she said his dick like this," Chante said holding up her pinky finger.

"Oh, he one of them," Legacy continued to laugh

"This stupid bitch said his balls had to come out in a single file line because his other shit was so small, she said that she couldn't see it no other way." Chante joined in with the laughter.

"She crazy as hell," Legacy stated.

"Aint she, but what chu gotta holla at me about?" Chante asked while inhaling the potent weed smoke from her blunt.

"I gotta go meet Train because it's almost time for me to go see the connect and he wanna go wit me, but I really don't want him in my business like that. That's my man's friend which don't necessarily mean he'll be a good one to me. I can say that because I know when I be serving these niggas, I can feel the resentment and I know it's because they buying bricks from a female and they know Boss locked up facing all that time, it won't be long before one of these fool azz niggas try me and make me have to kill they azz," Legacy said picking up the pistol that rested in between her legs.

"Leggy I feel you, niggas see you out here iced up, rollin 28s and they get on some Brandy shit, they just wanna be down and if not, they wanna take your shine and I'm not gonna let that happen to you so my question to you is, how do you want me to help you?" Chante asked while dumping her ashes over the tinted windows. Legacy looked at her sister and knew this was the person she wanted and needed on her team, so she spoke up. "I want you to be my right-hand woman and we gon' get this money and say fuck you to whoever got something to say about it." Legacy was very optimistic that Chante was ready.

"Bitch that's all you had to say in the first place, let me run in the house real fast and then we can rollout," Chante said while getting out of the car.

'I knew she wouldn't let me down, now I gotta see what this nigga Train talkin about,' she thought.

Thirty minutes later, Legacy and Chante pulled up into the Denny's parking lot on Brown Deer Road pumping "Right Now" by Kaylee Cross Fire and Kia Rap Princess. Finding a parking space, they exited the car, but not before Legacy armed herself. Boss told her never to leave home without her unit because you can never say what's in store for you. Going into the restaurant, they spotted Train waving them over from a corner booth.

"What's good wit it?" Train asked as they slid into the booth.

"Shit chillin," Legacy said noticing that his eyes were going back and forth from her to Chante, before realizing she had not told him that she was bringing somebody with her.

"Oh, this my right hand, so whatever you gotta say to me, you can say in front of her, aight?" she added as Chante flashed a fake smile. Train took everything in for a minute, then got right down to business.

"Aight shawty have it yo way. I got a duffle bag in the trunk wit two-hundred and thirty bands for ten of those thangs when you go meet dude. How many you are buying?" he asked in a whisper from across the table just as the waitress came to the table. Legacy grew even more suspicious of him after that question because he had never asked that before and besides, did he need to know how many she was buying? She made a mental note to watch him even closer.

"Hi, I'm Crissy and I'll be your waitress today, may I take your or. . . " the waitress was about to ask before being cut off.

"Ay, can you give us a second we tryna holla right now, damn," Train blurted out rudely.

"Okay," the waitress said before hurrying away pissed.

"Now, where were we?" Train asked

"That's what I wanted to holla at chu about. As I told chu, this my right hand and I'mma be taking her to make the drops. Now, I ain't got no problem wit taken yo money and gettin yo shit for you, it's just you got your way of doing things and I got mine. However, this works out best for me, you feel me?" Legacy stated. She really didn't give a damn how he felt about it, her decision was final.

"I understand shawty, you well within yo rights to do what's best for you. You my nigga woman and I'm gon' ' support yo choice, but don't hesitate to call me if you need me for anything," Train said seriously.

"I appreciate that," Legacy said trying to read him for sincerity, but she'd always keep her eyes open no matter what. "What's up wit that kush?" she continued.

"Four gees a ping for that depending on how many you want," he said.

"Twenty if you can get em for at least twenty-eight hundred apiece," she reasoned.

"That shouldn't be a problem," he responded.

"Aight, let me know when you ready, pop yo trunk so I can grab them funds," Legacy said as she and Chante stood up to leave.

"Y'all leaving already? We ain't even eat yet," Train said raising his hands.

"I know but we got some things we need to take care of, so maybe another time. Dude should be calling later today or tomorrow, so I'll hit you after that," she said.

"That's a hunnid, Y'all be smooth and remember what I said," Train retorted.

"Fo sho," Legacy said as she and Chante turned to leave. Stopping at the back of a white Dodge Charger SXT just as the trunk popped open, Legacy looked around to make sure nobody was watching her before reaching in and grabbing the duffel bag. Closing the trunk, she put the strap on her shoulder, walked to the MC, and put it in the trunk before getting in and starting it.

"You handled that well," Chante smiled.

"I'm learning as I go, I just hope I don't have to pay for any mistakes with my life, to keep it one hunnid," she stated seriously.

"We'll be good, I still can't believe he gave you all that money though," Chante said.

"I been takin his money and buying his work since Boss got knocked, he just wanted to start going to cop wit me, but I wasn't feeling that. I talked to Boss about it and he said if I really needed Train then I should take him, but I knew he was saying that to try and comfort me because that's his friend, but when Boss was out here he never took Train to meet Ant, so I wasn't about to, besides if something happened I ain't want no parts in it, so I'd rather take somebody I know I can trust, you feel me? Anyways, his money is in good hands and he know that. I ain't gon' take his shit and the nigga Ant havin so much money this is merely peanuts to him girl," Legacy explained.

"I might have to mix business with pleasure," Chante smiled.

"Bitch you a mess, we gonna get this money though," Legacy stated seriously

"That's what's up," Chante said leaning back in her seat as Legacy cranked the volume to 'I Fuck Wit em' by Party Boi feat. Amazin as they pulled out of the parking lot with the 2-15" JL Audio subwoofers blazing.

CHAPTER TWO

P ress one to accep..." the voice service said but was cut off.

"Hello," Legacy answered happily "What' s good baby?" Boss smiled.

"You, I love you and I miss you so much," she explained sincerely.

"I love you too sweetheart," he chuckled at her antics.

"I sent those magazines you asked for and I sent you a few thousand, so be lookin for all that," she said.

"Aight, how you holdin up out there?" he asked concerned. "I'm maintaining the best way I possibly can without you," she answered honestly.

"You can fall back from that yadig if you want to," Boss said letting her know that she didn't have to move the work if she wasn't up for it, he had other people in line if need be.

"Naw bae, it's reppin time so I got this," she retorted. Boss couldn't do anything but smile at the way his woman was taking care of business.

"How did things go for you this time around?" he inquired, wanting to know if the drug transaction went as smoothly as the last time.

"He ain't reach for me yet," she said. "Your lawyer called me yesterday, so I'mma go see him sometime this week and I'll be to see you tomorrow," she added.

"You have one-minute left," the voice service said.

"I love ya and I'll see you tomorrow, I might call back later on," he said.

"I love you to daddy, I'll talk to you later if not tomorrow," Legacy said as the phone call ended.

Legacy and Chante were sitting in Legacy's living room watching game two of the 2012 Eastern Conference semi-finals between the Miami Heat and the Indiana Pacers. The

Heat escaped game one in a nail-biting win, and game two was just like the previous game. Lebron James just hit a three pointer in Paul George's face to bring the Heat to within one point.

"That man ain't gone lose this time, if he do, them critics gon' be all over his azz," Chante said speaking of Lebron.

"Hell naw, he can't. It looks like him and D. Wade is turning the fuck up right now, and if Bosh do what he do, they'll get that ring this year," Legacy agreed as her text alert went off. After reading it, she texted back. Then told Chante "Let's go," before getting up and heading to the back room.

"Go where?" Chante asked puzzled.

"We gotta go meet Ant, now grab that bag out the MC and put it in the jeep," she said while making sure all of her money was intact before putting the duffel bag on her shoulder. Going in

the living room, she grabbed her gun and loaded the second bag into the back of the '07 Jeep Liberty, before hopping in and pulling off. Pulling up to the stop sign on

39th and Lloyd, a black Cadillac Escalade EXT with chrome 26" rims and music so loud that it felt like Legacy and Chante were playing it, stormed past them.

"There he goes right there," Legacy said making a left down the one-way street following the truck. Ant pulled to the right and let Legacy pull up to his window.

"Pull up in the back and back in," Ant said as the diamonds in his mouth danced to their own beat. Legacy nodded and pulled off to do as she had been instructed.

"Make sure yo gun ready to shoot if some shit pops off," Chante said sliding the hack back on her 9mm Taurus.

"Girl that weed got you paranoid as hell, now put that gun up and bring yo azz on," Legacy laughed as they got out of the jeep and grabbed the duffel bags, Ant came around the corner with the phone to his ear wearing so much ice that he could've easily been mistaken for Birdman from Cash Money. Ant hung up his phone and simultaneously the back door opened up.

"What's good my nigga?" Ant asked when the door opened as he ushered the ladies in.

16

"I can't call it," the fat man said while locking the door after everybody was in. The AR-15 in his hand let the ladies know he wasn't playing.

"Now, how can I help you ladies?" the 6'2, 210-pound Ant said wearing a goatee and 360 waves that would make an ocean jealous.

"I need twenty of em," Legacy said as she and Chante placed their bags on the table.

"Jeff, put twenty in a bag and bring it in here. Boo count that money in the money counter for me my nigga," Ant said firing off orders the only way a boss nigga could. "How my boy doin?" he added.

"It's still kinda early, but he might beat that shit, at least, I hope so," Legacy said.

"I hope so too because he a good nigga," Ant said seriously; he had seen Boss through his come up, from buying zips to four and a split and through continuously flipping until he was coppin' bricks. Boss was 14 years old when Ant first met him. Now at age 23, he had more game, brains, and change than niggas twice his age. Ant hated to see shit play out the way it did because he knew there weren't too many real niggas in life, let alone in the game.

"I'll tell him that you asked about him," Legacy smiled. She knew she had a good man because the people that he really messed with wanted to see him come from under the situation he was in and get back out there.

"My bad, who is this fine woman right here that you have with you? "Ant asked licking his lips. He already knew the woman was Legacy's sister because she had already explained the situation to him over the phone or she would've never been let in the house, he didn't give a fuck how fine and thick she was, he had come too far along in the game to slip now.

"This my sis…" Legacy said but was cut off by Chante interrupting her just as Jeff brought the bag in the room and put it on the table.

"Tay, I'm her sister," she said extending her hand. Chante was just as pretty as Legacy, much hooder, and with her 36C-25-44 frame, much thicker in the lower region.

Chante was also an inch taller, maybe because they had different fathers.

"Pleasure to meet you, my name is Ant," he said lighting up the room with his smile, Ant decided right then and there that he had to have her in due time.

"Likewise," she smiled.

"It's all there," Boo said after he finished counting the money as Legacy checked the cocaine.

"Alright Ant, I'll see you later," Legacy said while zipping the duffel bag up. "How was Jamaica?" she continued.

"Beautiful, enjoyed myself a lot, blew damn near a hunnid gees too," he smiled. "Boo take this bag to the car for them my nigga," he continued.

"Did you eat that curry goat soup?" she asked.

"What you know bout that? I got hooked on that the first time I went over there," Ant said while opening the back door.

"That shit is delicious," Legacy smiled.

19

"Bye, now y'all be easy out there, and I'll see you later Tay," he said with a smile.

"Bye," they both said in unison, but the way Chante said it meant much more. Boo put the bag in the back of the Jeep and went back in the house.

Legacy and Chante drove a few blocks away before Legacy pulled over, put the car in park, pressed a series of buttons and the brake pedal until they heard something pop. Legacy then climbed to the back, told Chante to drive while she put the bag in the safety of her stash spot, and locked in place. Then she made her way to the passenger's seat.

"What the fuck, the car got secret stash spots and shit?" Chante laughed with her face scrunched up.

"Yeah, you never know when you'll be riding around with twenty bricks in the whip," Legacy laughed while pulling out her phone and sending a few texts.

"Well I'm glad you got that with all the shit we are hauling," Chante said while keeping both hands on the steering wheel.

"I seen how that nigga Ant was looking at you, talkin' bout and I'll see you later Tay." she said as they both laughed.

"Girl he knows a bad bitch when he sees one," Chante said while moving her neck around. "His fine azz will definitely be seeing me again," she added with a laugh, but she meant every word. Legacy just smiled as she put her phone away and cut the volume up to 'So Cold' by Rikkashay before she leaned back in her seat deep in thought.

The next morning Legacy went to visit Boss in the county jail and Chante was hard at work on her stretch game. First, she cut the kilos with a liquid additive and thoroughly blended them in the blender, creating another brick and a half from ten of them. Then she spread each kilo out on its own cookie sheet with the biggest spatula she could find. Once it started to dry, she formed each brick into a mold until they completely dried out. She learned this trick from her ex-boyfriend Black who was now doing time in Fox Lake correctional institution on drug charges.

After that she cooked two bricks and turned them into three in the form of crack cocaine. While letting it dry, she cleaned up everything with some bleach, and wrapped the remaining 9½ kilo's individually in plastic.

Sitting down, she removed her gloves, surgical mask, and work goggles just as Legacy entered the kitchen and put her purse and keys on the counter.

"What's good girl? I see you in here puttin' that whip game down," Legacy smiled while sitting at the table.

"You already know how I do, Boss got yo' azz happy as hell," she giggled

"I just can't wait for this to be over with," Legacy sighed. "This nigga gone ask me to show him my titties on that video monitor," she added.

"Did you do it?" she questioned.

"Yeah," Legacy laughed.

"Yo nasty azz," she joined in on the laughter.

"How many did you bring back?" Legacy said getting down to business.

"Well, I used a little from each brick, put some 'Comeback 'on it and made another 1½, then I whipped 2 into 3 in crack. The other 91/2 right there on the counter," she stated.

"That's good shit, Boss said we need a spot to get some hand to hand action, so we can see more money other than what we get from the workers, but I don't wanna sit in no spot all day, that shit for the birds. We need to find somebody who wanna eat and hungry enough to stay down and don't pull no slick shit and make a bitch have to pop that azz," Legacy said seriously while in thought.

"What about Lil Chris?" Chante said enthusiastically.

"Hell yeah, I should've been thought of that," Legacy said. Lil Chris was Chante's 17-year-old brother on her dad's side. He and Legacy still said that they were brother and sister despite not being connected biologically. "Call his azz while I get in the shower and tell him we coming to see him, but don't tell him why yet," Chante said before heading to the shower. Legacy picked up her phone and scrolled through her call log until she landed on his number.

"What's good sis?" he answered.

"Boy take some of that bass outta yo' voice?" she joked.

"This what it is, I'm grown as hell now," he said confidently.

"Where you at?" she asked.

"In the Meadows, do I gotta fuck a nigga up or somethin'?" he asked seriously.

"Naw, you got bag?" she asked trying to throw him off from her real intentions.

"No doubt," he responded

"Me and Tay gonna ride down on you," she said while looking under the sink and grabbing the digital scale.

"Aight, one," he said hanging up the phone.

Legacy got four sandwich bags, doubled them up, weighed 28 grams of crack in each one, and tied them up. Cleaning the scale, she put it back under the sink before putting the 9 1/2 kilos in the duffel bag and putting them in the safe that was in the basement. Going upstairs, she wrapped up the rest of the crack and put it in the floor safe in the guest bedroom.

"You ready?" Chante asked coming from the back combing out her wrap.

"Let's roll, we gon' take the MC to give this nigga some admiration and enthusiasm to get money," Legacy said grabbing her keys and getting her gun out of her room. Hopping in the MC, she backed out of the garage and pulled off.

Pulling into the second lot on 91st and Brown Deer, she blared "Walk First" by the Bless Team out of the speakers. They spotted Lil Chris leaning up against a primed up El Camino talking to some big booty girl. Hearing the music instantly got his attention as Legacy pulled up and backed into a parking space. Lil Chris said something to the girl and then ran over to the car. Chante let the door up and raised the seat up so that he could get in the back seat before she got back in and closed the door.

"This muthafucka shakin' the shit out the ground, on my Mama," he said referring to the music. "That nigga Boss holdin," he continued after looking around at all the fixtures the car had.

"Never mind that, I see you still out here chasin' dem hood rats," Chante smiled.

"Neva that you don't have to chase what you can attract." He spoke confidently. "I see y'all ridin' these sixes, I hope y'all got a heater in this bitch," he added.

"Nigga get yo' ruler out, these 28s and the whole car strapped and I ain't talkin' seatbelts," Legacy said quoting Young Jeezy as she and Chante showed their guns.

"Y'all clownin and y'all ain't neva lied," he smiled while showing his 40 cal.

"That's what's up, but what you doing out here?" Legacy asked seriously trying to see where his head was at.

"I got that bag for…," Lil Chris started but was cut off.

"Naw nigga, how you livin? Is you eatin' out here?" Legacy asked while eyeing him closely.

"I'm doin' aight, it really seems like I'm hustlin' to re-up again, I can't get over the hump. I just bought that whip and it's gon' take some money to get that together and you know a nigga gotta stay fitted, but I promise once I make it to the top I ain't never lookin' back again," he said, meaning every word.

"Why you buy that ugly azz car?" Chante scolded him.

"Shit, ain't nobody in the city got a El Camino, when I get my money up, I'mma have that bitch sittin' pretty believe that," he said matter of factly.

Legacy could see the sincerity in his eyes and hear the drive and determination in his voice that he was trying to eat, and she was going to see what he was about. Reaching under her seat she grabbed two ounces and passed them to him through the middle of the seat. She figured if he fucked the two zips off, she'd know he wasn't serious about gettin' money, but if he did right, this could be the start of something beautiful.

"What's this?" he asked puzzled.

"A business proposition, that's two zips, bring me back twelve hunnid as soon as you can, and we'll go from there," Legacy said looking at him through her rearview mirror.

"That's it? I got you in a couple days. Y'all be easy, I love y'all," he said as Chante let him out of the car.

"We love you too," they said in unison and pulled off.

"I think that was a great business move, he ready and I can tell," Legacy said while texting Train the meeting spot.

"Only time will tell Leggy, only time will tell," Chante said while relaxing in her seat.

CHAPTER THREE

A month and a half later, Legacy was on her way to see Lil Chris. After she gave him the two ounces, he had called her five days later to pick up her money. She sent him on another test run with 4 zips and a pound of kush. Three weeks later, he had her money. Seeing he was ready, she had him get a hype to put a spot in the hype's name, so he could serve out of it, now it was time to see if he could handle some weight.

Pulling in the second lot of the meadows, Legacy called and let him know that she was outside while she backed into a parking space.

Lil Chris ran out of the house dressed in black, red, and green Gucci from head to toe with Gucci aviators on his face. Straightening the gold Cuban link chain around his neck with the letter 'C' charm, he walked towards the car. You could definitely tell that he was getting some money now.

"What's good, sis?" he asked while getting in the passenger's seat.

"I see you lookin' like new money," she smiled proudly that her little brother was on the come up.

"This shit just looks good, sis. I'm tryna stack and buy a few cribs, but this shit makes me feel comfortable," he said keeping it a hunnid.

"Stop buying all that shit, then you'll be able to translate into the real estate game," she said with her hands in the air.

"I know! I wanna save because I know I gotta solidify myself out here. This money can be plentiful, but it can also be short lived. I never want to assume that I will be here forever, so I'mma try to make sure I'm makin' the right moves to make myself fool proof and one of the ways to do that is by owning shit because that's guaranteed money," Lil Chris said seriously while removing his glasses.

Legacy was shocked to see that he was so mature at a young age and thinking about his future.

"Do what you gotta do to make sure you good out here, I got yo' back lil nigga," she said pushing his head playfully. All of a sudden, bass could be heard from afar, then a yellow H3 Hummer rolled up sitting on chrome 26-inch Lexani rims. Lil Chris and Legacy watched as the dude hopped out with a cell phone glued to his ear and went inside a house leaving the truck running with a chick sitting inside.

"Who is that?" Legacy inquired after seeing the look on her brother's face.

"My biggest competition, this nigga name Big Ball," he said through clenched teeth.

Legacy took in what he was saying before she spoke. "I'mma tell you something I heard Boss say to another muthafucka. Competition is good in any other game, but in this game, competition has to be moved around because how can you reach yo' full potential with a muthafucka in yo' way who ain't on yo' team? You can't, besides, when you climb that ladder of success muthafucka's gon' be tryna push you down any way they can and you gotta be prepared for that also, but any nigga ahead of you on that ladder who ain't tryna help you up the ladder has to be moved around because that's how the game is played, you feel me?" she said dropping some jewels on him.

"I'mma already on that," he said while watching the truck storm passed them.

"Here, this a brick and five pounds of weed, can you handle that?" she asked as she passed him the bag from the backseat.

"Oh, hell yeah, I got you," he said taking the bag, this was his first time seeing a brick, let alone having one.

"I need fifty off that," she said.

"Aight cool," he said while digging in his front pocket and passing her a brown paper bag full of money from his last consignment. "I'mma hit you up, you be easy," he added while putting his glasses back on. Legacy looked in the bag and said, "you can keep it."

"For real?"

"Yeah, I wanna see you get yo' paper up," she said.

"Aight sis, good lookin'," he said enthusiastically.

"No problem, I love you."

"I love you, too," he said while getting out of the car and making a call on his cell phone while walking to the house.

Legacy smiled as she pulled off. Pulling up to the apartment buildings on 95th and Silver Spring Drive, she did what was required to open her stash box, then she climbed in the back to retrieve the package before making a call.

"Hello," the male voice said.

"I'm outside, Shawn," she said then hung up. A couple minutes later a 6'1 bald-headed light-skinned man with a light beard and goatee stepped out on the porch wearing a pair of white gold

Versace frames, looking like a professor, but slangin' more than a little poison in the hood. He also wore a white gold chain with the Wisconsin Badgers 'W' charm flooded in red diamonds.

"What's good wit it?" Shawn asked getting into the passenger seat.

"Maintaining," she said accepting the large wad of rubber banded bills.

"That's what's up," he responded taking the two bricks and stuffing them down the front of his pants. "I'mma get up wit you," he continued before sliding out of the car.

"Fo sho," she said then pulled into traffic, while dialing on her cell phone and putting it on speaker.

"What up, bitch?" Chante answered.

"Shit, where you at?" she responded.

"Just got done bussin' a few moves, why what up?"

"I'm tryna hit the mall," she said hitting her turn signal and switching lanes.

"Aight, I'mma meet you at yo' crib," Chante stated.

"Fo sho," she said ending the call and sending a few texts. Legacy would drop the work off to Ben and Curt. The two worked for Boss when he was out, and they stayed true so far, so she kept fucking with them. After that her and Chante were going to do a little splurging at the mall.

∞

At around 12am later that night, Lil Chris and his best friend Dre stood in the cut dressed in all black waiting on the right time to strike their prey. They watched their soon-to-be victim arrive about 45 minutes beforehand; they had wanted to strike then, but they had noticed the two lurking cars from afar watching everything, which would have possibly lead to a shootout and they came for much more, so they held their positions.

"Fam, let's just kick the door in and take what we want," Dre said angrily because they had been out there so long.

"Nigga is you stupid? We gon' do this shit the right way, now come on," Lil Chris said, then they walked across the street towards the house.

"Look, his son right there watching T.V.," Dre said about to walk up to the window, when Chris abruptly stopped him and pointed to the motion-sensored light on the side of the house.

"I got an idea," Lil Chris said digging in his pocket and pulling out a band. "When I say go, hurry up and lay this money in front of that window and get out the way," he instructed Dre. This was the only thing he could think of at that time and it was so crazy that it just might work, at least he hoped it did.

Lil Chris picked up five small rocks with his baseball gloved hand and threw one at the window while watching the boy. **Tink**, the first rock hit the window, the boy didn't budge. **Tink,** the second rock hit and the boy looked.

"Go," Lil Chris said in a whisper and Dre quickly ran by the window, causing the light to come on, and spreading the money out, he got out of the way.

Noticing that the light had come on, the boy got up and looked out the window. He immediately saw the pile of money which made his eyes grow big. The boy quickly ran by the stairs to see if his mom or dad was coming, seeing they weren't, he hurriedly put the alarm code in, opened the door, and ran out of the house right to where the money was. Soon as he was about to reach down and pick it up, Lil Chris put his gloved hand over the boy's mouth, snatched him off his feet, took him out of the shine of the light, and put his gun on the boy's temple.

"Didn't anybody tell you all money ain't good money, lil nigga?" Lil Chris said as Dre positioned himself right next to Lil Chris after picking the money up.

"When we go inside this house, you betta not make a sound or I'm gon' have to shoot you, alright?" Lil Chris warned the boy. He shook his head up and down letting him know he fully understood him. "Now, who all in the house?" he added.

"My mama and daddy" The scared 12-year-old boy said through tears. Lil Chris and Dre then entered the house with the boy. Lil Chris told Dre to take the shoe strings out of a pair of shoes by the door and tie the boy up. "Bring that lil nigga and come on," Lil Chris said walking up the stairs with his .45 leading the way, looking in every bedroom along the way. Hearing moans and the sounds of Tank's song 'Sex Music', Lil Chris stopped in front of the door and pointed to the room. Dre nodded his head and Lil Chris opened up the door slowly to see Big Ball hitting his baby mama doggystyle with his back to the door. Lil Chris walked up right behind him and said, "hit that big ass for me too."

Big Ball pushed his baby mama from in front of him and made a dive for his gun on the dresser. Lil Chris grabbed his ankle and pulled him back making him fall short of the dresser.

"Nigga you go for that gun my partna here gon' blow yo' son head off," Lil Chris said with his gun aimed on Big Ball as Dre walked in the room with his gun on the boy's head. "Bitch shut the fuck up screamin' fo' I pop yo' stupid azz. Tie that bitch up," he ordered grabbing Big Ball's gun off the dresser.

Dre laid the boy down and pulled the duct tape from his hoodie pocket and taped the woman's hands, feet, and mouth.

"Now, I know you know why I'm here, we can make it easy and you tell me where the shit at or we can make it hard and do it another way, either way, I'm good with," Lil Chris said as Dre taped Big Ball's hands and feet.

"I aint' got shit here, man," Big Ball said looking shook.

"So, we gon' play that game," Lil Chris said and tucked his pistol away. He then turned on the light which made the ceiling fan start spinning very fast. Putting a piece of tape on Big Ball's mouth, he told Dre to help him lift the boy up. "So, you wanna play, let's play," Lil Chris said as he and Dre lifted the boy until his head was hitting the fan. Muffled screams filled the room as they lowered the now bleeding boy.

"You ready to talk now!" Lil Chris said pulling his pistol out and smacking Ball across the face with it. When Big Ball didn't reply, Lil Chris said, "round two." Then he started tucking his pistol away as he and Dre lifted the boy up just as the woman got hysterical.

"I think she got something to say," Dre said as they laid the boy back down and he went to remove the tape from her mouth.

"I can't believe yo' bitch azz gon' let them do that to our son, it's a safe in the basement, the combination is 20-18-12 and in the linen closet down the hall it's two bags under the floor." The woman spoke angrily before Dre put the tape back on her mouth.

"Go get that," Lil Chris instructed Dre before having a seat at the end of the bed. "Yo' woman got more nuts than yo' hoe azz. You was gon' let us kill yo' son rather than give us some shit you can replace. I gotta say that was some bitch azz shit!" Lil Chris said before striking him across the face twice with the pistol.

Getting off the bed, he started collecting jewelry off the dresser and night stand, including Big Ball's platinum chain with the #8 pool ball flooded in black diamonds.

"I got the shit, let's go!" Dre said running into the room.

Turning to leave, something Legacy said stopped him in his tracks. "Competition is good in any other game, but in this game, competition has to be moved around because how can you reach yo' full potential with a muthafucka in yo' way who ain't on yo' team? You can't besides, when you climb that ladder of success muthafucka's gon' be tryna push you down any way they can and you gotta be prepared for that also, but any nigga ahead of you on that ladder who ain't tryna help you up the ladder has to be moved around because that's how the game is played, you feel me?" He remembered her words verbatim and without a second thought, he walked up to Big Ball who was laying on the floor pissing on himself because he knew he was about to lose his life. "I'll see yo' bitch azz when I get there **Boc Boc Boc,**" Lil Chris said and fired three shots into his head, silencing him forever. Lil Chris knew Big Ball was well-established in the game and he couldn't take the chance of letting him live, possibly finding out who he was and coming after him, so he did what he felt was necessary.

Lil Chris walked up to the woman and put the pistol to her temple. "If I go to jail, you goin' in a box, you got me?" he said showing her her identification card that he found on the dresser. Her head went up and down vigorously as tears flowed down her face. With that notion, they grabbed the bags and exited the way they'd come in.

Running as fast as they could, they made it to the car, threw the bags in, got in, and removed their scream masks. Starting the car, they pulled off.

∞

Legacy laid in her bed, halfway sleep watching the Channel 12 news until 'BREAKING NEWS' flashed across the screen, which got her attention.

"Hi, I'm on the city's Northwest side in the eighty-eight hundred block of North Fairy Chaism where a heinous crime has just taken place in this house right behind me," the news woman said as the camera man zoomed in on the house. Legacy saw a few cars in the driveway. A 745, a Trail Blazer, a Chevy, and a yellow Hummer. This caused her to pay even closer attention to what was going on. "Police said there was a woman and a child in the house, but their condition is not known, what we do know is there is a deceased man inside, police have declined any further comments, but we do know there are no suspects in custody. I am Danielle White reporting live from JISN Channel 12 News," the News reporter signed off.

Legacy grabbed her phone and texted 'you good?' to her brother and waited on edge for a response. A sigh of relief left her body when the text came back 'great'. She knew that her little brother had dove head first into the game and she hoped like hell that he knew what he was doing.

Nevertheless, she'd take her secret to her grave. Legacy put her phone back on the charger and went to sleep.

∞

"My nigga, our lives finna change forever," Dre said hitting the blunt.

"Listen we gon' continue to live how we been living niggas already know we getting paper, so we gon' maintain for a while before we go hard. These niggas and bitches is watchin' because the streets gon' be talkin' believe that," Lil Chris said sipping from his bottle of Wasted vodka. He drank occasionally but did not smoke.

"You're right, but in a couple of months, I'm gonna shit on these niggas like Lebron James be doin," Dre said excitedly. "I'll be back, I gotta go catch this action from Mister down the hill," he continued.

"Mister, aint that the hype that be havin' the pistol on him and dem gloves in his back pocket like he bout to whack something?" Lil Chris asked remembering the name.

"Hell yeah, but Mister already know not to try no slick shit wit me. I'm always watching his hands anyway, one false move and instead of smokin' he gon' be smoked," Dre said seriously while pulling out his pistol, showing his quick draw before putting it back on his hip and leaving the house.

Lil Chris hit the bottle again and thought 'I'm never goin broke again.' He and Dre had made it out with $125, 000, 4 kilos, and 5 pounds of kush a piece. "With my brains and new change, I'm bout to sew the whole hood up," he said out loud to himself with a devious smile on his face.

CHAPTER FOUR

Three weeks later things where starting to get back to normal. After Big Ball's death, police chief Penn had squad cars posted everywhere in the hood and sweating everything movin', the block was on fire.

Lil Chris and Dre had been staying at the Courtyard Hotel down Brown Deer and catching action off their phones. They were yet to be labeled as suspects, which was great news, but they also knew that you could never get too comfortable with the circumstances at hand.

"My nigga, even though this shit coolin' down, we got too much money to be in idle mode. We need a change of scenery for a minute," Dre said while disconnecting the smoke detector and putting a wet towel under the door. Lil Chris had been thinking the same thing as he pulled out his iPhone and dialed a number.

"Hello," the female voice answered.

45

"What you doin', sis?" Lil Chris asked.

"Writing a letter to Boss, why what up? Are you okay?" she asked in a motherly tone.

"Yeah yeah, I'm straight. When the last time you seen yo' mom?" he asked beating around the bush.

"A minute ago, but we damn near talk every day," she responded wondering where this was going.

"Let's go down there for a week, I wanna get slugged up anyway," he said optimistically.

"I was thinking about going down there because the Stunt fest car and bike show is next weekend, when you talkin' about leavin'?" she asked.

"Oh yeah, you gon' put all them miles on that MC?" he asked thinking that she must be crazy.

"Hell naw, I'mma put it on the train and put insurance on it, it cost like $1,500," she said thinking that he must be crazy.

"Let's leave tomorrow, I'm takin' my whip too, so set that up. Call and see if Tay wanna go, I'm bringing' Dre and I know you don't wanna be kickin' it with us like that," he said. "What's up Legacy?" Dre said from the background. Unbeknowingly to her and Lil Chris, Dre had a major crush on Legacy.

"Tell that nigga I said what's up, I'm bout to call Tay on three way," Legacy said then clicked over.

"Hello," Chante answered.

"What's good, sis?" Lil Chris asked.

"Hey Tay," Legacy smiled.

"Damn, what the fuck is this a family reunion?" Chante asked making everybody laugh.

"Naw bitch, we tryna go to ATL tomorrow to see mama and Chris tryna get slugged up, so we wanted to know if you wanted to go?" Legacy stated.

"Hell yeah!" Chante said excitedly.

"Aight Leggy, get a big truck from the rental place and set that car thing up, I'll hit yo' hand when I get there. Get some snacks cause we sleepin' over and leavin' early so we can get there with time to spare," Lil Chris instructed.

"Nigga who you think you is firing off orders like you the man," Legacy joked.

"Y'all little brother, I'll see y'all later," he said before hanging up.

"My nigga, we gotta go to Magic City," Dre said putting his blunt out while thinking about the place he had heard so much about over the years, he couldn't wait to experience what the strip club had to offer first hand.

"No doubt," Lil Chris said gathering his things.

"It's going down," Dre said gleefully as Lil Chris pulled out his phone, dialed a number, then put it to his ear.

"Hello," a lady answered.

"Auntie let me speak to Ken," he said.

"Well hi to you too," she responded, but before he could say anything back, she sat the phone down and called out to Ken.

"Yeah," Ken got on the phone.

"Ay be outside, I'm gonna come through and holla at you," Lil Chris said business-like.

"Aight," Ken said then hung up.

Checking their keys into the hotel's front desk, they left. Pulling up to the apartments on 76th and Servite, Lil Chris saw Ken standing outside as he pulled up with Dre right behind him in the '03 Impala.

"What's good, cuz?" Ken said getting in the passenger's seat and shaking Lil Chris' hand.

"You wanna make some money?" Lil Chris asked.

"Yeah, hell yeah," Ken said while moving his head up and down.

"Here go my line and the charger. Take this 4 and a split and this pound of weed, bag up $10 bags of the dope in this size and $20 bags of the weed in this size," Lil Chris showed him with his fingers.

"You keep the Impala behind me and use that for your transportation, and if you feeling uneasy about a situation, use this and don't hesitate, please don't," he said giving him

49

a millennium edition. 380. "Stack that money and if somebody call you for some weight, tell 'em to call back next week and I'll plug 'em. If you fuck up my line, I ain't fuckin' wit you like that no more, you got that?" 'Lil Chris said trying to run the game down to Ken as he knew it.

"Yeah, I got you cuz," Ken said, he and Lil Chris were the same age, but lived two different lives.

"Don't tell auntie nothin' bout that, just tell her I let you borrow my car while I go out of town, I'll be back in a week, don't drive wit all that shit on you either, just a little over what they want. Meet them at a place with a lot of light too, okay?" Lil Chris said shaking his hand.

"Got it, I'll see you next week," Ken said before getting out of the car and accepting the keys to the Impala from Dre before he hopped in the car with Lil Chris.

"You think he gon' be alright?" Dre asked closing the door as Lil Chris pulled off.

"Yeah, he'll be straight. Niggas know our get down, ya feel me? Plus, we can trust him," Lil Chris said seriously

"No doubt," Dre said as they shook on that. They were headed to Chris' mama's house. then to Legacy's house.

Legacy pulled up in front of her house in a rented 2012 GMC Yukon Denali XL, followed by Chante in her orange 2009 Chevy Camaro on 22" Lexani chrome rims with the orange background. Getting out of her car, Chante hopped in the truck with Legacy just as she was finishing up her call with Boss.

"You drive the first half and I'll do the second half," Legacy said hanging up the phone.

"Aight, cause them lil niggas ain't about to be drivin' me on no highway at that distance," Chante said eating her Cheetos.

"On er'thang," Legacy co-signed just as the hard bass and crisp words could be heard to Feragamos hit single "How We Roll", as Lil Chris bent the corner in his El Camino. The used to be bucket was no more. The now cherry-red candy painted 1981 El Camino SS looked like it was dripping wet as Lil Chris drove down the block sitting on 30" gold DUB flash spinner rims. Stopping in front of

Legacy's house, him and Dre hopped out jackin' about cashin' out, both with a fist full of money, while the rims on the car were still doing 40mph.

"Boy, if you don't cut that shit down!" Legacy warned him.

"I'm practicing for Stunt fest, I'm finna turn the fuck up on these niggas," Lil Chris smiled while going to cut his music down. He had totally flipped the car, fiberglass throughout the inside, red leather swan seats, shaved door handles with remote door opener, 15" T'Vs in each door, 20" in dash TV with a custom red Xbox 360 mounted under the dashboard, Clarion radio with 3.5" LCD TV screen display. A 15" solobaric L-7 speaker under each seat powered by two Rockford Fosgate 800-watt amps that were also mounted under the seat, twenty tweeters throughout the car, a Plexiglas back window, and a chrome 350 engine under the hood. He had been working on the car since Legacy put him on, now to see it complete was something special to him, he knew the car was surely a pussy magnet in any state. Pulling the car into the driveway, he parked, and hopped out smiling.

"Bro bro, that ain't the car that I told you was ugly is it?" Chante asked knowing the car had come a long way.

"Hell yeah, now look at it, I told you I was gon' have that bitch sittin' pretty," Lil Chris boasted.

"You did that, it don't even look like the same car," Chante gave him his props.

"Leggy, when are we takin' the whips?" Lil Chris asked anxiously.

"Right now, I'm finna let Tay in cause she drivin' first and Dre can follow us in the truck to the Amtrak station," Legacy said going to open the door.

"Y'all want me to help y'all drive," Lil Chris offered.

"We good," Legacy and Chante said in unison.

"Now I ain't the smartest man in the world, but I'd say y'all already knew that I was gon' ask to drive and y'all agreed not to let me drive," Lil Chris said with one eyebrow up. Legacy and Chante looked at each other and started laughing as Chante handed Dre the keys to the truck and Lil Chris ran their bags inside the house.

After letting Chante in, Legacy backed the MC out of the driveway after Lil Chris backed his car out. Then Legacy pulled off followed by Lil Chris and Dre coming up the back; they were headed downtown to the train station.

∞

Boss was laid back on his bunk reading Loyalty before Royalty by G. Q. when his cellmate came into the small cell and pulled the door up. Cutting his eyes away from his book, he spoke, "what's good?"

"Shit, I was chillin' out there tryna read this Hip Hop Weekly, but these niggas pissin' me off talkin' bout how big they rims is, how many grams they buying, how much money they got, and how fine they baby mama is. If everybody fuckin' dimes, who got all these ugly bitches pregnant?" Larry said angrily, he was a smooth dude off 23rd and Locust, that Boss had taken a liking to, so he gave him a few words of wisdom whenever he could.

"What do you expect? Some niggas feel that's the only way they can make themselves relevant but let me tell you something despite all that shit," Boss said sitting up. "The

54

most luxurious possession, the richest treasure anybody has, is their personal dignity," Boss said quoting Jackie Robinson, one of the many books he'd read while incarcerated.

"I feel you my nigga, that shit be crazy thou. Keeping it hot, I really wasn't out there like that, I made a little two's and few's enough to stay afloat and keep me and my daughter straight. I had a whip nothing extravagant, just good enough to get me where I needed to go, but it seemed like something would happen every time I was on my way up on my feet that would knock me back down. Real niggas get money man, I gotta do something better to get something better," Larry said leaning up against the wall with his foot up on it while shaking his head. At age 25, he was two years older than Boss, but unbeknown to him, Boss was a big-time drug dealer and well respected in his hood. He never spoke about this to Larry because whenever people found out about money, it always complicated things, some people even tend to become different in efforts to fit in and Boss couldn't stand no cock jockin' azz niggas. Besides, it was none of his business what he was doing on the streets. He was glad that nobody on the pod knew him and as far as Larry knew, he just thought Boss was wise and witty for his age.

"Let me tell you something, first of all, you don't have to be a paid nigga to be a real nigga. Real niggas do real things if they are rich or if they're poor," Boss paused for a minute to let that sink in. "Being a real nigga is about being honorable and living with the choices that you make in life. And if you fuckin' wit the game, you know what yo' ultimate goal is, so plan wise and until you see it, sacrifices must be made for the greater good. Success is how high you bounce when you hit the bottom, feel me? Don't let nobody stop you from achieving what you know you can," Boss continued dropping some jewels on him.

"I feel you, you got a lot of game about yo'self too but before you get back deep in that book let me hit this toilet my nigga. That taco meat at the dinner runnin through a nigga," Larry said holding his stomach as beads of sweat formed on his forehead.

"I'm gonna hop on the jack anyway," Boss said getting off the bottom bunk, sliding on his sandals, and heading to the door. "Damn!" Boss added as Larry let out a vicious sounding fart. "Check yo' draws my nigga, that sounded like you left something in 'em," he continued before closing the door behind him.

"My bad bro," Larry yelled through the door. Normally, one would've took that as a form of disrespect, but he fucked with Larry, and he also knew how it could be when you got the B. G.'s (Bubble Guts) from state food. He had gotten them himself a few times, Boss laughed to himself as he picked up the phone and started dialing.

∞

"Time to get up, wash ya face, and brush ya teeth," Lil Chris said entering the living room where everybody slept last night banging two pots together.

"Nigga if you don't stop makin' all that noise, I'mma fuck you up," Chante spat tiredly.

"Then get yo azz up!" he continued banging.

"What time is it?" Legacy asked pulling the covers from over her head.

"6:49," Dre stated eating a bagel and drinking a glass of orange juice. He and Lil Chris had been up since 5 o'clock. They had done 500 push-ups, sit ups, and jumping jacks. This was a part of their daily regimen. They had already showered, dressed, and were ready to hit the road.

"Damn, was I slobbin' my face feel tight as hell," Chante said getting up and heading to the bathroom as everybody bursted into laughter. Unknown to her, since she fell asleep first, Lil Chris had put whipped Cream in her hand, tickled her face, and watched her smack herself a couple of times while Dre filmed it. Against Legacy's protest, they had then uploaded it to YouTube.

As Legacy was walking down the hallway on her way to the shower, Chante stormed out of the bathroom, past her, and into the living room. "Which one of you little muthafuckas did this?" she asked pointing to the dried-up whipped cream that was on the side of her face and in her hair. Seeing Dre chuckle, with the speed of a cat, she was up on him landing a right to his side, turning him around, she put him in a full nelson. Lil Chris was on his way to help when she pushed Dre into him causing them both to fall on the kitchen floor, then she seized her opportunity and hit them with a couple quick punches.

"You niggas betta recognize when you fuckin' wit a real bitch," she smiled before running to the bathroom and locking the door as they gave chase.

"I'm whoopin' yo azz for that! " Lil Chris barked through the door. "Man, how you let her whoop

you like that?" he asked Dre laughing. Legacy couldn't do anything but laugh at the three of them as she went into her room and closed the door.

Thirty-five minutes later, after putting Chante's Camaro in the garage, they were ready to go.

Getting in the truck with Chante behind the wheel, Legacy in the passenger's seat, Lil Chris in the back, and Dre on the third-row seat, they pulled off.

Chante pulled up to a pump at the gas station and looked in the rear-view mirror as she came to a stop.

"Boy, what the fuck is that on yo eyes?" she asked making Legacy turn around to see.

"These the iPod video goggles," Lil Chris said removing them.

"How they work?" she asked.

"It's a 24-inch TV right before your eyes, you don't need batteries because it's powered by yo iPod. I got 600 songs on my iPod and every time I listen to a song, I can watch the video," he explained.

"Let me see em," Chante said excitedly.

"Hell naw, you betta ask Dre to see his," he replied while moving them out of her reach.

"I can't stand yo azz, when we get half way there I'mma leave yo azz on the side of the highway," she said making everybody laugh as they got out of the car. Getting their snacks and filling up the tank, they hopped back in the truck, put Yo Gotti's mix tape CD 'CM7: Cocaine Muzik 7 in the deck and headed towards the highway.

∞

Ken sat in his bedroom counting the money he made all last night and in the wee hours of the morning. He had been hustling non-stop since he met up with Lil Chris and things had been going smoothly so far. The $1,435 that occupied his hands was the most he had ever had at one time. He counted it again for the fifth time since getting home and a smile came across his face. He could get used to this type of action and he was gon' holla at Lil Chris when he got back about staying on the grind. He looked over his shoulder at Big Booty Rudy, the neighborhood jumpdown who laid in his bed watching TV in a beige bra and thong set that used to be white, but Ken didn't care about that. He had been pressing her for some pussy for a while now and always came up on the short end of the stick. It's funny how a few dollars and a whip could change things, that and the low top pink and white Air Force Ones that he bought her persuaded her to give him what he'd practically been begging for.

Ken stripped down, turned off the TV, and helped Rudy out of her bra and thong. Big Booty Rudy was one of those light-skinned girls who always looked dusty, but she had a really big ass and a nice set of breasts which was always a plus for any female, especially when she was so generous with sharing it.

Ken looked over her body hungrily as he dove in face first and ate her pussy. Eating any girl out besides your wifey was a big no no, especially a jumpdown, but Ken wasn't used to getting action like that, so when he did, he enjoyed it any way he could. After Rudy came in his mouth, he swallowed it, scooted up, and slid his fully erect member inside of her bare. This was also a no no, but Ken was only hearing yes yes coming from Rudy. After he came 10 minutes later, he laid next to her with his chest heaving, staring at the ceiling, he couldn't believe after all this time he had finally hit her, he was happy to say the least. Turning towards Big Booty Rudy, he said, "you ready to go?" while hopping up and putting his clothes back on.

CHAPTER FIVE

12 hours later, Legacy saw a sign on her right that said, 'Welcome to the state of Georgia'. She turned up Cincere's hit "Good Time" featuring Corey Preper to alert everybody that they were there.

"Bitch you trippin," Chante said turning the music down.

"We're here!" Legacy yelled.

"Good Dre fye up some of that good and let me hit it," Chante said.

"I'm already a step ahead of you," Dre said sparking the already rolled blunt, hitting it a few times, and passing it to Chante.

"This what I'm talkin' about," she said as the potent weed filled her lungs and worked its magic.

A little while later, they pulled up to the Westin Hotel in downtown Atlanta. This was the second tallest building in the Western hemisphere.

Hopping out of the truck, Legacy opened the trunk, handed the keys to the valet with a tip as the bell boy helped them put their luggage on a cart. Walking into the huge spacious hotel lobby, they approached the front desk.

"Hi, welcome to the Westin Hotel, how may I help you?" the busty blonde said from behind the desk.

"Hi, I have a reservation for Legacy Duncan," she said placing her ID and credit card on the counter as the lady who's name tag read Cindy typed into the computer.

"Oh yes, I have it right here Ms. Duncan," Cindy said still typing. Picking up Legacy's credit card, she swiped it, and typed again. "Sign and date here please," she said passing her a paper on a clipboard and a pen. Signing the paper, Legacy passed it back, and Cindy gave her two key cards.

"Can I please have one more key card for each room?" Legacy asked politely.

"Sure, enjoy your stay and if you need anything, don't hesitate to call," Cindy said passing her two more key cards.

"Thank you," Legacy said accepting the key cards before walking off in the direction of the elevators while taking in the beautiful scenery of the hotel.

Getting to their rooms that were right next to each other's, Lil Chris tipped the bell boy and went into the room that he shared with Dre. The girls complained of being tired, so they all agreed to meet in the lobby in a couple of hours before Chante and Legacy retired to their room.

Lil Chris and Dre were a little tired as well, but being in a new city with new women, and bands on deck, they'd sacrifice their sleep to see what was in store for them. Since the cars wouldn't arrive until tomorrow, they had to find something else to get into because Legacy was not giving them the keys to the rental car. Lil Chris   watch read, 7:25pm, so they changed their clothes and headed down to the pool area.

Spreading their towels out on the lounge chairs, they got comfortable and enjoyed the sight of the swimming pool while relaxing under the umbrellas. Lil Chris flagged down a waiter and attempted to buy some alcoholic beverages, but he got carded, so he offered somebody a hundred-dollar bill to get them for them and they quickly obliged. There weren't a lot of people at the pool due to the time of day, however, they enjoyed themselves.

"My nigga this what I'm talkin about, this how we supposed to be living, like kings," Dre said smiling with one hand held out for some love.

"Nigga we are kings and don't forget it, when we get back to Milwaukee, we gon' take flight on niggas, but for now, we gon' show these southern niggas how the Midwest swag," Lil Chris boasted while shaking Dre's hand, then he focused his attention on a dark-skinned woman who was getting out of the pool looking stunning. The two-piece Casabella swimsuit that she wore left little to the imagination.

"I'll be right back, my nig," Lil Chris said getting up while Dre tried to see what had his boy's attention. Spotting the woman, Dre said, "yeah, get that my nigga she bad."

Lil Chris approached the woman from the back while she was drying off and the first thing he noticed was her voluptuous rear end, and the second thing was a tattoo of a small sand beach with two palm trees, water around the beach, and the word 'PARADISE' over it. Lil Chris had never seen a tramp stamp like that before, but he liked it, but only if it indicated what he thought it meant.

"Excuse me," Lil Chris said as the Zimbabwean and Jamaican-mixed product turned around and greeted him with a warm smile.

"Yahs," she said in a thick Jamaican accent which made her even more attractive to Lil Chris.

"How you doin? My name is Chris, and you are?" Lil Chris asked confidently smiling.

"Shelly, boy how old are you?" she replied in broken English flaunting her 36-27-44 crotch grabbing frame.

"Seventeen, but that's merely a number. I'm a man in every sense of the word and given the opportunity, can show and prove. Please don't prejudge me before you know the real me," Lil Chris said shooting his shot.

"Boy, you are so coot, but I too old for you," she said turning him down.

Rejection didn't sit well with Lil Chris, but he stayed composed and kept his game face on. He wasn't like most dudes who get rejected and slang the bitch word around, he just rolled with the punches. He'd see her later on down the line, and things may be different. He stood there and talked to her for about 10 more minutes and found out that she was 20 years old, originally from Jamaica, but moved to the U. S. (to Houston, Texas) at age 13. He found out that her and her older sister by a year where trying to transfer from the University of Houston, move to Atlanta and attend Clark Atlanta University. They were in town touring the school and the bright lights of the big city. Lil Chris told her that he would see her around and they parted ways.

Walking back to his seat, he spotted Dre by the pool talking to two white girls, and it looked like he was storing a number into his cell phone.

"What happened my nigga?" Dre asked coming back to his seat.

"She shot ya boy down, but it's all good," he said honestly.

"What! Oh well her loss," Dre said trying to keep his boys spirits up. "Don't even trip thou, if this

fall through we gon' be in some snow bunnies tonight. They say they gon' call when their parents go to sleep. One 17 the other is 19, so we should just chill for tonight, fuck wit them and let yo sisters sleep," Dre added

"That sounds like a plan, where they from?" he asked seeing the logic in what Dre said.

"Minnesota, and them hoes do drugs," Dre said gleefully.

"Let's go back to the room," he said pulling out his iPhone and texting Legacy to let her know that they could sleep in and they'd party tomorrow.

Getting back to their room, he got a text back from Legacy that said 'Thanx 143,' He smiled and texted back '143.'

"Come on, let me whoop yo azz in this," Dre said hooking up the PlayStation 3 and putting in NBA 2K12 - their favorite game.

Lil Chris rolled with the Russell Westbrook and Kevin Durant led Oklahoma City Thunder and Dre took the LeBron James and Dwayne Wade led Miami Heat. They battled back and forth only to have it tied up at the half as Dre's text alert went off.

"G-Ball, why the white bitch just text and ask how big my piece is," Dre said smiling.

"Text the bitch back my nigga and tell her what she wanna know," he stated as Dre did just that.

'9 inch with a curve,' Dre texted her.

'Um a curve makes it a challenge to deep throat LOL' she texted back, Dre showed Chris every text that came in.

'Everybody loves a challenge, are you ready for one?' he texted back.

'Absolutely! My sister said bring your friend, we think he's cute, what's his name?' she texted.

'Lil C, what room y'all in?' he texted ready to get down to business.

The girls sent their room number, told them to hurry and bring some MJ. They turned off the game, grabbed four bottles of Cîroc from the room's stock mini bar, the kush the girls asked for and left the room headed to the elevators.

Arriving on the floor, they found their room with no incident and were about to knock, but the door opened before they could. Lil Chris and Dre entered the room, greeted the girls, and took a seat on opposite beds. "Hi, I'm Kara," the young woman said sitting on the bed next to Lil Chris. He found her decent in the face with long brown hair. She had big breasts, thick thighs, and a nice ass to be a white girl, even though her body would definitely put shame to some of the black girls that he knew, her 34D-

28-36 was very enticing. She had to be the older of the two, Lil Chris thought as they engaged in small talk.

"Uhh, Kristen," Kara said to her sister who was sitting on Dre's lap kissing him. 'Uhh is right' Lil Chris thought, he was definitely going to holla at Dre about that when they got back to the room. Lil Chris blessed the bottle of liquor and cracked the seal before taking a gulp. He then took Kristen in, she was petite with a nice pair of 36Cs, she looked a lot like the beautiful Demi Lovato in the face.

"Can I have some?" Kara asked as he passed her a bottle for herself. 'Bitch must be crazy if she thinks she drinking out my bottle.' He thought.

Kristen went to the dresser drawer and pulled out a bottle with about 10 ecstasy pills and gave everybody one before taking one herself. Lil Chris had never done ecstasy before, but he was partying in another state, with potential pussy, and feeling good so he said fuck it, it's 2012 and tossed the Blue Toyota in his mouth and washed it down with a gulp of Cîroc. Ten minutes later, his body started to tingle. He didn't know what the fuck was going on, but it felt good.

"Dre roll that weed up," Chris said. He might as well do it all tonight. Dre rolled three pencil-sized blunts of kush, disconnected the smoke detector, put a wet towel under the door, and fired up one blunt after another. The girls were starting to get hot and removed pieces of their clothing. Lil Chris and Dre were shirtless and high as hell as Dre rapped a part of Young Jeezy's chorus on his song.

'Supa Freak' with 2 Chainz "Last night it was kush and Cîroc, I was supa geeked," he giggled, obviously the pills had him rolling hard.

Kara passed Lil Chris a bottled water that he drank down in two gulps. She then grabbed the remote and ordered a porno movie. Seeing Pinky's sexy azz go at it with Kelly Starr awoke a sleeping giant in Lil Chris. Just as he was about to make his move on Kara, she placed her hand on top of his hard dick and started massaging it through his shorts before whispering in his ear. "I wanna put this in my mouth and then I want you to fuck me with it," she said with a smile.

Lil Chris didn't hesitate as he scooted up in the bed after kicking his shoes off and had Kara unfasten his shorts, pull his fully erect member out of his boxers, and put his microphone to her mouth, but she wasn't testing, she was bobbing with a whole lot of spit. Lil Chris looked over to the other bed to see Kristen kneeling on the floor in front of Dre sucking his dick.

Lil Chris then looked back to Kara who's mouth was making love to his dick and smiled. This was his first time ever fuckin' with a white girl, not because he didn't like them, there just weren't many where he grew up. Chris could already tell the technique on her head game was different from the black chicks that he fucked with, not better, but different. Before he knew it, he had shot a load off and Kara swallowed everything that he had to offer.

Getting out of bed, she removed her bra, turned around and slid her boy shorts off, bending all the way over giving him a good view of her shaved pussy lips. Lil Chris grabbed the Magnum out of his pocket before taking the rest of his clothes off.

Kara got back in the bed and laid on her back, ready to be dominated. Lil Chris sucked on her neck, titties, and played with her pussy until it was nice and wet. Putting the rubber on, he slid halfway into her and instantly knew that she had a shot on her. He put her legs on his shoulders and stroked her with halfway quick strokes before he got a little bit deeper as she moaned out in ecstasy.

Turning her over, she got on all fours with her ass high in the air. He walked over to the dresser to get an X-pill while eyeing Kristen the whole time with his dick swinging from side to side. She licked her lips then put her finger in her mouth and sucked hard on it, letting him know that he could get it.

Getting back behind Kara, Lil Chris slid in her and she seemed to be even wetter. After a couple minutes of pounding, he spread her ass cheeks, soaked up some saliva on his index and middle finger, then he lubricated her asshole with it before sliding the X-pill down her rectum.

Ten minutes later, he was still hitting her from the back, but Kara turned up on him and got to bucking back hard causing him to lose his balance. Chris quickly got himself back in position and matched her aggression.

Sliding out, he laid down and Kara mounted and rode him reverse cowgirl style. Lil Chris looked over and saw Kristen on the same shit. 'These freaks planned this,' he thought as he smacked Kara's ass leaving a red hand print as she moaned. She was in a sexual trance as she turned around without taking him out of her, then she continued to ride him while facing him.

Lil Chris couldn't deny that Kara was riding the hell out of him. Speeding up, Kara was making it hard for him to try and suppress his nut. Not being able to take it anymore, he filled the rubber tip with his semen.

Going into the bathroom, he flushed the rubber, washed his hands, and looked at his reflection in the mirror knowing that he had just killed that pussy. The X-pill still had his dick brick hard. 'Round 2,' he thought heading out of the bathroom.

Seeing Dre fucking Kara on the bed he was just fucking Kristen on, he smiled and looked to the other bed to see Kristen waving him over with her finger. 'They definitely planned this,' he thought as he made his way over to her. She immediately started sucking him off. Now, she had some good head, but Kara's was better. Grabbing another rubber, he slid in her pussy from the back. She was just as wet as Kara, but her pussy was a little tighter. Bending her in every position known to man, he killed that pussy too. They then switched back and went at it some more. Little Chris and Dre finally made it to their room a little after 3am. 'If this is what Atlanta has to offer, I can't wait until tomorrow,' Little Chris thought as he dozed off back to sleep.

中

CHAPTER SIX

The next morning, Lil Chris was awakened by his cellphone's ring tone: Flawless and Snakebite's 'Mil nigaa alert'.

"Yeah," he answered still halfway asleep.

"Let's go get you fitted for yo grill," Legacy said as soon as he picked up.

Hearing this, Lil Chris got some energy from somewhere as he sat up in bed. "Give me ten minutes," he said, hanging up and heading for the shower. After washing off last night's session, he handled his hygiene, and got dressed. He put on a pair of grey Akoo jean shorts, a white short-sleeved button-up made by Akoo, and a pair of white, grey and black Air Max 95s with the Air Max 360 bubble. Putting his chain on his neck, and his watch on his wrist, he stuffed 15 bands in his pocket, grabbed his phone, and put his all grey Miami Heat fitted hat on his head.

Seeing Dre still asleep on the other bed snoring, he smiled knowing his friend was exhausted as he left the room.

Walking into the lobby, he spotted Legacy sitting in a chair reading the latest Jet magazine. Seeing him, she got up and hugged him. "You look nice, what's that, T. I. line?" she asked speaking of the Akoo outfit he had on that rap superstar T. I. brought out.

"Yeah, you look nice too," he smiled. Legacy had on a long white spaghetti strapped dress by Dior that came down to her ankles. She had her hair in a bun, white Christian Dior oval sunglasses sat atop of her head. White Dior sandals adorned her pedicured feet, white Kate Spade tote on her arm, and a diamond pendent around her neck that added a touch to her class.

Heading out of the hotel, Legacy sent the valet to get the truck. A couple minutes later, the truck pulled up. As the valet hopped out, she tipped him. They got in and pulled off after Legacy pulled her sunglasses over her eyes.

"What Tay on?" Lil Chris asked adjusting his seat to lean back.

"She went down to the pool in a skimpy azz two piece, got her titties hanging out and damn near a whole ass cheek," Legacy laughed.

"She clownin' ain't she?" he said joining in on the laughter.

"She talkin' bout that's her exercise for the day, bitch who you think you foolin' she knows she tryna catch," she smiled.

"If Black was out and she was fuckin' with him, she knows she would've never tried that shit," he smiled.

"Right," Legacy said looking over her shoulder while merging onto the freeway headed to Buckhead.

"Leggy, if I buy five of dem thangs, how much you gon' tax me?" he asked seriously.

"You tryna go hard lil nigga ain't you," she smiled." Well, I get 'em for 23 and that's a super plug, so I'd only charge you that, but when I go see my plug, I'mma see how many I gotta buy to get the numbers to drop a little more," she continued. Lil Chris sat quiet for a minute while doing some mental math in his head. "Alright, how bout when we get back to the Mil, a couple days later, I'll give you a hunnid and you add that to what you got, so when you go holla at dude and present that offer, it makes it that much sweeter," he said logically.

Legacy did the numbers in her head and said "Bet." She figured that by taking his money, hers, and Train's she was sure to get some type of deal, being that it would be at least 25 kilos she would be buying at one time.

Pulling up to Exclusive jewelry store, there was a few niggas out there sitting on their whips playing music and messing with chicks.

"You got yo heat wit you?" he asked. He had too much money on him and didn't know how A-Town niggas got down, so he had to be prepared.

"Always," Legacy said and passed him her .40cal in the .380 frame out of her purse. She was allowed to travel with her gun because she was licensed to carry it. Needless to say, Lil Chris wasn't. Tucking it on his hip, they exited the car, and walked towards the shop. Lil Chris tried to return every mean mug he got on his way in, he knew most of the stares were for Legacy because they probably wanted to talk to her but didn't know if he was her man or not.

Getting buzzed in, they approached the counter, and were greeted by a white woman wearing plenty of jewelry. Telling her why they were there, she asked them to please wait while she called who they needed to see. Legacy and Lil Chris looked around the store while they waited. They looked at most of the pictures on the wall of various rappers, singers, actors, actresses, and people that they did not know with a man they presumed to be the owner. There were pictures with T. I., Trae The Truth, Big Boi from Outkast, Monica, 2Chainz, Soulja Boy, Rocko, Gucci Mane, Young Jeezy, and Kim Zolciak from the Real Housewives of Atlanta, to name a few.

Walking to the counter, Lil Chris fixed his eyes on a black watch with big black diamonds in it.

"That's a Dunamis watch," the white lady said walking over to see what he was looking at.

"How much is it?" he asked looking in her face now, she was really pretty.

"That one there is $8,500," she said.

Lil Chris decided he had to have one in due time as the man in the pictures walked up to where they were standing and whispered something to the woman who nodded her head and walked off.

"Hi, I'm Frankie the owner and dental technician here," the white man said with a smile. He was about 6'2 in his mid-40s, balding and wore Armani slacks, shoes, tie, and shirt that was rolled up at the sleeves. The Audemar wrist watch on his wrist was so icy that it almost blinded Lil Chris and Legacy. "How may I help you?" he added with his hand extended, the man exuded money.

Lil Chris and Legacy introduced themselves with a hand shake and Lil Chris explained what he was trying to do and what he wanted to spend. After that, he was led into the back of the shop where Frankie washed his hands, put on a pair of latex gloves, and did what was required to prep for the golds. They talked in between him opening and closing his mouth and Frankie seemed to be real smooth to him. After about 20 minutes, he was done and told Lil Chris he'd have to at least put down five grand on his tab and the rest would have to be paid before the procedure was started. That wasn't a problem for Lil Chris. Walking back out front, he put 7gees on his bill in cash.

"Be here tomorrow at 8:00am," Frankie said.

"Alright what them custom pieces running?" he asked seriously.

"Depends on what you want Lil C," Frankie shot back.

"I want something that represents what you see when you see me," he explained. He decided that he would let Frankie's creativity take over.

"Your busting my balls here pal," Frankie said chuckling. "Give me 15 grand and I got you," he added.

"I'll tell you what, I'll give you 20 for you to put some extra D's in my shit and an extra 5 gees if you can have one of your jewelry techs finish it by the time you put my grill in," he bargained.

Frankie thought about this for a minute. He knew that trying to have the jewelry done by tomorrow was cutting it close, but he was in the business for the money and didn't mind working a little overtime to get it, he even had some equipment at his home for times like this.

"You know what I like you, so I'll tell you what, put 5 grand down now and I got you," Frankie said running his hand over his bald head.

Lil Chris dug into his pocket, counted it out and put it on the counter. Getting his receipt for his grill, he shook Frankie's hand and him and Legacy left the shop and hopped in the truck.

"That muthafucka's so crooked but he's also smart at the same time," Legacy smiled while driving off.

"Why you say that?" he asked curiously.

"Cause how the fuck can you go in there and drop that kinda money, you ain't got no job or check stubs. He probably buying most of those diamonds on the black market and when niggas come in there tossing all that money around he gotta hook them receipts up like they made payment to avoid the Feds investigating him and other niggas, I know the receipts never say what you actually paid, I guarantee you that. Did you see his face when you offered him that extra 5 gees, ain't no way he was turning that down, you gotta think, everybody who go in there got money, so they're more than likely doin' the same thing you did, and he's probably buying a new Benz every year just off the extra money that niggas spending with him. Not to mention, he doin' shit for celebrities. I ain't mad at him thou, that is the game, and I know that muthafucka richer than rich wearing that quarter of a million-dollar watch," she stated as they pulled up in front of the hotel, gave the keys of the truck to a valet, and went inside.

Legacy told Lil Chris to be down in the lobby in 20 minutes, so they could go pick up the cars, he agreed, and they went to their rooms.

∞

Ken stood in the bathroom over the toilet squeezing his dick. Every time he pissed, he moaned in agony, so by squeezing himself and letting a few squirts out at a time, he was able to piss a little better without breaking down and crying. "That dirty bitch don' burnt me," he said out loud to himself with his eyes closed tightly. He had been fucking big booty Rudy for the last two days raw and caught the clap.

He woke up this morning, went to use the bathroom and noticed something in his draws that he regarded as some cum that leaked out from when he was fucking Rudy, but after he tried to piss, he realized that it really was discharge, and he was burning. He thought about going to the clinic, but he'd be too embarrassed to show his face in front of the building because then everybody would know he had some type of issue and fuck up his credibility with the ladies before he had one if word got out. Instead, he tried not to drink a lot of liquid, so he wouldn't have to piss as much.

He thought about going to confront Rudy about his condition, but he didn't want her to get mad and stop letting him hit that, so he quickly dismissed that thought but he told himself that he wouldn't hit that without a rubber again. After he finished using the bathroom, he rolled up some tissue and tucked it in front of his draws and left it there to catch the discharge. Hearing the phone ring, he quickly washed his hands and went to grab it.

"Yeah?" he answered.

"Ken can I get six of 'em for the fifty?" the woman asked.

"Man," Ken said wondering why everybody wanted a deal.

"Come on baby I been shopping with you all day," the woman said after sensing he was going to say no.

"Aight Dee, meet me at the station," he said ending the call. Ken had been having damn near all of his clientele meet him at the gas station on 91st and Brown Deer. Business had been going good for him and he had 4 gees in the safety of his Air Jordan shoe box and still clockin'. His phone rang again, and he had that action meet him in the same place. Grabbing the work and weed he needed, he put the pistol on his waistline, and grabbed his keys.

Hoping in to the car he put a CD in that he burned himself and put on "Ricky da Ruler" by Tay 2 Cold featuring Petti Hendrix and hit the volume button up a few notches on the three twelves and pulled off. Seeing some girls standing on the corner by the bus stop, he pulled up, turned the music down and yelled out of the window.

"Ay Rudy, come ride wit me for a minute," he said as he turned the music back up. She got in and he pulled off to go catch his action.

∞

They took a taxi to the train station to get the whips, so they wouldn't have to drive three cars around. Now they were on their way to see Legacy and Chante's mother; she lived in Stone Mountain, Georgia.

Legacy pulled up on Bridle Bluff banging "With the Shits" by Songwritaz. Lil Chris was right behind her. Pulling up in front of her mom's house, they got out, and went into the house.

"Hey mama," Legacy and Chante said in unison while rushing over to hug her.

"My girls, how my babies doin? "she asked elated to see them. Mary hadn't seen her daughters since last Thanksgiving.

Lil Chris looked on and saw that Legacy and Chante were a splitting image of their mom - even in her early 5Os, she still looked good.

"Who are they, y'all boyfriends?" Mary asked, thinking that they looked a little young.

"Naw ma, this Christopher Junior and that's his friend, Andre," Chante explained.

Hearing the Man's name that caused her so much pain, she felt some type a way about that, but her facial expression never changed. She looked at Lil Chris and reached up to remove his hat to get a better look at him.

"Yeah, you yo' father's child, you look just like him," Mary said smiling while giving him a hug, then she placed his hat back on crookedly, turned around and mumbled, "with his no-good azz," thinking that Lil Chris didn't hear her, but he did. He just smiled and shook his head. "Hey baby, how you doin," she added, talking to Dre.

"I'm alright, how about you?" Dre said then chuckled because she sounded so much like the lady in the movie 'Norbit' when she said 'How you doin'.

"I'm fine," she responded.

"What's that smell, Ma?" Legacy asked smelling the soul food lingering from the kitchen.

"Oh, that's some baked chicken with barbecue sauce, cabbage, mac 'n' cheese, and cornbread. I got homemade apple pies in the oven and ice cream in the deep freezer, now y'all help ya 'self. Jeff be here after a while," she said going into the living room.

Jeff was Legacy, Chante, and Lil Chris' brother and at age 34, he was the oldest of Mary's four children. Their other brother Michael would've been the next oldest, but he was killed 14 years ago on Mary's front porch in Milwaukee. Mary was devastated by the tragedy, so she moved to Georgia, and never returned to Milwaukee.

Jeff, Michael, Chante, and of course Lil Chris all shared the same father, but none of them knew where he was, and neither did Mary or Claire, Lil Chris' mom. Legacy was a product of Mary's next marriage, but he died of cancer 7 years ago leaving Mary a widow.

Everybody fixed themselves a plate, said grace, and sat around the table eating and laughing as Jeff walked in smiling.

"Hey bro," Legacy said getting up to hug him, Chante did the same.

"What's happenin in here?" Jeff said surveying the room with his 6'4 frame, stopping on Lil Chris, he paused. Jeff knew those features anywhere because he had them as well, big nose and all. He had not seen Lil Chris since he was a little boy. "What's good lil bro?" Jeff said walking over, shaking his hand, and one arm hugging him.

"Chillin man, what up wit you?" Lil Chris said, he remembered Jeff, but not vividly. A part of the reason why Lil Chris hadn't seen him was because he did a twelve-year bid in a Federal Penitentiary for drug charges. Prior to his incarceration, Jeff was out in the city of Atlanta having plenty money from selling dope, but he was snatched from his fame because another nigga couldn't hold his weight and turned state.

The hardest thing for Jeff was trying to teach his son to be a man from behind those walls. Jeff vowed to do something different with his life because he had promised his son that once he got released, he'd never be away from him ever again.

Taking initiative, he enrolled in a welding program offered at the penitentiary and developed a knack and a passion for it, and since his release 3 years ago, he had a job working at a welding plant in Columbus, Georgia making $26 an hour. The other part was because they lived in different states and due to Jeff's parole agreement, he was not allowed to leave the state just yet. Lil Chris introduced Jeff to Dre before the two brothers got reacquainted with each other for a while.

"That's yo El Camino out there?" Jeff asked skeptically, not because of the car, but because he knew all too well how he got the car, and that was the 'Hustle'.

"Yep, you like it?" he smiled

"Yeah, it's hard, bro, let me see the inside though," Jeff said.

Lil Chris told Dre he'd be right back and followed Jeff outside. He knew Jeff did some time in prison, so he hoped that this conversation wasn't about him getting his life together because if it was, Jeff could save it because Lil Chris didn't wanna hear it at all. "Let me see yo keys," Jeff continued while holding his hand out prepared to catch them. Lil Chris was skeptical about giving him his keys because that car was his most prized possession and he didn't know what Jeff was on, but he tossed them anyway.

'If bro fuck my whip up, I'm gon' have to hurt his azz,' Lil Chris thought as they walked towards the car. They both got in with Jeff behind the wheel, he started it and hit the gas a few times.

"Yeah, this a runner," he said after hearing the clean flow of the dual exhaust, then he cut the car off. A sigh of relief left Lil Chris after he cut the car off. "Pop the hood," Lil Chris said getting out of the car and pulling the hood up with Jeff standing right next to him.

"You did that," Jeff said seeing the all-chrome engine as Lil Chris smiled proudly. "You got a stash spot in the whip," he added

"Nope," Lil Chris said thinking here we go with the bullshit, he was just about to tell Jeff to save the lecture, but Jeff spoke first.

"Don't you think you need one?" Jeff voiced his concern.

Lil Chris nodded his head in agreement. "Check this out bro, I'm not on no preaching stuff or nothing like that, but I don't wanna see you make the same mistakes in the game that I did, I ain't in the game no more, but I'mma try my best to help you avoid any situations that you can possibly get into. Obviously, you already all in, and I support you being your own man, because I can't tell you how to live your life, how could I? I can't, you gotta make your own decisions and be smart about what you're doing. Now, I'm not in the game, but you can always call me for whatever and I do mean anything, I'mma leave you my number, so don't ever hesitate to call, we ain't strangers' nigga," Jeff said shaking his hand and one arm hugging him.

"I appreciate that bro, I really do," Lil Chris said honestly after breaking their embrace. They exchanged numbers and locked them in their phones. "That's you over there, huh?" Lil Chris asked pointing to Jeff's 2010 silver Buick

Lacrosse sitting on 22" chrome wheels with the black 4" lip. The mirror tinted windows really set the car off.

"You already know a Milwaukee nigga love his car," Jeff smiled as they shared a laugh while walking back towards the house.

"Ay, you gotta always remember that the only financial security that you will ever have is the one that you create for yourself," Jeff said.

Lil Chris listened every time knowledge was being dropped because you never knew when it would apply to you and you would have to utilize it. Besides, you were never too old or wise to learn something.

They went back inside the house, chopped it up with the family, ate, and enjoyed each other's company for a little while longer.

∞

"Man, why you don't wanna go to Magic City?" Dre asked visibly upset.

"Cause nigga, when I step up in there, I wanna be turning heads and throwing bread. I get my grill tomorrow, we'll go the day after that. I didn't wanna go to this club, but I wasn't about to let my sisters go out by themselves," Lil Chris said pulling up to the light. They were headed to Club Crucial in Bankhead,

Atlanta which was popularly owned by rap superstar T. I.

"I feel you, I just can 't wait," Dre said rubbing his hands together.

The club's lights could be seen from afar. Lil Chris turned up "Airplane Mode" By B Justice featuring Travis Romell and pressed the gas pedal a little harder. When they pulled into the parking lot, Lil Chris got amped up. He swerved from right to left, stopping briefly only for people to see the big rims spinning. He had Luke's 'Peep Show' playing on his TVs. Niggas were giving him head nods like they knew him, and women were staring him down. Sure, they were fine and thick in all the right places, but he could hear a snake hissing two miles away. Even with that thought in mind, he saw someone that he couldn't pass up on.

"Excuse me shawty, can I have a minute of your time?" he asked in his best Atlanta slang while pulling up next to the woman who was walking through the parking lot. She was light-skinned with long hair and had Christina Millian facial features. She wore a sheer dress, high heels, and had a clutch in her hand. The dress material was so thin that every time she took a step; her bodacious ass shook. 'She either has a thong on or no panties at all,' Lil Chris thought, he wanted to reach out and touch it, but he didn't want to be disrespectful.

The woman turned her head and said, "boy, how old is you?" with one of the prettiest smiles he'd ever seen.

"Seventeen, but that's merely a number," he said smiling while driving on the side of her.

"I got a little brother your age, I'm 27 with a daughter, and I need a man who don 't play games," she stated

"Well here I go, they say anything that is worth something is worth waiting on, so this is your opportunity to get me while I'm young." Lil Chris ran his script, seeing her smile, he pushed the envelope further. "What's yo name sweetheart, you are too fine to be out here by ya 'self," he added putting emphasis on the word fine.

"Stacy, and yours?" she asked.

"Lil C," he said thinking that he was finally getting somewhere just as a red Maserati sitting on 24" chrome rims pulled up on the other side of the road.

"Get in the car, Stacy," the man in the car said. Lil C could barely see him, so he knew he was short.

"I'm through fuckin' with you Miles, go get the bitch who's face you was all up in," Stacy said, never losing her stride.

"Don't play with me, Stacy," Miles responded.

"You heard what the fuck I said," she retorted as the dude stopped the car, hopped out, and walked over to her. Lil Chris and Dre looked on in amusement. The man said what he had to say, they went back and forth for a minute, then Stacy gave in and walked to his car. She looked at Lil Chris, who winked at her and she responded with a shaky wave. He knew if the circumstances were different, he'd have her.

"Say lil partna, you can gon' ' head bout yo bidness, you can't afford her no way," Miles said looking towards Lil Chris. "Ay man, this ain't what you want, that's between y'all and I'd advise you to keep me the fuck up out it cause you don 't know what the fuck I can buy, nigga," Lil Chris said checking him, he was slightly offended at how Miles came at him.

"What, nigga I'd advise you not to be advising me shit, yo money ain't long enough," Miles said.

Lil Chris threw his car in park and hopped out with Dre who had the pistol in his hand and Lil Chris with the bandz in his hands that he had in his pocket.

"See I was tryna be a player, but I see yo punk azz ain't one, so I'mma treat you like the bitch you is," Lil Chris said and threw the money on the car which slide and hit Miles in the face. "Now get the fuck up outta here before a muthafucka see what yo life worth, Kevin Hart lookin' azz nigga," Lil Chris said menacingly as Dre came around the car and flashed the heat just as the Monte Carlo rolled up with Legacy and Chante hopping out, guns in hand.

"You good, bro?" they asked in unison ready to pop something.

"Hell yeah, just tryna move this lame azz nigga around before I do something to him," Lil Chris said watching the Maserati as it sped away. After Miles saw the guns, he thought better of trying to defend his honor, hopped in his car got up out of there. "Young and gettin' it for real nigga!" Lil Chris continued with a yell. "Sis, this bitch azz nigga just blew me with all that hoe shit, let's just get up outta here, grab something to eat, and retire for the night, I promise I'll make it up to y'all," he added, visibly upset. They agreed and went to get something to eat at Krystal's where Lil Chris told them the entire story about what happened at the club. After that, they went back to the hotel and called it a night.

CHAPTER SEVEN

The next day, Legacy was awakened by the hotel's front desk calling her room. She had requested a wake-up call for 6:30am and they were letting her know that it was that time. She sat up and yawned while stretching. Making her way to the bathroom, she used it, and then showered. After showering, she handled her hygiene, oiled her body down, and dressed in an identical Dior outfit she wore the previous day, only this time it was black. Picking her phone up off the dresser, she called Lil Chris.

"Sup, Sis?" he answered.

"Oh, you up?" she asked surprised.

"Yeah, I'm ready," he responded, he had been waiting years for this day.

"Okay, I'll meet you down in the lobby in five minutes," she said before hanging up. Transferring everything from her white bag into her black one, she left the room. Exiting the elevator, she walked towards the lobby to see Lil Chris and Dre sitting down talking.

"Oh, my goodness," Dre said under his breath when he saw Legacy, she was secretly his dream girl.

"I see you ready to go get the golds, huh?" she smiled. "You already know," he responded elated. "Dre tryna get a piece made too," he added.

"It's about time you spend some of that money, I know you got plenty of it," Legacy said playfully pushing him.

"I spend that money, I got my Magnum gettin done right now, it just wasn't done before we came down here, I definitely spend it on what I like and who I like," Dre secretly flirted with her.

"Okay nigga, get out here then, the sun is bright, so shine shine," Legacy smiled, she totally missed Dre's flirting, or she disregarded it as they left the hotel, got the truck from the valet, and headed to Buckhead, Atlanta.

Pulling up outside of Exclusive Jewelry, Lil Chris passed the pistol to Dre and he tucked in his waistline and they exited the truck.

Getting buzzed in, they were met at the door by Frankie and the white woman who worked the counter. Lil Chris was escorted to the back after he paid the remaining money on his tab as Legacy and Dre looked around.

∞

"Ken, I got two hunnid, what can you do for me?" the hype said as soon as Ken answered.

"I got something for you, Greg, meet me at the station," Ken said after recognizing the voice, then he hung up. Greg was this dude that Ken went to school with pops. Ken didn't judge him though, he knew there was a fiend in every family. After throwing on some clothes, he grabbed his keys, sack, phone, and pistol. Hopping in the car, he pulled off. A few minutes later, he pulled into the gas station on 95th and Brown Deer bumping Phatboy's "Trained to Go" and parked by the pay phone.

"Where the fuck is this nigga at?" Ken said out loud to himself. Then he spotted Greg coming across the street.

"What's up, Ken," Greg said getting in looking nervous as hell. Ken disregarded his look as he just needed his fix.

"Shit chillin," Ken said as he passed him 23 dime bags without getting the money first. Greg cuffed the bags, handed Ken a wad of bills, then he hopped out of the car. Something didn't sit right with Ken, so he quickly flipped through the bills and counted out $123. Ken then stuck his head out of the window.

"Greg! Greg!" Ken yelled, but Greg acted like he didn't hear him and quickened his pace. Ken dropped the gear shift into drive and smashed out into traffic, almost hitting another car. Seeing Greg run in between some apartment buildings, he stormed down 95th Street, made a right in the alley, quickly threw the car into park, and hopped out as Greg tried to hop the fence. Ken ran up behind him and grabbed both his legs and yanked him off the fence, making him hit the ground with a hard crash. Greg was hurt briefly until his hype intuition kicked in.

When a hype felt like they were in danger, they'd go to great lengths to get out of any situation, even kill somebody, just to assure they had their fix. Ken saw his opportunity to get his dope back, so he reached down and tried to go in Greg's pockets. Unbeknowingly to Ken, Greg was laying there playing possum, soon as he felt Ken's hand by his pocket, he turned on his back, sat up, and before Ken could react, he was hit in his eye with a right jab. Ken stumbled back and held his left eye which immediately

began to swell. Greg had already started running down the alley as fast as he could. Ken snatched the .380 from his waistline and trained it on Greg with his good eye and fired two shots. One hit a parked car and the other hit Greg square in the ass, causing him to fall on the ground.

"Ahhh!" he yelled as Ken ran over to him and pointed the gun at him while he laid on the ground.

"I should kill yo dope fiend azz for doin that hoe azz shit," Ken said then kicked him twice in the side, something like what he saw on Menace to Society.

"I'm...sorry...man," Greg said in between coughs.

"Not sorry as you gon' be if you move," Ken stated while going in his pockets and taking his dope back and the rest of Greg's money. "If you tell somebody I shot you, I'm gon' kill you and Lil Greg. And if you get on some slick shit, I'mma have somebody else do it," he added then kicked him again before running back to the car and pulling off. Ken would learn another valuable lesson, get the money first, count it, and then give the product.

∞

Boss stood by the phones enjoying his conversation so much that he wasn't even paying attention to the new inmate who had just come to the pod.

"Send me some pictures too, and don 't smack the MC either," he laughed still unaware of the guy walking up behind him staring.

"I got you, and I will definitely not wreck the car, I don't wanna know how you'd act after that," Legacy giggled. "You have one-minute left," the voice service said.

"Aight baby, have fun and I love you," he said seriously.

"Okay, I love you too, call me later," she said before hanging up.

Boss hung up the phone feeling good about Legacy enjoying herself, she had been a soldier to him on the streets and since he had been down. He knew it was stressful at times because he was away, but he was glad she was doing things to occupy her time. In the county jail, you can only have two visits a week and she'd come every weekend, leaving one day for his mom to visit as she often did, sometimes with Train.

He really loved Legacy, he just hoped things never took a turn like how most niggas' girls do them during their man 's incarceration with all the lying, games, and disloyalty. He did not ever want to go through that shit and he wouldn't tolerate it by any means, he was a man first before anything. Walking back to his cell, he heard somebody call his name.

"Boss, what's good my nigga, I knew that was you," the Man smiled. Boss looked at the man and smiled back.

"Wayne, what up cuz?" Boss asked, shaking his hand and one arm hugging him. Wayne was 6'5, 225 pounds, brolic, and black as the night with dreads, he was Boss's older cousin who he had not seen in a while.

"Shit, I was hoping I was gon' run into yo azz down here, look cuz, I want to let you know that I appreciate how you looked out for sis, I…" Wayne was interrupted by Boss speaking.

"Cuz, don't even mention that, just know she family too, and you already know what that mean to me," Boss said letting him know that he didn't need to say anything else about the situation that occurred, which was also the reason why he was locked up and the case was still pending. Wayne got the hint and changed the subject.

You right," Wayne said. He and Boss's fathers were brothers.

"I thought you moved to Houston with Debra before I got locked up," Boss said as they walked to the nearest table and sat down.

"I did, but I been back for a couple months now, me and the bitch split because I got caught fuckin off, them bitches thick as cornbread in Texas," Wayne smiled trying to make light of the situation. Boss nodded his head knowing how his cousin felt because he knew how close of a relationship he had with Debra.

"That's fucked up cuz, but what the fuck you doin in here?" he questioned.

"Got caught with some dope and some percs," Wayne said looking around to make sure nobody was in ear shot because niggas in the County Jail be nosey as hell, snakes, quick to jump on a nigga case to free themselves, but they all claim to be real street niggas, so if anybody was looking like they were listening, Wayne would've surely addressed it.

"How much?" he inquired.

"Two zips and twenty percs," Wayne said still upset with himself for the mistake of getting caught.

"Damn, you should've got the fuck up outta there," Boss said.

"I did, but I was droppin the shit off on 5th and Locust, and you know the police station right around the corner, so it ain't take no time for them to corner me and take a nigga down, it wasn't even my whip thou, but I'm glad that I ain't have that heat on me because I definitely woulda got trigger locked," Wayne said as Boss shook his head in agreement.

"When you start fuckin with that dope anyway? I been tryna get you to get down since we were younger, and you wouldn't fuck around for shit," Boss said only loud enough for him to hear.

"I couldn't get no gig in Houston, the nigga next door to me was doing good, so I bought a split, and started doing my thang that way," Wayne said simply as Boss nodded.

"You got a lawyer yet?" he asked.

"Nope, I ain't even holla at nobody yet," Wayne stated. "I'm finna hop on line in a minute and have my lawyer come see you and give me the number that you want on and I'rnrna have my lady get the line on for you, aight," he explained as his cell mate Larry came out of the room and noticed him sitting at the table with a nigga he'd never seen before in the pod. More importantly, he hadn't ever seen Boss in the dayroom except for chow, going or coming from the shower, going or coming from visits, the second half of any sports game, and using the phone. But never sitting down talking to a nigga. Knowing this, Larry slid over there to get a feel for what was going on.

"Yep, that's one hunnid cuz," Wayne said shaking his hand showing his appreciation.

"What's that then, Boss," Larry said walking to the table while watching Wayne as he sat down.

He didn't care how big he was, he was never the one to hoe up in any situation, if Boss went, he went. Boss instantly peeped Larry's demeanor and put things to rest.

"I'm coolin, this my blood cousin, Wayne Wayne this my boy, Larry," Boss introduced the two. "What's good, fam," Wayne said with his hand extended. If Boss introduced them, he knew that Larry must be good peoples.

"Chillin bro," Larry said shaking his hand, he was now at ease, but he was ready to get down with Boss if he had to, and Boss now knew that.

"Cuz, you still got that MC on dem sixes?" Wayne asked switching subjects. Boss wasn't with that jacking shit, he felt like whatever you were doing, the real would show, besides, Larry knew nothing about the life he lived on the streets, but after what he had just displayed, Boss didn't mind giving a little insight as to who he really was. However, Boss wouldn't put him in his business like that.

"Hell yeah, but my lady put it on eights now," Boss said nonchalantly while catching the look from Larry out of his peripheral vision.

"I know you got some flicks on it, let me see 'em," Wayne said knowing he had pictures of the car. Boss smiled although he was deep in thought, then he went to go get the pictures, "Lil cuz was out there eatin' good, lil Fam," Wayne added talking to Larry while Boss was walking away. He had no idea that Larry didn't know that since him and Boss seemed to be tight, he was just proud of his lil cousin's success.

Boss came back and sat at the table with five pictures and handed them to Wayne. One of them was a side view of the car displaying the 28" gold Asanti rims, one with the trunk open displaying the audio equipment, one of the navy-blue Ostrich leather interior seats that also displayed several TVs, another from the front showing the custom gold Asanti Billet Grille, and the last one was a picture with the hood up showing the engine.

"On my mama, this bitch smakin'," Wayne said after going through the pictures. "Look at this muthafucka Larry, that muthafucka wet, ain't it?" Wayne continued while passing the pictures to Larry as Boss watched him go through them. Larry hadn't seen any of Boss's pictures before and Boss never asked to see his. Larry looked at the pictures, looked at Boss, then back to the pictures.

"Yeah, it is wet," he responded, sliding the pictures back to Boss before getting up to leave.

"What the fuck he on?" Wayne snapped slightly offended at how he slid the photos back to Boss. Wayne was rising from his seat about to go holla at Larry when Boss stopped him. "He good, I just never told him how I was livin' out there, you know me. My silence speaks volumes, I'll holla at him later," Boss

said calming Wayne down. Wayne was five years older than Boss at the age of 28, but he was still a hothead.

"I was finna introduce that lil nigga to a knuckle sandwich," Wayne stated seriously while kissing his fists, making Boss laugh.

"Chill out my nigga, you a fool thou. Let me hop on line and handle this business for you, write that

number down and bring it over," Boss said before walking over to the phone, picking it up, and calling

Legacy.

∞

"Bite down, now open wide, bite down again. Does everything feel normal?" Frankie asked while turning the overhead light off.

"Um huh," Lil Chris mumbled.

"Alright, we're done. You may be numb for a while and experience some sensitivity to cold and hot things for the first week or so, but it should go away after that. Here's a bottle of Tylenol for any pain you may have after the numbing subsides, here you go," Frankie said passing him the bottle and a mirror as he removed his surgical mask, gloves, and washed his hands. "Also, no solid foods for a week," he added.

Lil Chris looked in the mirror at his swollen mouth, then he smiled and realized the drilling and pain wasn't all in vain as the 10 on top, 10 on bottom gold teeth with the VS2 diamonds all through it shined. The $25,000 he had put in his mouth was well worth it.

"Gargle this and spit it in the sink," Frankie said handing him a cup with some type of solution in it after he got out of the dental chair. After doing that, he looked back into the mirror and it seemed his diamonds were shining even harder.

"Brush and floss often to prevent that smelly breath and your teeth from rotting, and you should also get your teeth cleaned every four to six months to keep them healthy, now let's go get your chain" he added smiling. Frankie stayed up most of the night and was proud about the work that he did, also the money that he was going to make from doing it. Walking back out front, he saw Legacy get up and walk over to him.

"Let me see, Bro," she smiled. When he opened his mouth, the diamonds glistened to their own light. "Damn nigga, yo shit shining hard as hell, dem hoes gon' eat you alive," she continued before walking off as her phone rang. A moment later, Frankie came back with his chain.

"You said come up with something that represents what I see when I see you, and when I see you, I see money, so check this out," Frankie said passing him the necklace. Lil Chris stared at the 26" gold chain and charm of a gold 4-inch coin with his image on the coin wearing shades. You could even see the waves in his hair on the coin with VS2 diamonds all around it. But the thing that caught his attention the most, was at the top of the coin where it had the words 'C-Money'. Lil Chris was amazed at the piece and chain, unbeknowingly to Frankie, he had just given Lil Chris his new nickname.

"Frankie, you did yo thang with this here, I'm at a loss of words right now," Lil Chris said while wiping his mouth because he was still numb, and he didn't know if he was still slabbing before he handed Frankie the rest of his bill.

"I'm glad you like it my friend," Frankie said while walking to the back-security room to ring up the necklace.

"Let me see your mouth, honey, " the white woman who worked the counter said. Lil Chris opened his mouth and gave her a smile. "You look very handsome," she added.

Lil Chris faced the full-length mirror, put his chain on, and admired his 6'0ft,190-pounds athletic build frame with his brown skin, and 360 waves. He knew that he was too much for them nigga's and three much for them hoes, his smile just set everything off, he thought as Dre walked up.

"My nigga you icy as a bitch. I put in to get my piece done too, they said my shit gon' be done the day after tomorrow, then let's hit Magic City and jack on a bitch," Dre said shaking his friend's hand.

"You already know my nigga," Lil Chris said turning back towards the mirror. "From now on thou, I'm goin' by the name CMoney, that's what my neck says," he added showing Dre the coin. "Damn, dude cold as a bitch," Dre said elated as Frankie came back and gave CMoney his receipt. CMoney thanked him and they left the store.

"My nigga, that shit we did to Tay got over 90,000 views already," Dre showed him his phone.

"That shit crazy," CMoney smiled seeing Chante smack herself in the face with whip cream. "I was talkin' to Kristen and her and Kara want us to come through on the late-night tip," Dre smiled knowing what the night would consist of with the two boss freaks.

"Who is them hoes?" Legacy asked nosily.

"Damn, cut the water on cuz, she nosey as hell and I need her off my lawn," CMoney said laughing. "We could do that thou," he added talking to Dre.

"I'm just saying, ain't nothing but legs open on the late-night tip," she giggled

"You clowin', pull up to that Shell gas station so I can get some ice because my mouth swollen as a bitch," CMoney stated from the backseat.

"Alright, we bout to go get Tay and go to Greenbriar Mall and do a little shopping," Legacy said. "I'm wit that, but please let me get some ice first," CMoney said making everybody laugh out loud.

CHAPTER EIGHT

Two days later, CMoney was feeling good except for a little sensitivity that he was experiencing, but other than that, he was good. He had just gotten out of the shower and handled his hygiene. They were going to Magic City tonight, so he started getting dressed.

CMoney dressed in triple black True Religion shorts, a red short-sleeved True Religion button-up, and his black and red patent leather retro #11 Air Jordan's. Putting his gold Brietling wrist watch on, his all black Milwaukee Bucks fitted hat on his head, he stuffed 20 bandz in his pocket, put his pistol on his hip, grabbed his phone, and wiped his teeth off with his jewelry rag before putting it in his back pocket.

Lastly, he put his chain on which complemented his ensemble well. He and Dre brought 100K apiece to Atlanta with them and CMoney had a little over 20 left, not including the 20 in his pocket.

Dre came out of the bathroom wearing dark indigo blue jean True religion shorts, royal blue short-sleeved True Religion button-up, and his black, royal blue, and white Nike Air Penny #1's. He had an all royal blue Orlando Magic fitted hat on, his 26" gold chain with the Baking soda box charm in VS2 diamonds that he just got from Frankie that day, VS2 diamond buggers in his ears, and his gold Brietling wrist watch with the VS2 diamond bezel, also with 20 bandz in his pocket, he was ready to do the damn thing tonight.

"My nigga, I'm finna act a fool tonight," Dre said enthusiastically shaking CMoney's hand.

"You already know!" he said smiling while pulling out his phone to call Legacy.

"We ready bro, we'll meet y'all in the lobby in five minutes," she said ending the call, before applying her lip gloss to her full lips in the bathroom mirror. Legacy didn't hold back tonight, she wore a black single-sleeve form fitting dress by Roberto Cavalli that flattered her hourglass figure. She wore black calf tie open toe 3-inch heels made by Cavalli, a Diamond Time watch by Cavalli, and a black clutch also be Cavalli. The gold diamond pendant around her neck set her outfit off perfectly. She then ran a comb through her freshly permed wrap that hung to the middle of her back. She finished up and left out of the bathroom to see Chante in a sleeveless leopard print button-up blouse, red mini skirt all made by Dolce&Gabbana, which hugged her frame snuggly. She wore 3-inch leopard print Christian Louboutin red-bottom heels. she put on her Dolce&Gabbana watch, and grabbed her Dolce&Gabbana clutch, Chante also had a freshly permed wrap that hung to the middle of her back. The two women looked flawless and were definitely worthy of stopping traffic in any city.

"I can't believe I let these fools talk me into going to a shake dancer joint," Legacy laughed.

"You'll be alright, I guarantee you that," Chante smiled while adjusting her skirt.

"I know you know, you used to work in that building," Legacy said remembering her sister's days as a stripper.

"That was a long time ago, I done moved on to bigger and better things," Chante said checking herself out in the full-length mirror.

"I know that's right, you ready?" Legacy said grabbing her phone, keys, and her .40, CMoney had her Berretta.

"Let's ride," Chante said grabbing her phone off the charger before they left the room.

CMoney and Dre waited in the lobby for the girls while they talked about how each other was going to stunt tonight.

"Hay, lil C," Shelly said in her thick accent, she was the Jamaican chick he met by the pool the first day they arrived in Atlanta.

"It's CMoney now shawty, but how you doin' sexy?" he said flashing his 25K smile.

Shelly's smile quickly faded and looked to turn into a look of lust as she looked him over, he was indeed shining in a new light.

"Okay CMoney, see ya lader," she said while looking over her shoulder at him as he stared at her backside, he still wanted to hit that.

"Y'all ready?" Legacy asked breaking their stare.

"Yep," CMoney said.

"Damn!" Dre said. "How y'all looking right now, they might just throw the money at y'all," Dre said looking Legacy over lustfully wishing he had her, then he wondered what she looked like naked.

"Shut up boy and come on," Legacy smiled.

"What's that?" Chante asked.

"A navigation system in case we run into some action and need to find our way around," CMoney stated.

"You so nasty, come on," Chante said as they left the hotel and walked through the parking lot to where their cars were parked. CMoney got in and turned on a movie called 'I Love Haters' on his TVs and started the car as Legacy started hers. He whipped out of the parking space, put the car into park, and hopped out with a pack of Armor All wipes to wipe his tires off and add that extra shine.

"CMoney," he heard somebody call his name, and when he turned around it was Shelly.

"What' s good, baby?" he asked knowing what this was about.

"Here me number, call me lader," Shelly smiled while handing him a piece of paper with her number on it, then she turned to leave. CMoney programmed the number into his phone while shaking his head at how women these days acted, but it was official; Shelly was a gold digger. After finishing wiping his tires, he hopped back in the car and smashed off behind Legacy.

They drove the short distance being that they were already downtown before they spotted the big neon blue letters of 'MAGIC CITY', which was directly across from the downtown Greyhound bus station. Magic City was home to Atlanta's finest selection of exotic all black strippers, maybe a couple white ones, but nevertheless, they were all bad and it always went down there. CMoney pulled into the parking lot behind Legacy as Petti Hendrix's 'Married' blared out of his speakers while he and Dre bobbed their heads to the music. They pulled up in front of the entrance where people were going in and coming out. They stopped briefly, sitting stupid high, while CMoney let his rims spin for a minute jacking it down for the people that were out there before pulling off behind Legacy to find a parking space.

Finding two vacant spots right next to each other, they both backed in. CMoney slid his pistol under the seat because he knew he was not getting in that building with it, then he checked himself in the visor mirror before exiting the car and walking to the building with Dre and his sisters.

"Seduction, what's good girl?" the beefy security guard said.

"It's Tay nigga, get it right," Chante snapped, correcting the man. It had been a long time since she heard her old stage name and it brought back memories "But how you doing anyway, Sam?" she asked, passing him her ID card.

"I'm alright, I ain't seen you in a while, you look like you still doing good thou," Sam stated.

"Thank you and believe me when I say, I am," Chante responded as CMoney and Dre stepped up and produced the fake IDs that Chante had taken them to get. The security guard took them and looked at the two men questionably as CMoney handed him everybody's entry fee.

"Aight, y'all go ahead," Sam said before stepping aside to let the two flashy young men through after they had the metal detector wand waved over them by the other security guard. They walked into the dimly lit room as Baby Drew's 'Shake Something' was pounding out of the speakers, they smiled at the sight of beautiful black women butt naked performing lap dances, on the pole dancing, and just doing their thing.

The two found a table to sit down at and the two heavily jeweled young men were immediately swarmed by four strippers wanting to perform their services for them. The strippers could smell the money on them and had to have it since that was their hustle. CMoney and Dre gave the four ladies $100 dollars apiece and watched them do their thing.

"This what I'm talkin' about my nigga!" Dre said excitedly giving his boy some dap while the two girls did their thing in front of him.

"You already know," CMoney smiled while summoning over a waitress. It was time for them to 'Order up' which was when they would give the amount of money they were going to spend to the waitress to procure $1 bills in order to give them to the strippers. Once the waitress came over, they told her what they wanted, then they both handed her two large wads of bills, and she rushed off to meet their demands.

CMoney soaked up everything that was going on in front of him as a stacked dark-chocolate woman wearing nothing but her high heels and a garter belt on her thigh full of money bent over and showed him the inside of her pink pussy from the back while the petite brown-skinned chick with micro braids grinded her ass on his lap.

She wore a red leather halter top dress with a black stripe down the middle, but when he gave her the money, she popped her 36C titties out, and raised her dress up, exposing that she wore nothing underneath it. CMoney enjoyed the show as did Dre who had a stripper in his lap wearing crotchless panties facing him and smacking him across the face with her titties.

Shortly after the waitress returned with the $2,500 apiece that they had given her, now in single dollar bills and spread out on two trays that were used for carrying drinks. She had another waitress with her who had two bottles of Moet Rose and three bottles of Ace of Spades on another tray. The Armand de Brignac Ace of Spades was $1,000 dollars a bottle, but they didn't care, the gold bottles matched their jewelry.

They paid for the liquor, gave the waitresses tips, and sent them on their way with a bottle of the $1,000 champagne to take over to Legacy and Chante's table.

CMoney and Dre both popped the corks on the expensive bottles of liquor, sipped, and enjoyed the show as the club's DJ put on 'Wet Wet' by Soc Sosa. CMoney noticed the twenty second delay in between songs to give the girls enough time to find their next potential clients. Clever, he thought.

The girls got geeked when that song came on, they both got on all fours in front of him and bounced their asses in unison, then they created the wave with their butt cheeks like the crowd does at sports games.

CMoney was starting to feel the effects of the bubbly, so after the song, he sent the girls on their way, grabbed the tray of money and made his way to the stage as the onlookers and spectators whispered, some hating and some not. Nevertheless, they were not going to stop his shine.

Getting front and center at the stage as Party Boi and N8 Official's 'Bands on You' came on, there were a couple of different women doing their thing on the pole, but one in particular stood out to him, she had the biggest ass he'd ever seen in person. He smiled, tossed some money on the stage and watched the show.

She interlocked her legs around the pole, then she bent backwards and slid slowly into a handstand. Using the pole for support, she started pussy popping upside down. Bills flew onto her from everywhere and 'Oh's' and 'Damns' could be heard from the audience. She then spread her legs into an upside-down split, showing her phat camel toe with a landing strip of hair. She flipped down and surveyed her audience to see CMoney smiling at her, obviously pleased with her show, but the look in his eyes said so much more to her and she hadn't seen a look like that in a while. Maybe it was the way diamonds in his mouth and chin danced in the light, she didn't know what it was. But he intrigued her.

She crawled ever so seductively to the part of the stage where CMoney stood, sat down and faced him. Opening her legs, she leaned back and made her pussy pulsate like it was blowing kisses right before him and she was rewarded with more bills.

CMoney looked over the 5'6 36D-27-46 light-skinned beauty who had one side of her hair cut low and wanted her right there on that stage. The next thing she did drove the crowd bizarre. She moved each one of her breasts up and down using no hands like a guy would do his pecs, showing great muscle control over her body before she turned around and bent over in a split and individually began to make each ass cheek bounce to the music while looking back at it.

CMoney really liked that, so he made it rain all over her ass with two handfuls of money as the song ended. The beautiful dancer turned around, scooped up all the bills, and winked at CMoney before rushing off the stage. CMoney made up his mind that he had to see her before he left. Going back to his seat with the tray in his hand, he spotted Chante.

"Nigga I seen yo' azz over there in a trance staring at Butter Pecan," she laughed

"You know her? Shawty bad as fuck," he responded shaking his head now knowing her name.

"Yeah, we go way back, she cool as hell, we used to work together," she explained.

"Sis, I want her! I'm gon' shoot my shot but put a good word in for me," he stated seriously.

"Alright, I got you bro," she said before walking off.

Making it back to the table, he sat down, and sipped from his bottle while in deep thought about Butter Pecan.

"ol girl was supa bad, wasn't she?" Dre asked smiling, he saw his friend at the stage watching her

perform in amazement.

"Man, wasn't she, I want her," CMoney responded as a tall Amazon chick walked past wearing a fishnet catsuit with the titties and pussy cut out. She had long curly hair, a pair of 4-inch heels on, and she was accompanied by a phat ass. CMoney was feeling himself and couldn't help but slap it.

"Ay ay, look for free, touch for a small fee," the cute woman said standing with her hand on her hip.

"That ain't a problem," he said and handed her a fist full of bills and she began to bounce and grind on him to Steve White's 'Calm down'. She was doing her thing as CMoney tried but failed to palm all that ass she had, so he opted for a few light smacks here and there until the song went off. "Don't be no stranger now," he added passing her some bills before she left as another stripper walked by looking good, so he reached out and grabbed her hand.

"What's yo name sexy?" he asked the caramel-complexioned petite woman who wore a thong, thigh high boots, a garter belt, and pasties on her nipples, only the darkness of her areolas could be seen.

"Flirtatious," she responded with a smile. CMoney stuffed some bills in her garter belt and watched her do her thing to 'Damn daddy' by Kaylee Crossfire. Although she was petite, shawty had a serious bubble but. What he found peculiar was the tattoo on her lower back of a dog chasing a cat, but she was dead on with that one.

She slid her thong off, turned around and gave him a good view of her pierced clitoris. He noticed that her pubic hair was in the shape of a diamond, but her lips were cleanly waxed.

CMoney looked over the table where Legacy and Chante were sitting and saw Chante talking to the girl named Butter Pecan who was on stage earlier. He saw Chante point in his direction, so he quickly turned his attention back to Flirtatios who was grinding in his lap.

Where he looked back over there, she was gone as the lap dance came to an end. CMoney sipped from his bottle while searching the room with his eyes to see where Butter Pecan could have gone, but before he knew it she was right in front of him opening his legs with her knee.

"Can I have this dance?" she asked with a pleasurable smile. Up close, she heavily favored the very sexy and beautiful Lauren London.

"No doubt, I been waiting on you all night and you did yo thang up there on that stage tonight," he smiled happily.

"Thank you I try" she said modestly and turned around dancing to Mr. Competition and Erl Will's 'We get to it'. The way she moved her body in that thong was like no other woman in the building. When the part came up and they rapped 'Bust a move, bust a move, bust a move...' she placed her hands over her head and made her ass clap loudly, getting the attention of other patrons and strippers over the loud music and she wasn't using her hands.

This drove CMoney crazy, 'That ass is colossal' he thought, knowing that he was definitely in the presence of a bad bitch without a doubt.

She sat down in his lap to dance and he took the opportunity to whisper in her ear what he had to say.

"How old are you?" she asked curiously.

"Seventeen," he said lighting up the room with his smile while wondering why all girls always asked that question. "But that's merely a number, I put on for mine in a major way," he added seriously using his favorite line before whispering in her ear again. Butter Pecan listened to what he had to say before she replied.

"Listen CMoney, despite what you think of dancers, it ain't that type of party with me. This art is on display and not for sale, Tay know how I get down, so you can ask her. I do this to reach the ultimate goal of what I really wanna do. I know my body's not going to look like this forever, so I take advantage of it right now. Only people who are special to me get to share what I have with me, so I ask, are you ready for the challenge?" she stated getting up from his lap. Butter Pecan was not at all offended by CMoney's comments, she had heard it all before. She took in several things and one was his age, she knew there was more to him from how he looked at her, but the first thing any guy saw when they walked in the club was her bodacious body, so she gave him the benefit of the doubt.

"So, this is possibly something that we both can build on together?" he asked even more interested in her than before after she passed his test.

"Play your cards right and we'll see," she responded as he handed her the tray with the rest of the dollar bills on it. "What's this for?" she asked.

"Your dance, it was the best of the night, now come and ride wit me for a minute," he smiled so brightly

"Ride wit you, huh? How I know you ain't no crazy stalker type of nigga?" she inquired with her hand on her hip.

"That's two bandz, that should cover the rest of your shift for tonight, I'll be waiting on you outside so don't be long," he said confidently.

"Aight, let me grab my things," she said after a long pause that seemed like forever, before turning to leave. 'I gotta have her,' he thought while watching her walk away before he leaned across the table to tell Dre who had a stripper on his lap what the biz was.

"That's what's up my nig, I'm bout to leave with this stripper named X-Tacy," Dre said

"Aight, check it, get a room in her name on a different floor at the same telly we stayin' at and make sure you get her phone as soon as y'all get to the room, tell her you gotta use it cause yo battery dead, if she won't give it to you, leave. Don't take all them pieces either, give 'em to sis to hold down, and do not fall asleep, you got me?" CMoney said trying to make sure his boy was fool proof.

"Got ya my nigga," Dre said shaking up with him.

CMoney texted Legacy to let her know their plans and assured her he'd be good. He told her to tell Chante when she saw Butter Pecan, let her know that he'd be sitting out front.

"My nigga, sis gonna hit it, grab that heat, they going straight back to the telly, so they straight. And remember, head up eyes open," he said seriously while grabbing a bottle of Moet Rose for the road.

"Gotcha," Dre said then turned his attention back to the stripper who was grinding on him.

Leaving out of the club, alert to his surroundings, he hopped in his whip, circled the parking lot once, then pulled up in front of the club. He did that to make sure he was spinning when she came out. About two minutes later, Butter Pecan came out, he hit the horn, and she came to the car, threw her bag in, then she hopped in.

"Could this car be sitting any higher?" she asked sarcastically while closing the door.

"I like to ride high because the sky is the limit for me, for you, and possibly for us," he said meaning every word.

"I guess" she said blushing as he turned up 'Smoother by the minute' by Topnotch J-Wingo but not too loud so that they couldn't talk while he pulled out of the parking lot.

"You gon' have to help me out here, I don't know where the fuck I'm going, I got the navigation right there under the armrest in case I need it. Otherwise, I don't know shit about this city except that it has some beautiful women here," he said then looked at her licking his lips. Even dressed down, her beauty couldn't be denied.

"I gotcha, just drive," she said getting comfortable in her seat watching TV.

"I cannot believe that you're only seventeen, you seem so mature, confident, and driven within yourself," she added with a smile.

"Thank you, I had to grow up fast with no dad around, I basically had to get it how I live, so I stayed on my grind. I've learned that tough times never last, but tough people do," he said making a left turn.

"So, do you always pick up strippers and ride them around in your tricked-out car tryna gas their heads up?" she asked wanting to really hear how he was going to respond to that question for her own personal reasons. He looked at her like she was crazy, but he knew where she was coming from, she wanted to know his intentions.

"First of all, that was my first time ever in a strip club. Secondly, absolutely not, I respect time too much to waste mine. This is far from a hobby of mine, plus, I don't see you in that way. Real niggaz do real thangz, but I wouldn't be real if I didn't tell you that when I first saw you, I was captivated by you because your aura is powerful. Then I looked in your eyes, and there it was. I definitely see what most people don't," he said pulling up to the lights.

"What do you see when you look in my eyes?" she inquired while turning to face him.

"A person who loves to love, but holds back, not wanting to give too much of herself that she gets lost in her lover and gets hurt again," he said looking directly into her eyes.

She turned away from his stare shocked. 'How could he read me like that? It's as if he could see into my soul. This nigga can't be seventeen,' she thought, but she had to admit that she was impressed by his mindset. She just sat there quietly because he had just fucked her head up with that one.

"Where the hell is we at?" he said looking out of the window at a church called Georgia Baptist. He changed the subject because he knew that once she turned away and didn't respond, he knew that meant that he was dead on with his assessment of her, even silence has a volume.

"We're on the East Atlanta side of town, the boulevard is just up ahead" she said coyly.

"What's the Boulevard, a club?" he asked knowing nothing about the place as she laughed.

"No, it's what the whites call the center of poverty, but it's what we call the hood," she responded. "Can you please put on some softer music?" she asked nicely.

"What you wanna hear, I got Fourtune, Travis Romell, Jacob Latimore, Cincere, Rico love, a Rob K mix, anoth. . . " he said but was cut off.

"Rob K would be fine," she said cooly as he slid the disc in. 'Freak' came through the speakers.

"So, tell me more about yourself, starting with your real name, and why you work at that club," he asked inquisitively.

"So, you took it there, huh?" she asked as they shared a laugh. "Well my real name is Esther, and . . . I…" she said but was cut off.

"You mean Esther like the Jewish Queen of Persia who saved her people from massacre?" he questioned.

"Exactly, how the hell you know that?" she asked smiling, she was really feeling his swag.

"It's more than meets the eye wit me, and if you choose to stick around, you'll realize that," he stated seriously.

"You is too much, anyways, to finish your questions. I'm 25 years old, I attend Georgia University, go bulldogs! I'm working on my master's degree, I want to become a doctor. I have my associates in business management already! have no children, I'm goal-orientated, ambitious, loyal, trustworthy, honest, smart, dedicated, and loving. I've been working at the club for 6 years to help fund my college tuition and live comfortably, I don't like it, but I gotta do what I gotta do. I grew up with both parents, my mom is white Jewish lady, hint the name, and my daddy is black. I have two siblings, a brother and a sister, me and my sister are roommates. I'm single, been that way for 5 months because the guy I was with cheated on me and cheating kills the trust and undermines the love and respect so critical to everlasting happiness, so I broke it off. I think that's about it," she smiled.

CMoney paid close attention to everything she said, he loved her qualities. They rode around til the wee hours of the morning talking, laughing, listening to music, and getting better acquainted with one another.

CMoney dropped her back off at the club where her truck was parked. He carried her bag to her truck for her, hugged her, and told her that he'd call her later. He turned to leave, but she grabbed him, turned him around, and gave him a peck on the lips.

"I enjoyed myself with you tonight, well, day too," she laughed. "Thank you, I really needed that piece of mind, it's been a long time. I'll be looking forward to that call," she said smiling while she handed him his 2 gees back.

"What's this for?" he asked puzzled.

"You don't need to pay for my time, I'm not money hungry, besides, I like you, and I hope to see more of you," she explained.

"Don't worry bout it, buy yourself something nice wit it, it's on me," he said gaining a new respect for her as he slid her the money back while she got in her truck.

"I'mma hit you up, be safe," he said before closing her door and walking off to his car. Hopping in, he pulled off, and headed to the hotel to get some much-needed rest.

CHAPTER NINE

Three days later, the day had finally arrived for Stunt fest.

CMoney had gone to the South Dekalb Mall yesterday with Esther, got him a fit, and went to the barbershop to get his hair cut, he also got his car washed and detailed for today. He had been spending a lot of time with Esther. He had yet to fuck her, but he'd be lying if he said that he didn't enjoy her company often. However, he did fuck the Jamaican chick - Shelly, the day before yesterday, and she was a boss freak. CMoney nutted all over that tattoo of the small sand beach with the palm trees and the words 'PARADISE' over it, that she had on her lower back. She took it in the butt, swallowed, let him bust in her face and all, she did the whole shabang. CMoney didn't know what would happen between him and Esther since he planned on heading back to the Mil tomorrow, but he'd see how the situation played out though. But for now, it was stuntin' time.

Fresh up out of the shower, he got dressed in all white Louis Vuitton shorts, white belt with red LV's all over it,

and big gold LV belt buckle. Red three button polo style shirt made by Louis Vuitton and all white custom Louis Vuitton Air Force Ones with Red LVs all over the shoe. Putting on all of his jewelry including the gold diamond pinkie rings for each pinkie that he bought at the mall yesterday, he ran the brush over his waves.

CMoney had about 31 gees left, so he stuffed the odd 11 in his pocket, put his pistol in his waistband, grabbed his phone, hit his teeth with the jewelry rag before stuffing it in his back pocket, and put on his gold Louis Vuitton Millionaire sunglasses. He was ready for his presence to be felt today.

Dre came out of the bathroom tucking Chante's pistol into his waistband. He was Gucci down in white and yellow, he had his jewelry on and Big Ball's #8 pool ball chain. The white and yellow custom Gucci Air Force Ones on his feet set his fit off perfectly.

"You ready to roll, my nig?" Dre asked anxiously.

Hell yeah, let me see what they on," he said before calling Legacy.

"We already in the car, I just came back from getting it washed, and gassed up," she said enthusiastically.

"Aight, we on our way down," he said hanging up.

Leaving the room, they hit the elevator, then walked through the lobby, and out the front door.

Legacy and Chante sat in the car with the tinted windows halfway down bumping 'To be honest' by GP El Magico featuring Skillz. The bass-filled track vibrated the trunk hard.

CMoney walked past them and threw up the deuces, he was unaware that Legacy was snapping pictures of them or he would have given her one of his patent player poses. CMoney and Dre hopped in his car and put his '53206' DVD in his X-Box, then he turned up '32 Bars' by Bless and Team Big C as his text alert went off, it was Esther. *'What up bae? I'm on my way there'* she texted.

'C-U there sexy' he texted back before pulling his gear shift into drive and pulling off behind Legacy and Chante.

∞

They pulled up to Stunt fest Car and Bike Show, held at Atlanta Motor Speedway. The event was packed, there were people there from all over the country showing off their whips. We know where there's whips, there's money, and money brings the honeys. There were all types of different themed cars, there was a Sprite box Chevy, Lucky Charms box Chevy, a peach bubble Caprice with a 'peach' painted on the trunk on 26Ll rims since Georgia was known as the Peach State. There was a Herds box Chevy, an ATL-themed box Chevy with 24" spinning 'A' rims, Dreign cars were galore, and all types of different cars and trucks on different sized rims. There were also a lot of motorcycles, some with spinning rims, and some just candy painted.

CMoney fit right in with the jackaz and the stunnaz as he turned up 'All I know is Milwaukee' by Big Rick featuring Coo Coo Cal and started swerving right to left, stopping briefly so it was known that he was spinning.

"It's going down, my nigga," Dre said shaking up with his boy before hanging out of the window jackin'.

CMoney smiled and shook his head at his friend as he pulled up on Legacy's passenger side turning his music down.

"This muthafucka jumpin' ain't it?" CMoney said

"Hell yeah, lets pull up over there," Legacy said pointing.

"I'm behind you," he said and pulled off behind her after she did while turning his music back up. Driving behind Legacy, he saw a black Cadillac SRX truck coming from the opposite direction. He hit the horn a few times trying to get Legacy's attention to stop, but her music must've been up as he stopped with a car's distance in between his car and the SUV.

"What's happenin, baby?" he asked smiling to everyone's enjoyment except for the one that was already used to it.

"You don't be getting in no trouble out here honey," Esther said jokingly in her southern accent as he put the car in park, put the pistol that was on his lap on the seat, and hopped out looking over his shoulder to see if his

rims were still spinning, and they were doing about 25 mph as he got to her window.

"It's plenty in quantity out here, but I recognize the quality in you when I see it, you feel me?" he said while brushing the back of his index finger down her cheek, making her blush in a schoolgirl way before removing his glasses.

"Awww," all three of her friends in the truck said in unison. CMoney smiled as she blushed even harder. He didn't know who the girl was that sat in the seat directly behind Esther, but he noticed that she was staring daggers into his face he started to ask her can he get his face back.

"I feel you," Esther smiled.

"Get out once," he smiled while noticing Legacy pull back up.

"No, why?" she asked as he opened her door after putting his glasses back on.

"I wanna see how you look," he responded as she stepped out of the truck. "Um!" he added as he spun her around. She wore a red Louis Vuitton halter top dress that stopped just before her knees. The dress hugged her curvaceous body like a second skin. She wore red 3-inch Jimmy Choo stiletto pumps, a gold locket around her neck, gold hooped earrings, and her hair was laced, she looked beautiful as usual.

"All, that's cute, they match," one of her friends said from the car.

"You did that on purpose, huh?" he asked just now realizing that they matched after her friend said it.

"Nope," she snickered while wrapping her arms around his neck, and him with his around her waist.

"So, what up, we kickin' it tonight?" he asked seriously.

"It'll have to be after I get off work," she responded.

"You ain't even gotta go," he said breaking their embrace, going in his pocket, pulling out 11 bandz, and shuffling through the large stack. "How much you gon'

make tonight,4 gees,5 gees,6 gees? I got you," he smiled as all the girls in the truck smiled with their eyes big.

"Whatever, I'll see what I can do," she responded.

"That's more like it," he said hugging her and kissing her lips. "Now you be safe, I'm bout to show these niggas how we do it Midwest style," he said watching her get in the car before walking off.

"He fine as hell," he heard one of the girls say, he just smiled and kept it moving.

"Let me find out you in love with a stripper," Dre teased him as soon as he got in the car. He smiled, put the pistol back on his lap, turned the music up, and followed Legacy. She turned, then pulled to the side signaling that she wanted him to pull up next to her. CMoney pulled up to her passenger side window as a white '08 Audi A6 pulled up sitting on chrome 24" Davin's, playing some song about getting off the wall. CMoney grabbed his heat because he didn't know the nigga or what he was on, but Legacy started talking to him, so he laid the heat back on his lap.

"What up, girl?" the man asked.

"Shawn! What you doing down here?" Legacy asked smiling. Shawn was one of the niggas she sold brick too. He was the one with the Wisconsin Badgers 'W' piece. He had that chain on and an iced-out Milwaukee Bucks piece on as well, which was crazy because she heard that he was from Mississippi, but to each it's on.

"Partying one time for the one time," Shawn responded smiling while adjusting his white gold frames. "That's what's up, I'm on the same shit," she said

"Aight, I'mma catch up with you when we get back to our stomping grounds," Shawn said before pulling off playing that wall song.

"Who dat?" CMoney asked curiously.

"One of my guys, he from the Mil," Legacy responded.

"Aw, what up, thou?" he asked.

"Let's go down the line," Chante said excitedly.

"Let's go!" he smiled.

The line was two long rows of cars parked on opposite sides with plenty of room in between, so people who wanted to could drive through the middle showing off their cars, stunt, and see who was all there.

CMoney put on one of his favorite songs to stunt off of. 'Glazin' by Party Boi featuring B.E and Kia Shine came blasting through the speakers. As they got to the beginning of the line. CMoney swerved from side to side as he and Dre bobbed their heads. He had a porno called 'Nuttin Butt Pinky' playing on his TVs, and he was feeling good while driving down the line as the hoes looked at him ready to take their panties off right there and fuck him or at least give him some head. And the niggas, they wished they could be behind the wheel of the 30" spinning rims at the least.

CMoney saw somebody that he had to stunt on, so that's what he did. He sat up in his seat and turned his volume up a little more as he approached the group of niggas and hoes that were standing by a black Maserati sitting on 24's and another Maserati that looked identical, but it was red on 24's. CMoney took his shades off and locked

eyes with the nigga named Miles, then he hung out of the window letting his pieces and grill catch the shine of the sun rays to blind a bitch.

"And my rims way bigger than yours!" he yelled, stopped and let his rims spin for a second, then he swerved on him. 'Hoe azz nigga' he thought as he slid back in the car and continued down the line when all of a sudden, a loud noise sounded, and his back window came crashing in. You didn't have to tell CMoney or Dre what that noise was, they had been using them since they were 12, and with the back window in between them, it only validated what they already knew.

Sliding down in their seats, CMoney threw the car into park as two more shots hit the car. Dre started bussing through the back window which was a cover for CMoney who grabbed the 17 shot Berretta off his lap, opened the door, and hopped out blasting Denzel style on 'Training Day'. **Boc Boc Boc** Boc Boc Boc Boc Boc Boc, he shot at both Maserati's flipping two niggas in the process as Legacy and Dre hopped out letting their pistols ride too.

CMoney saw a nigga leaning against a car with a choppa in his hands, he couldn't shoot him because he was shielded by the car, so he did the next best thing he could do at that point.

"Get down!" CMoney yelled as the choppa sprayed bullets.

When he saw his best friend fly off of his feet, he turned to Legacy and saw her laying on the ground with blood around her, something in him just snapped. CMoney grabbed Legacy's gun and stood up letting both pistols ride **Boc Boc Boc Boc Boc Boc Boc**. Out of his peripheral vision, he saw a light-skinned bald-headed nigga with what looked like a Mac bussing at the same niggas that he was bussing at. He recognized that the nigga who was bussing was the nigga in the Audi who Legacy was talking to earlier. The Mac he was spitting definitely helped CMoney get them niggas up off of him as the Maserati's sped away.

"Help me get them in the car!" Chante yelled after backing the MC up and hopping out. They put Legacy in

the car, but they couldn't tell where she was hit because her shirt was, soaked in blood. Shawn put Dre in the El Camino and everybody scattered to their cars, hopped in, and smashed out.

Pulling up to the Emergency Room entrance, CMoney hopped out and ran in the hospital with his phone ringing every two seconds as he ran up to the counter and snapped.

"I need a muthafuckin' doctor, we got two people shot out here, and if I don't get no help soon, it's gon' be three maybe four up in this muthafucka," he said lividly as the nurses scrambled out to get Legacy and Dre.

CMoney couldn't believe the nerve of that hoe nigga Miles, that night at the club he wasn't on shit, then he pulled this stunt. 'I'm gon' kill that nigga if it's the last thing I do,' he thought, pissed off as Chante came rushing in.

"Nigga you betta get the fuck up outta here, you know these muthafuckas finna call the police and you got that hot azz gun in the car too, you gotta go lay low. I already wiped the other two guns down, they registered, so they good, I'mma call you later, okay?" she said then hugged

him before he ran out of the hospital to his car, and pulled off not knowing where he was headed, but knowing he had to get away from the hospital. He looked at his phone that had yet to stop ringing to see Esther's phone number.

"Yeah," he answered.

"Thank God, why you ain't been answering the phone? I thought you were dead," she broke down. CMoney could tell that she was crying.

"Naw I'm good, but I'm gon' need you to come through for me, can you handle that?" he asked optimistically because his back was to the wall and his options were limited, so he had to trust her. If she ever had what it took to be with him, this was her time to show and prove. Being that this situation was a part of the game he was in, he needed to know that she was a ridah and not a hider.

"Without a doubt," she responded sincerely. Hearing her response with sincerity in her voice, he knew she was definitely a ridah.

"I need you to show me the way off these streets, I'm sure my whip hot by now, and when you come, don't bring nobody with you," he instructed her.

"I already dropped everybody off, now where you at?" she asked sniffling.

CMoney told her what the street signs said at his location and she was there in no time.

"I didn't think I was gon' see you again," she said sorrowfully after getting out of her truck, walking up, and hugging him.

"I'm still here baby" he stated hugging her back. 'Shawty really feeling a nigga,' he thought. "Let's get out of here," he added breaking their embrace.

"Okay, we going to my house thou," she stated, and he had no complaints with that. He advised her to take the back cuts to her house and he followed close behind her.

He parked his car in her garage and they entered her plush home on the West Side of Atlanta.

"You got some bleach?" he asked as soon as they entered the house.

"Yeah, it's in here" she said as he followed her into the kitchen and got the bleach from under the kitchen sink. He put his arm over the sink, then poured the bleach on it, and scrubbed it with a green scrub pad that was on the sink before repeating the same process on his other arm in efforts

to wash away any gun powder residue. Feeling satisfied, he washed his arms in dish soap, and put the bleach back under the sink after he doused a dish towel with it. "I need some plastic bags, some gloves, and a drill if you got one," he said sitting down at the kitchen table.

Esther went to get everything he asked for, came back, sat down, and watched what he was doing. CMoney put the plastic gloves on used for doing perms with, pulled the pistol from his waistband, and laid it on the table. Opening the tool box, he pulled the big drill out, and

squeezed the trigger to see if it worked. Satisfied with that, he picked the pistol up, hit the button to release the clip, pulled the hack back, and caught the bullet before it hit the table. Then he put a long wide drill bit in the drill, and drilled it down the barrel of the gun, making sure it hit and destroyed the firing pin while scraping all around the barrel in efforts to mess up the ballistics. After doing that, he broke the gun down into two pieces.

'He know too much to be so young,' Esther thought while watching everything he did.

After wiping everything down with the bleached towel, he doubled three bags. Placing the clip in one, the hack in one, and the handle in the other and triple tied them down, he'd get rid of the pieces later. Then he flushed the four remaining bullets down the toilet one by one before Esther led him to her bedroom where he removed his shirt knowing it had gun powder residue on it.

He sat at the foot of the bed with his beater on and was about to text Chante, but thought better of it, he knew them people were probably there by now grilling her, but

Chante was thorough and could hold her own, he had witnessed it on several occasions, but he promised himself that he would definitely check up on his people a little bit later.

"Damn! Hoe azz nigga," he yelled outraged while slamming his phone on the carpet before putting his head in his hands. "I'm sorry if I'm scaring you, it's just my sister and my best friend laying' up in that hospital shot and I can't help but to think that it should be me there instead of them," he continued knowing that they were there because he took that fuck nigga lightly, but that would never happen again with nobody, he vowed to himself.

"Please don't say that, Chris," she said wiping the tears from her eyes.

"That's how I feel, all this was because of my carelessness," he said plotting. Miles had to die for the shit he pulled, he couldn't see it no other way.

"I just want you to know that you won't be the only one affected by your decisions," she said sitting with her

back on the headboard and her arms wrapped around her legs that were pulled to her chest.

"I know that, but what's gon' happen when I go back to the Mil and it's a million miles in between us?" he asked seriously while turning to face her, he really wanted to hear her response to that question.

"We'll both have to do some traveling in this long-distance relationship until we can be together in one state," she said after a brief pause while turning to meet his stare.

'Good answer,' he thought, but he was hoping for more. "Well, I was thinking more along the lines of you coming back with me," he said putting his cards on the table face up.

"As much as I would like to do that, how can I when I got a life here?! Got school, family, and a job," she said compassionately. CMoney wasn't trying to hear that she wasn't coming as he had a semi sucka attack. All real niggas go through that with that one 'Special Chick' in their lives whether they want to admit it or not. This just

happened to be his time, so he fought for what he wanted.

"As you said, we can travel back and forth to see yo' family together. You can go to school up there, I'll even pay for it, it's nothing, and you won't want for shit. How we gon' grow and flourish so far apart? Now, I don't know how you feel about us, but to keep it a hunnid with you and myself, I want you in my life and in order for us to be together, sacrifices must be made on both of our behalf's," CMoney paused to let that sink in before driving back on her harder. "You know y'all women kill me talkin' that love shit, but yet, y'all can't see it when it's right in y'all faces. Do you know what love is? Love is power, a testimony to compassion, and empathy beyond human understanding. The embodiment of a sacrifice that staggered the mind and humbled the heart. It's being in love with a woman, and always loving and respecting and protecting your woman and the women in your family, I..," he said but was abruptly cut off by Esther hopping up and kissing him passionately.

"No man has ever said what you just said to me. The fact that you're willing to fight for me speaks volumes to my heart and it shows that you care. I can't deny we have incredible chemistry, and I would definitely like to build on that," she paused. "Let me tie up some loose ends, then we can leave," she continued sincerely.

"So, you gon' come with me?" he asked.

"Yeah," she smiled as he grabbed her and kissed her passionately while palming her plentiful ass. They undressed each other as their tongues explored each other's mouths until they were both as naked as the day they were born. CMoney laid her down and looked over her body hungrily. This wasn't his first time seeing her naked obviously, but her body looked like somebody sculpted it with their bare hands because it was so flawless. He laid on top of her and kissed her as his hands roamed her body. While kissing her neck, soft moans escaped her lips as he worked his way down to her breasts and put her right nipple in his mouth as his finger entered her sugar walls.

"Uhhh," Esther moaned in pleasure. CMoney then switched and started sucking on her left tittie while he worked his finger expertly. Satisfied that she was nice and wet, he got between her thighs and was about to enter her, when she stopped him.

"Be gentle, it's been awhile," she said seriously.

"Aight," he said and kissed her once more before he slid halfway into her bare. This was his first time ever bare in some pussy, but the first thing he noticed was how tight she was and how good it felt. The second thing he noticed was how wet she was. She was so wet, that it felt like somebody pushed her off of a boat or something he thought as he thrusted in her with slow halfway strokes.

"Ummm ahh," she moaned and immediately began to claw at his back. Once she adjusted to his size, she opened her legs wider and allowed him to go deeper. Now, she wasn't no slouch in bed, but he came to put in work as he filled her with long, slow, and hard strokes.

"Ah shit, ohh...oh...," Esther moaned throwing it up at him as he beat it back down. Putting her legs on his shoulders, he was able to get even deeper, and take over her body as if they were one.

"I'm cu... cu... cumin!" she managed to scream out. CMoney looked down never stopping his stride to see the creamy white substance all over his dick and her pussy lips. Feeling his own nut nearing, he sped up the pace as Esther went crazy.

"Ah...ah...ah ah, oh shit," she said while clawing at his back as his strokes became more forceful. The last stroke before he came, he pushed himself deep inside of her, and filled her up with his hot thick nut.

Stroking a few more times to assure he was empty, he let her legs down, slid out, and laid next to her spent.

Esther put her head on his chest rubbing his abs satisfied sexually and with her decision to leave with him. CMoney was sure not to fall asleep until he heard from Chante and got rid of that gun. He just laid there thinking that Dre might've been right when he said that he was in love with a stripper.

∞

Boss laid back on his bunk with his hands behind his head while deep in thought. He'd been calling Legacy all day to no avail. He didn't know what was going on as a million things ran through his head. First, he thought her phone died or she lost it. Then he thought she met a nigga and ran off with him, but he quickly dismissed that notion because that wasn't in her character nor did he ever see that in her or he wouldn't have wifed her. He thought that she may had been involved in an accident and was scared to tell him. Even worse, he thought she could've gotten robbed and car jacked, but where was her brother at that time? He cursed himself for letting her take that damn car to Atlanta. Times like this made the predicament that he was in even tougher, but not one to wear his emotions on his sleeve, he hid it well.

His thoughts were interrupted when Wayne came to his cell door.

"What up fool? Come holla at ya big Cuz," Wayne said looking in the door.

"Aight, here I come," Boss said sitting up, sliding on his shower shoes, and pulling the orange shirt over his head before leaving out of the door. Getting to the table where Wayne was, he took a seat.

"Cuz, I just got off the line wit Moms," Wayne was cut off.

"How she doing?" Boss asked sincerely about the woman he'd known as an aunt his whole life.

"She good, she just reminded me of some things. It's going from sugar to shit wit the niggas in our family. I'm locked up, you locked up, C died in a car accident, uncle Rob died of a stroke, the nigga Brandon got killed too. That really fucked me up cause he was a good nigga, still young, and he was eatin' good. The nigga was only like three four years older than me," Wayne said reminiscing on the past.

"Yeah, that fucked me up too," Boss said meaning it, but he was plagued by the newest thing on his mind.

Wayne knew his cousin too well and no matter how much he tried to mask it, he knew something was wrong with him. "What's on yo mind my nigga? You know you can talk to me about anything," Wayne explained seriously. After a brief delay, Boss told him what was on his mind.

"Damn my nigga, that's fucked up. Did you call Auntie? If Legacy can, she sure to call yo' moms to let you know what's up with her," Wayne said logically. Boss was so distraught in the head that the thought didn't even cross his mind.

"I'm gonna call right now, I'll be right back, Boss said getting up and walking over to the phone to call his mom. "Boy, what took you so long to call me? Legacy's sister called over here and said that girl got shot down in Atlanta," Boss' mother said as soon as the call went through.

"Shot!" was all Boss could say as he stood there with his mouth wide open in a state of shock.

"Lando, Lando, you still there?" his mother asked, but he couldn't answer her, he was too grief stricken.

CHAPTER TEN

A week had gone by and CMoney had yet to run into the nigga named Miles. He damn near rode around the whole Atlanta and a couple of outskirts with the help of the navigation system, looking for both Maserati's every day. And today was like the previous days as he rode through the streets in a Chevy Equinox SUV that he had Esther rent for him. Dressed in all black with an MP5 smg laying on the floor in between the seats, the 30 round clip said that he had revenge on his mind.

The past week or so of his life had been a blessing and a curse. On one hand, he had met a beautiful compatible companion in Esther and things were on the up and up with them. But on the other hand, his sister and best friend had both taken bullets at the hands of a hoe nigga, but by the grace of God and the hesitation of a trigger finger, they survived.

Legacy had taken a bullet to the arm that turned out to be a flesh wound, so she was stitched up, and released from the hospital a day later with her arm in a sling. CMoney was elated hearing that news and thanked God

that his sister would make a full recovery. He met up with her and Chante before they headed back to the Mil and Legacy was on some let's ride on this nigga type shit with one of her arms in a sling. He understood where she was coming from, but he assured her that he'd make the nigga pay for what he had done when he caught him. He hugged her and apologized to her wholeheartedly and was glad that she had not become bitter over the whole ordeal. They kicked it for a little while longer, then he loaded up their bags in the truck for them and left. As for Dre, he wouldn't be so lucky to walk away with only minor injuries. He lived and CMoney was ecstatic for that. Dre had been his nigga since Happy Hill elementary school where they met. They went back to the days of red light green light, tea cup saucer, pitty pat, and shit like that. But unfortunately, the AK-47 bullet that he took to the stomach would have him wearing a colostomy bag, otherwise known as 'The Shit Bag'. Dre was getting released from the hospital today and CMoney was relieved to have his boy back around.

He sent Esther to pick him up because he didn't want to be nowhere near that hospital. Chante told him while the detective talked to her concerning the shooting, he pulled out a small notepad, and was distracted by another detective walking up and whispering something in his ear, which gave her a chance to get a good glimpse of what was on the notepad. She said they were looking for a black Man with dark skin driving a red convertible. That wasn't his description, but it was still too close for comfort, so he wouldn't risk it. She also told him that when she was questioned, she told them that they were from out of town and came to Georgia to visit family. They heard about the Stunt fest event and decided that would be a nice place to have fun and mingle. Upon getting there, they were having fun, but it was people there with a different agenda and caused her sister and her God cousin bodily harm by shooting them in an attempted carjacking, so they fired their weapons trying to protect themselves, it all happened so fast. Chante said what she told them and let the tears flow. She said she didn't see who it was or anything else.

They questioned Legacy and Dre as well and they gave an identical story coerced by Chante before the doctors led them away. The detectives figured that was how things went, so they confiscated their registered guns, gave her their card, and told her they'd get the guns back to her in a few days pending investigation and if she remembered anything else, she should give them a call, and then they left the hospital.

Turns out seven people were shot that day including Legacy and Dre, with two people meeting their final resting spot.

"I don't know nothin' bout no murda I was way in California wit Bun B ridin dirty blowin' purple all that morning," CMoney rapped the lyrics to 'Mind your Business' by Webbie with a smile as his phone rang.

"Hello," he answered.

"Hey bae, when you comin' home?" Esther asked happily.

"I'll be there in a minute, how my nigga doin'?" he inquired.

"He alright, he sleep right now. You know this nigga had the nerve to open that damn bag. I started to put his azz out," she said jokingly.

"He clowin' ain't he?" he laughed.

"Clowin' ain't the word, when we were leaving the hospital, he in there cursing the nurses out, talking about they stole his watch and chains. I told him that you put that stuff up for him, so he calmed down a little," she explained.

"Tell him to fall back, I got that shit put up, I'll see you in a minute sexy. "He stated

"Alright bye" she said then hung up.

CMoney had been spending every night at Esther's house since the day of the shooting. When he heard Dre was getting released from the hospital, he was about to rent a hotel room for them to stay in until they headed back to Milwaukee, but Esther wasn't having that. She talked to

her sister and they gave him their blessing to bring Dre over until they left. He declined, but they insisted, so to show his gratitude and appreciation, he gave her sister the rent money for the next two months. They wouldn't be there that long, but it was a nice gesture on their behalf's, so he didn't mind.

Pulling up to the light, he spotted a red car a few cars ahead. Reaching in between the seats, he gripped the MP5, switched lanes, and zoomed up towards the car.

"Damn, I'm trippin" He said looking at a new bright red Honda. He wanted Miles so bad that he was hallucinating. Laying the gun back down, he answered his ringing phone.

"Who dis?" he said.

"Cuz, what's happenin' man?" Ken asked anxiously.

"I' don't know, why? what up?" he asked casually.

"I ain't got no more of that shit, I need some more," he came out and said.

"Ay, don't be talkin like that on this line, now I'mma have somebody come see you, aight?" he said wondering just how much money Ken fucked off, and better yet, how much did he have.

"Aight bet, get at me when you get back," Ken said with excitement.

"No doubt," he said hanging up while pulling up in front of Esther's house. Texting Legacy, he explained what he wanted her to do, then he tucked the gun under his hoodie, got out of the truck, and went into the house.

∞

Back in Milwaukee, Chante and Legacy were getting back to the money. As they moved swiftly through traffic in the Jeep, Liberty making drop offs and pickups. Hearing her text alert go off, Legacy read it, and responded letting CMoney know that she would handle that.

"Pull up by Ken's house, Tay," Legacy said from the passenger's seat. She was supposed to be resting, but the

streets kept calling, so she had to give 'em what they wanted. Texting Ken, she asked him what he was working with, so she could get it ready, she had 9 zips of yay and a pound of kush in her stash box and didn't think he would need more than that. Needless to say, she was shocked and impressed when he texted her back that he had 10 thousand dollars. Ken really didn't have to spend any money because his mom kept him clothed and fed. He wasn't drug or alcohol dependent, so besides gas, and a few fits he bought for him and Big Booty Rudy, he stacked everything.

Pulling up on 76th and Servite, Chante made a left turn into the parking lot behind Menards and pulled into a parking space. Doing what was required to open the stash box, Chante went to retrieve the bag while Legacy texted Ken to let him know that they were outside. A few minutes later, Ken came out, and got in the truck.

"Tay, Legacy, what up?" Ken asked closing the door.

"Shit, what happened to yo' eye?" Legacy asked after turning around in her seat to face him.

"This hoe azz nigga snaked me, I had to put one in his as for that shit too, literally. But the swelling going down now," Ken explained, leaving out the fact he got into it with a dope fiend who tried to play him out of some money.

"Okay lil gangsta," Chante teased.

"I didn't bring a lot of shit, so give me 7 gees for these 255 grams and this pound of kush, and that's a plug lil nigga, but the 9 already hard or else I would've taxed yo' azz. I know you ain't got no wrist game in the kitchen anyway, so take this and count my money out," Legacy said seriously and handed him the bag as Ken shuffled through the stack of money and handed her what he owed, knowing he had to learn how to cook up dope.

"I heard what happened in Atlanta cuz, I wish I was there to help," Ken spoke sincerely.

"Aww, I appreciate that cuz, but that shit gon' get taken care of," Legacy said knowing that CMoney would make good on his promise to her.

"You be safe Ken and tell Auntie that I said hi," Chante said.

"Y'all too, I'm out," Ken responded getting out of the truck, putting the bag on his shoulder, and heading back into his house.

"That lil nigga something else, aint he?" Chante asked while backing out.

"Hell yeah, he hustlin' good too, who would've ever thought that," Legacy laughed while tucking the money away. "Go to Walgreen's by my house, so I can get these pictures developed from Atlanta and send 'em to Boss," she added.

"Alright," Chante said pulling out of the parking lot playing 'B.A.B' by Nu Money, heading to Walgreen's on 76th and Mill Road.

"Bro, I got you," CMoney said into his cell phone.

"Aight, one," Jeff said casually.

"One," CMoney responded and hung up. CMoney had been talking to Jeff a lot lately, he was almost uncontrollable when he found out that Legacy had been shot, he damn near turned green like the Hulk. He had even rode around with CMoney a couple of times looking for Miles. That fucked CMoney up to see Jeff heated up and ready to lay something down because he was pretty sure that during Jeff's prison sentence, he vowed to himself not to go down this rode again. 'First things learned are hard to forget' CMoney thought. The fact that his baby sister had gotten shot prompted his return to the streets to declare justice. Jeff put word out on his end about Miles and took CMoney to one of his homeboys who had artillery for sale. CMoney bought two AR-15s, two MP5 smg's, seven Walther P99 handguns with three extended clips, two FN Hertal 5.7 tactical pistols, two Glock 9mms, two boxes of bullets for everything, two silencers, and three level 4 tactical bulletproof slim vests.

He bought a lot of artillery because the dude said that he could get it shipped wherever he needed it to go, so when he got back to the Mil, he'd be ready for anything that ever came his way.

CMoney looked at the clock, it was 8:21 am. He had already been up for a little over an hour doing his 500 pushups, sit-ups, and jumping jacks. Esther had to be at school by 11:30 am to finalize her transfer to the university of Marquette, but they had also planned to go to breakfast, so they had to get a move on it.

"Sleepy head, get up," he said shaking Esther awake.

"Good Morning" she said turning over while stretching. "Top of the morning to you sexy, it's time to get up," he said kissing her on the forehead before she got out of the bed heading to the bathroom that was connected to her bedroom, wearing nothing but a sports bra. CMoney smiled at the sight of all that ass, then he left the room to go holla at Dre.

"What up, fool?" CMoney asked entering the guest room.

"Coolin," Dre said opening his eyes from his thoughts.

"We gonna go grab some breakfast, you wanna roll?" he asked sitting at the foot of the bed.

"Naw I'm good my nigga, just bring me something back," Dre said turning over and putting the covers over his head.

"Gotcha," he said before leaving the room. He started to make Dre get his azz up, because he knew him better than anybody else and he could tell that he was in a funk over being shot and wearing 'THE SHIT BAG', but ultimately it was about him not being in a position to body the nigga who shot him, and the fact that the nigga was still walking the streets was devastating to Dre. CMoney understood that fully, but in due time, Miles would get what he had coming.

Walking into the bathroom where Esther was showering, CMoney quickly undressed, and slid the shower door back. "You got room for me?" he asked while looking over her voluptuous figure hungrily.

"Always," she responded coyly while waving him in with her index finger. CMoney smiled, stepped in, and

slid the door closed. Soaping up her towel, he washed her gently while getting his feel on, "Are you gon' wash me or grope me?" she smiled.

"Both," he replied with a smile.

"How would you like it if I did this?" she said reaching out and grabbing his semi-erect member. His silence told her that he liked what she was doing as he started stroking her while watching it rise to its full potential. CMoney turned her around, bent her over, and since she was his lady, he ate her pussy from the back much to her delight. At the age of 17, this was the first time he ate pussy, so he darted his tongue in and out of her while rubbing her clit just like he saw in the porno movies he watched. Satisfied with that, he got up, and wiped his mouth.

"Now I know why your name is Butter Pecan," he smiled making her laugh. Not to be outdone by her man, she got down on her knees and blessed him with the best head that he ever had, deep throat and all. CMoney was getting weak in the knees and her mouth was the reason

why, so he pulled her up before he exploded everywhere. Turning her back around, he bent her over, spread her ass cheeks, and slid into her hot dripping wet pussy from the back. Moans immediately filled the entire bathroom. If the walls could talk they would've told you that he beat that thing up as he pounded away at her sweet pussy with long hard deep strokes while holding her jiggling ass in his hands as the shower jets sprayed all over them.

After 10 minutes of moaning and skin clapping, he pushed deep inside of her and filled her inside up with his semen, then he smacked her on the ass hard. Pulling out, he then washed her up, played with her titties, and then washed himself up before they got out of the shower. They dressed and CMoney grabbed 5 gees, his phone, and his brand-new Walther P99. Leaving the house, they hopped in the rental and pulled off.

Arriving at the Waffle House, they went in, and took a seat in the back of the restaurant.

"Hi, may I take your order?" the funny-looking waitress asked smiling.

"Yes, can I have pancakes, scrambled eggs, hash browns, and bacon with a large orange juice," Esther said.

"And I want French Toast, scrambled cheese eggs, and bacon with a large orange juice too," CMoney said while finally figuring out that the waitress looked like she could be Flavor Flav's sister.

"Coming right up," she said before walking away.

"Bae, I wanna ask you something," Esther said reaching across the table and taking his hands into hers.

"Shoot," he said eager to hear what she had to say.

"I wanna know what do you expect from me?" she inquired while thinking. CMoney thought for a minute before he responded. "I expect to full trust you firstly, because without trust, we have nothing to build on. I expect you to be honest with me about any and everything no matter what. I expect for you to love me, show me loyalty, stay ambitious, perfect your craft, if you feeling a certain way about something, talk to me

don't just assume, so we can put it behind us, communication rules the nation. And last, but definitely not the least, I expect to be the only one in between those thighs, but then again, I already know you knew that," he explained seriously while looking in her eyes,

"How do you feel about that?" he added after giving her enough time to take in what he just said.

"I understand exactly what you mean bae, and I feel the same as you do. I will support you in all situations because I know you must honor who your partner is now, as well as the potential of what he or she hopes to be, you have to support each other's decisions. I will be your love, I will be the shoe to your foot, the glove to your hand, and the Bonny to your Clyde as long as you put me first, respect me, show me love, be there for me, and bring your azz home to me every night I guarantee you that I will be everything you need and more," she stated meaning every word as the waitress brought their food over and walked away,

"And as long as I'm with you, the Va Jay Jay will be on lock, I promise you that," she added while cutting her pancakes.

"Who said sexy can't be sophisticated?" he asked as they shared a laugh, but they had just found something in each other, and they both knew it. That something was a genuine love. They talked more, ate, and laughed before CMoney paid the bill, gave a tip, and they left.

They pulled up to the University of Georgia and CMoney took in the college life as all the students walked about going wherever they had to go. He wondered after his senior year in high school that was coming up, would he attend college. 'I'll cross that bridge when I get there,' he thought.

"Pull up right there, bae," Esther said pointing up ahead as he pulled up to where she requested.

"Where you want me to park at?" he asked prepared for the wait as she kissed his lips.

"I don't know how long I'm gon' be, so hit the Lenox or something and I'll call you when I'm ready," she said grabbing her book bag and folder before she closed the door.

"Aight baby, I got you," he said before she walked away. He stayed parked until she got in the building, then he pulled off. Arriving in the parking lot to the southeast's premier shopping destination, otherwise known as the Lenox Mall on Peach Tree Street, he found a parking space, and parked. 'This mall bigger than all the malls in the Mil,' he thought while walking through one of the entrances.

Strolling through the mall, he spotted Candice from The Real Housewives walking through the mall looking super good while trying to hide her identity behind a pair of designer shades, but he knew her sexy self anywhere. He approached her gentleman-like and asked her for a picture, which she was cool with, so he asked her friend to snap it on his iPhone. He talked to her about the show and her music. He was going to ask her about the instant

success of her pleasure line, but he didn't want to make her feel uncomfortable or disrespected because she was his TV boo in his head, so that was out of the question. She was real down to earth, not stuck up like some people can be when they become wildly successful. He asked her for a hug, she gave him one, and with that, he left, but not before a look over his shoulder at her ample behind. 'She so bad,' he thought and kept it moving.

He went into several stores and was about to make his way back to the college, but he wanted to check the Louis Vuitton store out before he left. He bought a fit belt, and sunglasses for himself. A dress and sunglasses for Esther, paid for that, and left the store. While walking out of the store, he saw a familiar looking woman leaving out of the Kate Spade store with plenty of bags in her hand.

He quickly realized the woman was Stacy, Miles' bitch from that night at the club. 'His hoe azz gotta be here,' he thought while following her from a distance as she walked into Mayor's jewelry store. CMoney stood from afar watching the store like a hawk while acting like he was doing something else. His face instantly

frowned up with pure malice as his suspicions were confirmed. Not too far away from him, Stacy and Miles exited the store arm in arm not even knowing the danger that they were in. CMoney started to pull the P99 from his waistband and leave him and his bitch's brains all over the shoe store window that they were passing, but there were too many witnesses, so he had to be smarter, and plus he made a promise to Jeff, but that promise was fading by the minute as the exit that they were heading out of was hearing.

"Hold up boo, let's go in here," CMoney heard Miles say as Stacy became visibly upset. "You can go wait in the car, it's right there, you in here actin' a damn fool, embarrassing me and shit," Miles added pointing in the direction that he was talking about, then he walked in the store. But Stacy didn't leave, she walked in the store right behind him. Hearing that, CMoney quickly speed walked past the store looking in the opposite direction, so he wouldn't be recognized. Getting outside he ran like he had just stole something to the rental, hopped in, and peeled off to where he saw Miles point and pulled into a

parking space as a car was leaving, He was close enough to see the door that they were about to come out of.

CMoney searched the rows of cars with his eyes looking for the Maserati, but they had to be in a different car because he didn't see it.

Miles and Stacy came out of the mall and walked directly down the row of cars were CMoney was parked. CMoney could see the bulge in his waistline which meant that he had a pistol on him. They were getting close, so CMoney scooted down in his seat slightly so he wouldn't alert any suspicion, even though they were on the opposite side from where he was parked.

CMoney watched closely through the rear-view mirror as they passed him. A few more cars down, they loaded their bags into the trunk of a hardtop convertible Mercedes Benz SL5OO. Getting in the car, he dropped the top, pulled out, and smashed off as CMoney's phone rang. He looked at the phone to see that it was Esther.

"Fuck!" he yelled. He knew that she was ready to get picked up, what should he do? What would you do? He

hit the ignore button and pulled out following the Benz from a distance. 'I'm wit you baby, but I gave my word on this, so I gotta handle it,' he thought while pulling up to the light three cars behind Miles.

C Bands and Rickie Blow's 'Paper Long' bumped out of the speakers as Ken drove on his way to catch some action. He was feeling good and looking good in his True Religion outfit and freshly twisted cornrows. He didn't know why he hadn't been started hustling a long time ago. He loved everything about the game: the money, the sense of power, and the way the women looked at him. Even though he had been only fucking Big Booty Rudy faithfully, he promised himself that he would get some more bitches on his team. Big Booty Rudy had damn near became his wifey, they did almost everything together, like go to the movies, restaurants, and just kick it, which would lead to Rudy on her back or bent over and him getting some of that good pussy, with a condom on of course, but he loved hitting that.

Ken pulled up in the Meadows parking lot on 91st and Allyn, parked, and hopped out. Walking up to the house, he knocked on the door, got let in, counted the money, gave the dope, and left. Hopping back in the car, he pulled around the corner in the first parking lot on 95th and did the same thing. Then he drove a couple of parking lots over to what was known as 'Murda lot' to serve one of his decent-looking hype chicks.

"What up, Crystal?" he said when she opened the door.

"Hey Ken, come in," she responded smiling. Crystal was 32 years old with an 8-year-old son, but she was a functioning smoker. Meaning she kept herself up appearance wise, she worked, and her house was never in disarray like that of a traditional hype. She just simply liked to get high, occasionally. She'd call Ken one day and might not call him back for a week after that. However, the potent drug had yet to take away her looks and body and Ken was seeing that first-hand. Crystal wore a pair of black stretch leggings, a baby tee, and a

pair of flip flops. The leggings that she wore fit snuggly over her plump ass, prompting Ken's next move.

"How many you want, Crystal?" Ken asked while looking over her body lustfully as she was digging in her purse.

"Let me get something nice for this fifty," she said holding the fifty dollars bill out.

"I'll tell you what, I'll give you six for this fifty, or I'll give you ten for this fifty, and we can have a little fun before I go," he propositioned her while stepping so close that he could smell her body wash as he grabbed a handful of her ass.

Crystal thought about this for a minute, she'd be lying if she said that she never took the drug in exchange for a sexual favor, being that she had done it twice before. She did find Ken attractive, but he was so young, she didn't know if she should take it there. 'Fuck it, I'mma fuck the shit out his young azz,' she reasoned with herself after wrestling with her thoughts.

"You know I don't usually do this, but since you so cute, I'mma give you something to remember," she said grabbing his hand and leading him upstairs into her bedroom where she peeled her tight pants from her body and took everything else off while Ken did the same.

Crystal being the experienced one pushed him back on the bed, dropped to her knees, and wrapped her lips around his fully erect member.

"Ahh," Ken moaned as Crystal did her thing on him. She bobbed her head sensually with a death lock grip on him. Three minutes into the session, he was cumming down her throat. "Ah shit," he added after busting his nut.

"Ken, you eat a lot of sweets, don't you?" Crystal asked after swallowing his seed while jagging him off in an effort to keep him hard.

"Ye...yeah...why you say that?" he barely got out with his chest heaving.

"Because your cum tastes sweet, I could drink that shit all day," Crystal smiled. Hearing this, Ken's dick got right back on brick in her hand. "We'll talk about that

later, come on and let me get some of that good stuff," Ken said passing her a condom. She opened it, put it in her mouth, put his dick back in her mouth, and deep throated it slowly with short bobs of her head all the way down. That impressed Ken so much, that he got aggressive as he raised up, laid her down on the bed, got in between her legs, and entered her. She was a little dry at first, but Ken kept right on pumping until her water gates opened.

"Slow down nigga, this pussy ain't going nowhere," Crystal said, but Ken kept right on fucking like a jack rabbit as he pumped furiously inside of her. Crystal put her legs on his shoulders and tried to match his pace, but he was pumping too fast, then Ken couldn't take it anymore.

"Arrghh," he grunted as he came in the rubber, so he thought. Ken kept right on pumping until his dick became flaccid, then he pulled out and noticed the whole condom was at the base of his dick.

"Damn," he said knowing he just nutted in Crystal, but not knowing the significance of what he had done.

"What, that's all you got nigga?" Crystal smiled.

"For now, you got a good shot on you, had me bussin' everywhere, and the rubber popped too," Ken said nonchalantly.

"Did it? Yo azz betta not be tryna trap me," she said. "Yo azz was bussin' like that because this here is grown woman stuff, right? Nothing like dem lil girls you be messing with. I know what to do," she boasted.

"You definitely do too, and that mouth ain't nothing nice," Ken admitted.

"Here you go, that's you," he passed her 12 bags,

"When can I come back and see you?" he continued, he wanted some more of what she just gave him.

"Whenever my son ain't here, I'mma teach yo young azz how to fuck, all that bumpin' you doin' ain't bout shit. You will be turnt out," she said intending on making

good on her promise as she got up and walked him to the door after he got dressed.

"Aight, matter of fact, call me tomorrow when he's not here and I'll come through then," Ken said palming that ass one more time before he left.

"I'mma do that" she said before closing the door. Ken was all smiles, he now had four hoes under his belt. 'It's only gonna grow from here,' he thought while on his way to the car, when he saw a nigga limping through the cut which made him laugh.

"Greg! Greg!" he yelled. Greg was the hype who hit him in the eye, in which he shot him in the ass. Greg turned around, saw Ken, and turned back around with more pep in his step. "Fuck you then, hoe azz nigga! I was gon' tell you that I got that good if yo money right," Ken added while laughing before getting in his car and pulling off feeling good after a nice sex session. He contemplated on not messing with Big Booty Rudy no more, and just fucking with Crystal because Rudy never gave him no head before, but he'd asked on several occasions and she

wouldn't go, meanwhile, Crystal had just given him the total package. 'Naw, I'mma keep fucking both of em, but Rudy gotta step her game up,' he thought as he drove down Brown Deer.

∞

CMoney followed Miles and Stacy to a house in Decatur, Georgia, not too far from Columbia middle school. CMoney pulled up to the corner and watched the Benz drive slowly into an opening garage where he saw a red car inside. He'd bet a thousand dollars to a bucket of shit, that the red car was the Maserati.

He also saw an Acura truck in the driveway. Once Stacy hopped out of the car and grabbed a little girl that seemed to be maybe two or three years old from another girl who CMoney presumed to be the baby sitter. CMoney remembered that night at the club when Stacy mentioned that she had a daughter, so everything taking place led him to believe that this was their home. CMoney grabbed his phone, took a picture of the house, and the street signs around it before he pulled off.

"Gotcha bitch," he said to himself as his phone rang. "What's up baby?" he answered.

"I'm ready, but why haven't you been answering your phone?" Esther asked sternly.

"I fucked around and left my phone in the dressing room at the Louis Vuitton store and didn't know where I put it, I just found it, thou," he lied, but what was he gon' say? I saw the nigga who shot my sister and best friend, so I followed him? Some things are better kept unsaid, and this was one of those things.

"So why didn't you call me back when you seen my missed calls?" she asked puzzled.

'Damn, great question,' he thought. "I don't know, I just got the phone right now, I'm on my way right now, I'mma make it up to you," he smiled knowing that he'd finally met a woman that could challenge him mentally.

"You better, bye," she said hanging up. CMoney couldn't help but smile as he strolled down his call log.

"What's going on lil bro?" Jeff answered.

"Bro, you ain't gon' believe this," he said excitedly.

∞

Two days later, CMoney and Jeff sat parked down the street from Miles' house. The upstairs light had just went out, signaling that it was bed time for Stacy and her baby.

Miles wasn't home yet, he'd be arriving in the next 20 minutes or so, alone, and entering the house through the front door. They had been sitting on the house the previous two days and learned his routine quickly. I guess he didn't know routines got people killed, set up, or possibly both.

"Bro, you sure that's gon' work?" CMoney questioned.

"I did ten with the best of em, it's gon' work," Jeff said pulling his hood over the mask that sat on top of his head,

"You ready?" he continued while putting the small nap sack across his chest diagonally before making sure his P99 with the silencer was ready to fire.

"No doubt," he stated while putting his P99 with the silencer and extended clip in his hoodie pocket and pulling his hood over the mask that sat on top of his head. They had already taken the fuses out for the vehicles interior lights, so they didn't arouse any suspicion when they got out of the stolen car.

Getting out of the car, they ran through a yard in the crouching position and into the wooded area. They walked through the woods, careful not to snag any of their clothing as they approached Miles' house from the back. Suddenly, Jeff took off in a full sprint to the back door and quickly unscrewed the motion sensored light CMoney then met up with him at the back door as Jeff looked through the back-door's window, then he dug his gloved hand into the nap sack he carried. Pulling out a suction cup and a glass cutter, he placed the suction cup against the window, pushed it down until it was flush against the glass, then he cut around the suction cup leaving a hole at the top of the door's window.

Jeff then passed the suction cup that was holding the glass to CMoney, who took the glass of the suction cup, and slung it in the grass. Jeff dug back into his sack and pulled out a stick of gum and two pieces of duck tape. Putting the gum in his mouth, he slid the silver wrapper through the hole at the top of the door and placed it between the sensor and the door to complete its circuit, so when he opened the door the alarm wouldn't go off.

'The things you learn in prison,' CMoney thought as Jeff then taped the gum wrapper in place to assure it stayed there before getting the suction cup from CMoney and cutting a piece of glass out of at the bottom of the window, not too far from the knob. Placing the suction cup back in his sack, along with the cutter after taking the glass off and handing it to CMoney, who slung it in the grass, they were now ready to enter. Jeff reached through the window, unlocked the top lock, then the knob lock and opened the door slowly in efforts to not disturb the gum wrapper.

Upon gaining entry into the kitchen, CMoney had pulled the P99 out after he pulled his mask down over his face. Closing the door, Jeff fixed the curtains on the door's window, and pulled out his pistol as well after pulling his mask down.

Walking through the house lightly, they checked the entire first floor before they proceeded upstairs. Opening the first room door, they saw a little girl sleeping. CMoney held up one finger and pointed down the hall, meaning continue in that direction. After closing the door slowly, they came to another room, which was empty. Again, CMoney gave the signal to continued. Getting to the last room, they opened the door slowly to see Stacy laying on her stomach with a teddy on, and her whole ass out, she was obviously waiting on Miles, but he wouldn't be getting any of that apple bottom tonight or any other night for that matter.

Jeff, with duct tape in his hand, walked over to Stacy and quickly covered her mouth while trying to manhandle her, but she sprung to life, rolled over, and caught him

with a wild punch that caused him to take a step back, then she immediately started screaming.

"Shut the fuck up bitch," CMoney said sending a hard-right cross crashing into her jaw, knocking her unconscious. Jeff then taped her spread-eagle style to all four bed posts. CMoney peeked through the window to see if any lights suddenly came on from the neighbors hearing her scream. Seeing none, he looked at the clock that was on the dresser and grabbed the two watches he noticed and put them in his pocket. Then he peeked through the blinds once again, Miles was 15 minutes late, but headlights could be seen coming down the street. CMoney smiled when he heard the garage door opening, Miles was home.

"Here he come," CMoney said then took his position in the closet with the door cracked and his pistol in front of him. Jeff took his position behind the bedroom's door with pistol in hand.

About two minutes later, they could hear Miles running up the stairs, stop and check on his baby before making his way to the master's bedroom.

"Damn, you ready alrea...," Miles started, but was abruptly interrupted by the hit to the back of the head by Jeff's pistol knocking him out. CMoney darted out of the closet, helped pick him up, put him in the chair, then Jeff duct taped him thoroughly after they searched him and removed his .45 cal.

"Get yo' hoe azz up," CMoney said before slapping him across the face with a vicious blow. Miles woke up, looked at the masked man in front of him, then to Stacy laid out on the bed, and started to panic.

"What y'all want man?" he asked obviously scared.

"You know why we here, give us what we came for and you live," CMoney stated firmly.

"I ain't got shit here, I..," Miles started but was cut off.

"Wrong answer," CMoney said landing a vicious three-piece combo to his mid-section, making him gasp for air as Jeff left the room.

"I'm ...not...bullshitin man," Miles said in between coughs.

"Do you wanna die over some shit that you can replace?" CMoney asked him, getting no response as Jeff came back into the room with a pair of flat irons used for straightening hair and some Crisco cooking grease, Jeff then plugged the flat irons up.

"He ain't cooperation'?" Jeff asked. CMoney shook his head no, then Jeff came over and unleashed a barrage of punches to Miles' mid-section, breaking three ribs in the process,

"Talk punk or die," he added. Even in this hostile environment, Jeff stayed true to not cursing. Jeff then put a piece of tape over Miles' mouth, walked over to the flat irons, broke them in half, dipped them in the grease, then took a seat on the bed next to Stacy,

"You still don't wanna talk wit yo punk azz self?" Jeff said almost slipping up and cursing. Getting no response, he put the flat iron on Stacy's stomach. She woke up with a horrified scream coming out of her mouth as Jeff pressed it down even harder until it sizzled against her flesh. Even though her screams were muffled, it still said that she was in a lot of pain, Stacy then passed out from that pain.

Miles closed his eyes as tears ran rapidly, CMoney stood there watching his coward azz cry like a bitch, then he noticed what smelled like some fried but burned bologna as Jeff raised the flat iron from her stomach. Her skin was sticking to them along with puss and blood.

"You gon' talk now punk?" Jeff said punching him, then he removed the tape from his mouth.

CMoney got an idea, so he left the room, and when he returned, he had Miles' sleeping daughter in his arms. When CMoney looked at Miles, he saw defeat in his eyes.

"Aight man, in the living room, slide the table over, move the rug, and it's a floor safe. 25-17-13 is the combination, just please don't hurt my daughter man," Miles said finally giving in at the sight of his daughter.

"Go get that, while I handle this. Put her back in the room and hit the floor as soon as you get the safe opened," CMoney directed Jeff while passing him the baby, then Jeff left to go retrieve the money.

"Now, do you know why I'm really here?" CMoney asked.

"The money right," he said puzzled.

"Wrong answer," CMoney said and punched him in the mouth, breaking his jaw. "I'll ask again, do you know why I'm here?" CMoney said getting agitated at the sight of him.

"Naw Man," Miles managed to get out because his jaw was hanging as the knock on the floor came letting CMoney know that Jeff had the safe open.

"See Miles, the money was just an extra incentive, I'm here for a much deeper reason. You and I, well, we got unfinished business," he said while pushing his mask back on top of his head.

Miles looked as if what he was seeing was phantom, he couldn't believe that his shit caught back up with him, he also knew that he fucked up badly. See CMoney wasn't going to reveal himself to Miles until he knew that the safe was open because once Miles saw him, there'd be no way he was going to tell him the combination to that safe because he would've known he was going to die, therefore keeping his silence.

"Man, you gotta believe me, I ain't have shit to do with that, I got a kid and a family," he lied trying to plead for his life, but his plea fell on deaf ears.

"Bitch azz nigga, you wasn't worried about my family when you shot 'em, and now you in here tryna play that, I ain't got shit to do with it card. Nigga fuck you, and you deserve to die," CMoney said pointing his gun at Miles.

"You said if I give you the money, you was gon' let me live," Miles said on the brink of tears.

"I lied, I'll see you when I get there "Pst Pst Pst Pst Pst," CMoney said pumping five rounds from his silenced pistol into Miles' face and body. Miles shook and convulsed before he slumped over dead. The five bullets symbolized two for Legacy, two for Dre, and one for making him chase his azz all over Georgia. Then he walked over to the bed Pst Pst Pst, he put three holes in Stacy, she was guilty by association. CMoney ran out of the room and down the stairs just as Jeff was tossing an army-sized duffel bag over his shoulder.

"Everything good?" Jeff asked.

"Yeah, let's go," CMoney said as they exited the same way they came in. Making it back to the stolen car, they got in, put the car in neutral, and let it roll down the hill not even closing the doors yet. Getting a decent distance, CMoney started the car, and pulled off closing the doors. They would drive not too far, burn the car, and hop in the rental.

A devilish grin came across CMoney's face because Miles was gone, and he made good on his promise to Legacy.

CHAPTER ELEVEN

Two days later, CMoney, Dre, and Esther were on their way to Milwaukee, Wisconsin. They were already seven

hours into their eleven to thirteen-hour road trip in a rented Ford Expedition truck. With Esther behind the wheel, CMoney sat in the passenger's seat listening to Rob K's 'Movie' while deep in thought. He had plans to take things to another level and become rich in the streets. He told himself that when it came to that bread, he didn't want a slice, he needed a loaf, and thanks to the $650,000 he got from Miles' house, there was no doubt that he was on his way to the top. Jeff wouldn't take any of the money at first, he just wanted Miles dead, but after a lot of persuading by CMoney, he took $50,000 which left CMoney with $600,000 of Miles' money. He planned to give Legacy, Dre, and Chante a hundred gees apiece for their pain and suffering. Most niggas would've been greedy and kept everything or bird fed them, but CMoney was a different breed from most niggas, he loved his people, and loyalty

meant everything to him. Besides, without them, he wouldn't even be in the position he was in now.

CMoney sat up and looked in the backseat to see Dre sound asleep. Since he told him that Miles was no longer walking the streets, Dre's spirits had risen drastically.

"You want me to drive the rest of the way?" he asked skeptically.

"I can make it baby," Esther said keeping her eyes on the road.

"You know I love you, right?" he asked smiling while looking at the side of her beautiful face. If she had a flaw, he surely couldn't see it.

"I love you too," she smiled while turning to meet his stare briefly before turning her attention back to the road. This was his third time telling her that, but she knew he meant it wholeheartedly every time. His actions displayed that he loved her even when he didn't say it, and that was the most important thing to her.

"I just want you to know that, because when I get back in these streets, I'm finna go hard in the paint and I don't want you to think for a second that I'm switching up on you because I can assure you that will never be the case. I will put you first, come home to you every night, and whenever you need me, I will be there. If there's anything you want us to do as a couple, just let me know a day in advance, and we'll make it happen. I don't you on this block I'm on at all without me because niggas gon' envy what I'm bout to put down, and I couldn't bare it if something happened to you because of me. I know you said you don't need a gun, but I prefer you let my sisters take you to get your CCW license because that would make me feel more comfortable when we're not together. We gon' buy a crib in a couple of months, so you can start looking on the internet for one now, but I gotta make this money baby, you feel me?" he asked seriously.

"As long as you uphold what you told me, I can't say anything. I understand you're going to be in the streets, just be careful and remember what you have at

home. I will get the CCW if you want me to, we gonna be fine baby," she said with a smile while puckering her lips up as CMoney leaned in and kissed her.

"That's all I needed to know," he said leaning back in his seat satisfied with the bond between them. He knew the street life could come between a man and his significant other at any given time, and because most niggas never have that talk with their women, she was often left in the dark, thinking the worst and ultimately finding her way into the arms of another man. CMoney had witnessed it first-hand in his own circle, in which he developed an understanding of how important communication really is, so he'd keep it one hunnid between him and her. 'Real niggas do real shit,' he thought.

∞

"Shawn, I'm outside," Legacy said into her cell phone from the passenger's seat of the Jeep Liberty.

"Aight, here I come," Shawn said hanging up. A few minutes later, he got into the backseat.

"What's good wit y'all? I'm glad you good girl, shit was not lookin' good at first," Shawn stated seriously as he dug in his pocket and handed Legacy two large knots of money for the two kilos he usually bought.

"I'm good, thanks," Legacy said taking the offered money. "I want you to know that I really appreciate what you did for us in Atlanta, cause you ain't have to do that, but you did and that says a lot about you," she added knowing Shawn was a real thoroughbred nigga.

"Thanks for that Shawn, real talk," Chante chimed in. "Y'all ain't gotta thank me for that, I fucks wit y'all the long way, so if I ever see some shit goin' down that I don't like, I'm gon' do what I gotta do. How could I call myself a real nigga if I turned my back on y'all like I didn't see what was happening? I can't, so I had to exercise what I preach," he stated seriously.

"That's what's up, I know you asked for two, but this is three for the price of two, just to show how appreciative we really are," Legacy said passing him the bag with three kilos in it.

"Nice lookin', but y'all ain't have to do that, I'll just take what I paid for, I did what I did because that's who I am," Shawn reasoned.

"Naw you good, that's you," Legacy assured him while gaining a new respect for him.

"If you insist," Shawn smiled.   "What happened to ol' boy?" he added.

"Dre, he gotta wear 'THE SHIT BAG' for awhile, but other than that, he'll be alright," Legacy responded.

"Ouch, at least he alive thou, I'mma get up wit y'all," he said getting out of the truck after dapping Legacy and Chante.

"Legacy, he a real nigga by all means, you don't meet too many like him no more," Chante said while pulling off.

"Who you telling," Legacy retorted.

"Did you get the keys from the landlord for Chris? Cause they should be here any minute now," Chante said making a left turn.

"Yeah, I got 'em already," Legacy stated. CMoney had her look for him and Esther an apartment to move into and he'd give her everything she paid when he got back into town.

"Where to now?" Chante asked.

"Go down there to see Curt and Ben," Legacy said. She had to go pick up the money and drop the work off to the workers.

∞

CMoney was elated to be back in Milwaukee as they exited the expressway on 8th and North Avenue. CMoney gave Esther the directions to his mother's house, which was in Lapham Park projects. Pulling up in front of her house, they parked and got out of the car, but not before CMoney grabbed his duffel bag, and went inside the house using his key.

"Chris, is that you?" Claire asked while walking into the kitchen.

"Yeah ma, how you doing pretty lady?" CMoney responded as he was now face to face with his mother. Seeing her, he hugged her and kissed her on the cheek.

"When you get back?" she inquired noticing that there was something different in her son's demeanor.

"I just got off the freeway," CMoney stated as Claire grabbed his chin.

"Open yo mouth," she said as CMoney did what she asked him to do.

"Boy you done lost yo damn mind, you think you that muthafuckin' Lil Wayne or Birdman, don't you? That shit shinnin' though," she said letting his chin go.

"Naw ma, this who I am, I don't follow no man, I do what I like," he said seriously even though he wanted to laugh at how outdated his mother was.

"I ain't gon' even ask you how you paid for that. Hey Dre, and who is this pretty girl standin' there," Claire smiled for the first time.

"That's my girlfriend," he smiled proudly because Esther was gorgeous.

"Yo' girlfriend?! she questioned, then looked to Esther.

"What is yo name sweetie?" she added.

"Esther" she responded.

"Y'all talk,   I'll be   right back,   come on Dre," CMoney stated before he kissed Esther and headed down to the basement. Turning the TV on, Dre sat down while CMoney went to his secret stash spot in the back of the basement. Getting there, he shimmied the two bricks out of the wall. Then he took the 4 kilos, 8 pounds of kush, and his .357 out, leaving the $45,000 in there. Taking $150,000 out of the duffel bag, he stashed that behind the wall, bringing the total to $195, 000, then he put the two concrete bricks in place. Stuffing his .357 automatic in his waistband, he put 5 gees in his pocket, and went back to the part of the basement where Dre was.

"Here you go my nigga," CMoney said throwing him a book bag, then placing $100,000 on the table in front of him.

"What's this fo'?" Dre asked puzzled while rubbing his hands over the money.

"That's for you, it's a hunnid thousand, courtesy of that fuck nigga in Atlanta for that shit he pulled," he said casually.

"You always come through for a nigga, don't you?" Dre responded before getting up and showing him some love.

"You my nigga, so I'mma always come through for you when I can, we bout to go super hard out here," he smiled.

"That's one hunnid," Dre said seriously as he stuffed the money in the book bag.

"Ay, I got a crib wit Esther, you movin' wit us or what?" he inquired not wanting to leave his boy out because he always had his back since elementary.

"Naw, that's you and ya girl crib, I'mma get me a bachelor's pad, but nice lookin on the offer, bro," Dre responded.

"Anytime, now let's get outta here," he said then turned the TV off, grabbed the bag, and headed upstairs.

"Aight ma, I'm outta here, call me if you need me," CMoney said.

"Okay baby, you betta have yo azz in school when it starts too, I don't give a damn about what you doing in them streets, this yo last year, so get it done," she said seriously.

"I'm definitely going to school, ma," he assured her.

"You ready baby?" he added, talking to Esther.

"Yeah," Esther said getting out of her seat and following him to the door.

"Chris,   come here   before   you leave," Claire yelled. CMoney sat the bag by the door and went to see what his mother wanted while Esther and Dre went to the truck.

"What up, ma?" CMoney asked casually.

"Don't do that girl wrong, say she came all the way from Atlanta to be with you, and I think she's a keeper, trust me, mama's know. She reminds me of that one girl, um...," Claire said snapping her fingers trying to jog her memory. "The girl that played in the movie ATL," she added.

"Lauren London," CMoney said smiling because he knew exactly who his mother was referring too.

"Yeah, that's her, very beautiful. Now you be safe out there," Claire said hugging him.

"I will, I'll   call   you   later," CMoney said   before turning to leave. On the way out of the door, he put the 5 gees in his pocket on the kitchen table, picked up his bag, and left. On his way to the truck, he texted

Legacy about the apartment while he got behind the wheel, then he pulled off while calling Ken.

"What up cuz, you back yet?" Ken answered.

"Yeah, where   you   at?" CMoney said nonchalantly. He heard that Ken had been doing good in his absence, but he didn't know the extent.

"I'm bout to leave the house right now and drop my bitch off at Ebony 2 to get her hair done. I got something for you too," Ken stated enthusiastically.

"Did you get that package I sent?" CMoney inquired.

"Yep, you want me to bring it?" Ken asked.

"Hell naw, I'll get it later, but bring whatever it is that you got for me, and I'll meet you at the shop," he said realizing that his cousin was still green in a lot of aspects of the game.

"Bet those," Ken said hanging up as CMoney's text alert went off. It was Legacy saying that she had the keys to the apartment and where did he want her to meet him. He texted her back and told her to meet him at Ebony's.

"Dre, Ken said to meet him at Ebony 2 because he gotta drop his bitch off to get her hair done," CMoney laughed.

"What! I bet she popped," Dre smiled knowing the girl was probably ugly.

Pulling up on 60th and Fond Du Lac he made a right and pulled up behind a car on the block where Ebony 2 hair Salon was. Hopping out of the truck, he walked around it and stepped on the side walk just as Ken got out of an GMC Envoy truck.

"What's happen, cuz?" Ken asked happily.

"Shit, what you on?" CMoney asked as Dre walked up. CMoney could tell that Ken had become a whole different person in the short time that he had been gone.

"Tryna get this money, I see you shinning hard as a bitch," Ken said referring to CMoney's grill.

"Fo' sho, who truck is that?" CMoney asked skeptically.

"That's mine, I just copped that," Ken said proudly. Seeing the look on CMoney's face, he spoke up. "Don't trip thou, I got 10 gees for you in the truck right now and yo' whip parked in front of mom's crib," he added. CMoney would be lying if he said that he wasn't impressed, Ken had been holding shit down correctly.

"Aight, but I wanna see this chick you got up in here," CMoney said as the three young men headed to the salon door and got buzzed in. Two minutes later, they were back outside laughing hard as hell.

"Fam, Big Booty Rudy yo bitch?" CMoney said in disbelief.

"Man, we done fucked her, got sucked, and passed her on to some we know and you wifed her? Shit, I put the rubber on tighter," Dre laughed.

"You betta not be kissin' that bitch," he added laughing even harder. CMoney could see the look of embarrassment all over Ken's face, but he had wifed a jump down and no respectable man would go that route knowingly unless he was a sucka azz nigga.

If she has no self-respect, how will she ever be able to respect your relationship? You cannot wife what isn't truly yours. CMoney would school him on the things he needed to know in due time.

"Cuz, I know you know she goin' like Davin's, nigga that ain't yo bitch. She may be yours right now because you wit her, but later on today she'll be the next nigga's. You can't wife no bitch like that, why buy the cow when you can get the milk for free? You gotta step yo game up my nigga, you havin' bands now. You aint a regular nigga no more. You gotta fuck bad bitches and wife bad bitches that's on something and just not on their backs, you feel me? Let me give you an example of what I'm talking about," CMoney said waving his hands in the air to get Esther's attention. Once he did, he told her to come here. Esther stepped out of the truck in a pair of skin   tight   medium   indigo Luxirie jeans by LRG, white short-sleeve polo, tight   fitting Luxirie shirt by LRG, and a pair of white open-toe ankle strap sandals by Sergio Rossi. Ken's mouth flew open as she walked up and kissed CMoney on the lips.

'She thick and bad as fuck, she looked like she walked straight off the pages of Straight Stuntin magazine, I don't know   how cuz got   that, but   he definitely did that,' Ken thought. He was mesmerized by her beauty and he immediately knew that he had to indeed step his game up in a major way.

"Baby this   my cousin   Ken, Ken   this   the wifey, Esther," CMoney said casually just as Chante and Legacy pulled up.

"How you doing, Ken?" Esther asked with a smile and a wave of her hand.

"I'm aight," Ken responded thinking that she looked like Lauren London up close.

"What's good family?" Chante said smiling as she and Legacy walked up.

'Damn,' Dre thought as he looked over Legacy's sexy azz, he wanted her bad, but he doubted that he could get her, so he never pursued her. After greeting and hugging everybody, CMoney pulled Ken to the side while the others talked.

"Come holla at me, my nigga," CMoney told Ken as they stepped away and hopped in the rental truck.

"What you wanted to holla at me about?" he continued.

"I want in my nigga, I'm ready to get on my grind," Ken stated seriously.

"You realize that its rules to this shit that must be followed and if they're not followed, even I can't save you," CMoney stated firmly after a brief pause.

"Save me," Ken said with both index fingers pointed towards himself.

"Cuz, I don't need nobody to save me from shit, and I'm fully aware of the fact that there's rules to this shit, do I know them all? No, but between you and experience, I'm sure to get it right as I possibly can. And don't ever imply or indicate me wit no snitchin' shit, if you wasn't family, I'd take that as disrespect. Whatever happens, I'm standing ten toes down on these feet, that part of the game, I do know," Ken said slightly offended that CMoney came at him like that.

CMoney was shocked that Ken responded like that. He knew Ken didn't have the knuckle game to beat him or the heart to pop him being that they were family, but he did like his fearlessness, the fact he didn't nut up or stand down to somebody he had no wins with told CMoney that Ken was serious and ready to ball in this game.

"Aight nigga calm down, I see you a lil mercenary like myself, I just needed to know that we see eye to eye because I'm bout to put this post game down on niggas in the paint, Shaq style," CMoney said while acting like his was dribbling and backing someone into the post.

"I feel you my nigga, I want in," Ken pleaded.

"You say you got 10 gees in the car for me, right?" CMoney asked while thinking.

"10 gees," Ken boasted. CMoney was taken back at first, he didn't expect him to advance that much, but he had 10 gees for him, riding a new whip, and sporting what CMoney estimated to be about a thousand dollars' worth of clothes including the shoes. He definitely had a lot of hustle in him, and CMoney knew he was ready to eat on the mean streets of Milwaukee.

"Aight nigga," CMoney said reaching in the back seat and unzipping the duffel bag, he made a mental note to get a car with a stash spot in it because he was riding around hot as hell.

"Can you handle that?" he added placing a kilo and five pounds of kush in Ken's lap.

"How much is this?" Ken asked puzzled, he still didn't know everything he needed to know yet.

"That's a kilo and five pounds," CMoney explained. Then he realized that Ken didn't know shit about what he had just given him.

"Listen, call me in the morning, I'mma have you come by the crib, and I'll teach you everything you need to know, cooking and all," he added.

"Aight cuz," Ken said elated, he had been wanting to learn how to cook crack ever since he started hustling.

"The phone is yours, just direct all weight orders to my line," CMoney explained.

"And I need 50 gees back," he added.

"Aight," Ken said while taking off his button-up shirt and wrapping the drugs in it.

Getting out of the truck, Ken jogged to his truck, hopped in, and came back to hand CMoney a brown paper bag with   10   gees   in   it. After   saying   his goodbyes, he hopped back in his truck and smashed off.

"Where my house at?" CMoney asked Legacy when he walked up to where everybody was standing.

"84th   and Grandtosa, apartment   number   103," Legacy responded.

"I'll follow you there," CMoney smiled.

"Aight," Legacy said as everybody piled into the cars they came in, then Chante   pulled   off   with CMoney right behind her. They made a right on 84th and Grandtosa and pulled   up in   front   of   the   second apartment complex. Getting out of the truck, everybody grabbed bags except Legacy who led them to Esther and CMoney's new apartment. Opening the door to the two bedroom, one-and-a-half-bathroom apartment with a good-sized kitchen, it was indeed very nice and more spacious than they initially thought.

"Y'all like it?" Legacy asked with a big smile.

"Yeah, it's real nice," Esther replied smiling.

"Oh yeah, this'll work right here," CMoney chimed in while standing next to Esther with his arm around her waist. The look she gave him let him know that she was going to put it on him later. CMoney and Dre went to go get the rest of the remaining bags after CMoney put the duffel bag in the closet that he and Esther decided would be their bedroom.

"Legacy, let me holla at you upstairs for a minute," CMoney said grabbing two bags of clothes before heading upstairs with Legacy in tow.

"Sis, I need y'all to take Esther to the furniture store, Wal-Mart, and to the car lot for me please, because I gotta get out here right now," CMoney said as soon as they got into the room while he dumped the clothes out of the bag onto the floor.

"Aight, I got you, bro," she stated watching CMoney slide the closet door back, unzip the duffel bag, and throw several large wads of money into one of the bags.

"This three hundred and five gees. A hunnid for you, a hunnid for Tay, and a hunnid for my work which I need ASAP and 5 gees is for your troubles in getting this apartment for us. This all from that hoe nigga in Atlanta, ya feel me?" CMoney explained.

"Yeah, I appreciate that too," Legacy said sincerely knowing that he was talking about the nigga that shot her, but what's understood need not to be said. Using her good arm, she flipped the bag on her shoulder. CMoney counted out twenty gees, put three in his pocket, put his chain on his neck, and stuffed the two kilos and two pounds of kush in the other bag. Zipping the duffel bag back up, he placed it back in the closet, then him and Legacy left the room, and went back downstairs.

"Esther, come here baby, let me holla at you in the kitchen," he said.

"What is up?" Esther said walking in the kitchen behind him.

"I need you to go with my sisters to the furniture
store and buy whatever you like. Then go to Wal-Mart
and get some cleaning supplies, dishes, hygiene products,
a few TVs, DVD players, and whatever else
we gon' need. And get me a key made to the house.
Then she gon' take you to the car lot, I know yo truck will
be here tomorrow, and I got another whip, but I think we
still gon' need another whip, so get something tinted up
that we'll both like, you feel me?" he asked knowing she
did.

"Of course, I always feel you," she smiled
while leaning in and kissing him on the
lips. CMoney gripped as much of her plentiful ass as he
could with his hand that wasn't loaded with money.

"You gon' get it tonight when you get home, so don't stay
out too late," she added after breaking their embrace.

"I already know," he smiled happily.

"Take this, it's seventeen thousand, it should be enough to
get everything, and if not, we'll get whatever

else tomorrow," he said passing her the fat wad of money.

"Baby, I'm not no broke bitch, I got money too, so whatever we need, I'll buy," she said passing him the money back. "I know you got money, I love the fact that you got yo own, but a man is a provider for his home or he cannot call himself a man, you feel me?" he stated seriously while looking into her honey-brown eyes.

"Yeah," she said coyly with a smile.

"You can buy the other shit for our next house," he said as they shared a laugh. CMoney went to get her the navigation system just in case she needed it, then he kissed her, told her he'd see her later, and to call if she needed him. After that, him and Dre hopped in the rental with their bags. Dre with the hunnid gees and CMoney with the drugs. They were headed to Dre's mother's house, so he could stash his money and get his work. Then they were off to the Meadows to open up shop.

∞

"What you gon' do when you get back out there, besides the obvious?" Wayne asked casually.

"I don't know my nigga, I'm thinking about opening up a clothing and shoe store," Boss said thinking. He was due to start trial in one week and he had high hopes that he could beat the case.

"You gon' marry Legacy?" Wayne smiled.

"Don't know yet, that's a big step, and I gotta make sure I'm ready for that, shit, she gotta be ready for that," Boss said honestly while leaning back in his chair.

"What? Nigga you was in shambles when you found out that she got shot, since you found out that she good and she been comin' to see yo azz, you been cheesin' hard as hell every day. From what I know, she's a good girl and she bad, shit, I don't know what the problem is," Wayne gave his view point on things.

Boss shook his head up and down in agreement knowing that his cousin was right. He was about to respond, but his thoughts were interrupted.

"Mail call!" the deputy yelled and then read off the names of inmates that had mail.

"SChad, Ferguson, Jackson, Dallas, Paul...," he continued.

"Which one?" Boss and Wayne said in unison.

"Orlando Paul," he replied, and Boss went to retrieve his mail. The guard handed him three envelopes, one from Train, and the two others were from Legacy, both with pictures in them. Getting back to the table, Boss sat down, took the pictures out, and quickly went through them before passing them to Wayne. He just wanted to make sure it wasn't any sexy lingerie pictures in there because he didn't want his cousin lusting over his girl because she was bad and thick as hell. He read Legacy's letter while Wayne went through the pictures.

"Who dis?" Wayne asked puzzled looking at a picture of CMoney standing next to his El Camino with his chain on after he got his grill done. Boss looked up briefly.

"That's her lil brother," he said and went back to reading his letter.

"Lil nigga eatin' good," Wayne said going through some more pictures.

"Who dis?" he asked again. Boss looked up from his letter.

"That's Legacy and her sister, Chante," Boss said casually, then continued reading.

"Her sister bad and thick as a bitch," Wayne said, Boss just smiled as Wayne went through more pictures until one prevented him from going through the rest as he stared deeply in to the picture wondering if what he was seeing was actually real, because he couldn't believe it.

"Cuz, who the fuck is dis?" he added visibly upset. Hearing the tone in his voice, Boss looked at the picture.

"I think that's her lil brother's best friend, why?" Boss inquired still not knowing what was going on.

"Cause that's the nigga Brandon's piece and chain he got around his muthafuckin' neck," Wayne spat. Hearing this, Boss snatched the picture out of his hand as Wayne walked off. Boss looked at the picture and saw Dre wearing the platinum chain with the iced out #8 pool ball in black diamonds. Yeah, Brandon was indeed Big Ball, and he was Boss and Wayne's cousin. Wayne came back to the table with Big Ball's obituary in his hand and showed Boss the picture in it of him wearing the chain. Boss looked at the obituary, then to the picture, and repeated the same process once more before he laid them both on the table. He just sat there stone-faced for a minute wondering if Legacy knew about her little brother and his best friend killing his cousin? If so, why didn't she try to stop him. She couldn't have known, he reasoned. Chris was from the Meadows which was close to where Big Ball lived, but did he really do it or was it a coincidence? If Chris or Dre did have anything to do with Brandon's death, Boss was sure to avenge that if he beat his case. He just sat there

becoming more and more livid by the minute because he
knew the inevitable.

CHAPTER TWELVE

F ive days later, CMoney was back in the swing of things, he hadn't heard anything about the Big Ball situation in the streets since he'd been back, which was good news for him and Dre. Right now, he was headed to Auto Customizations on South 27th Street in his new Buick Riviera that he bought two days ago from a nigga that he knew named Boo Boo in the Meadows. Esther followed close behind him in the new car that he sent her to buy, which was a gray 07 Monte Carlo SS behind tints. CMoney wanted to just wait til next summer and pull out something stupid, but it was August, which meant school started next month, and he had to pull up jackin' in style for the first day. He had left his El Camino in Atlanta in Esther's sister garage after it was shot up, so when he saw the two door Riviera sitting in front of Quick Pantry on 91st and Brown Deer with a for sale sign in the window for 3 gees, and in mint condition, he jumped all over it, and was now taking it to one of the hottest places in the city to have some things done to it.

Two days ago, Legacy went to go see her plug and talk to him about the proposed business plan that she had for him. After some number crunching and bargaining, he dropped the price down to $20,000 a square, and that was a super plug, but they had to at least buy 25 at a time, and anything under that, the original price would be restored. That was fine by Legacy, he had just cut $30,000 from every ten kilos' that they bought. Legacy bought 10 for her, 10 for Train, and 10 for CMoney and Dre to split. The plug wasn't losing though, he was still seeing over a half million from them. Since CMoney had gotten more bricks, he had been in the streets hustling even harder trying to double what he already had. He was trying to cop 15 squares at a time, bullshit ain't about nothing, so he was putting his best effort forward to make sure that he'd achieve that goal, all the while progressing in his relationship with Esther and getting ready for school himself.

Pulling up in front of Auto Customizations, he got out of the car, waited on Esther, and they entered the shop together.

CMoney talked to the owner who was a Puerto Rican man who went by the name Javier, Javi for short, he was the one that did CMoney's El Camino, and Dre's Magnum, he was a monster with the painting. CMoney explained to him exactly what he wanted and how he wanted it, then he put a down payment on his tab, so they could get started on the transformation. Giving Javi his keys, he got his receipt and left.

"What time the movie start?" CMoney asked as they got into the car.

"4:30," Esther responded while putting her seatbelt on in the passenger's seat. CMoney looked at his watch and he had about an hour to make it to Mayfair Mall where there was a movie theatre inside. Esther told him a day in advance that she wanted to go see Tyler Perry's new movie 'Madea's Withess Protection', so as promised, he was honoring her wishes as her man. This was actually their first real date, so they dressed to impress in the Louis Vuitton outfits that CMoney bought at the Lenox

Mall in Atlanta the day he had seen Miles, and of course they were matching.

"I guess we better get a move on it then," CMoney said pulling off heading to Mayfair Mall.

∞

"Why you acting like that, Ken? I still can't believe yo azz left me at the hair Salon," Big Booty Rudy said with an attitude.

"I ain't fuckin' wit you like that no more, you betta be lucky that I paid for yo hair when we first got there, or you really would've been azz'd out," Ken spat into his cell phone while standing in front of CMoney and Dre's spot in the Meadows. He had left Big Booty Rudy at Ebony 2 the day CMoney met him up there. Never had he been that embarrassed in his life, he knew he was dead wrong in the first place for trying to cuff her tramp azz, so now he was trying to shake her, but she wouldn't go easily.

"Why you don't want to fuck with me no more? Cause I ain't suck yo dick?" she asked apologetically. "Cause if that's why, you can come get me right now, and on my mama, I'll suck it and swallow you," she pleaded in true jump down form.

As much as Ken wanted to feel her mouth, he knew he had to cut all ties with her. He had finally realized that he had been a complete sucka fuckin' wit her. She burnt him, used him for his money, had niggas laughing at him, and to top it off, she was not wifey material. Now that he was through fucking with her, she wanted to do everything to keep him around. 'Typical bitch,' he thought.

"Naw I'm straight, I got somebody else taking care of that," Ken said, and he meant that. Crystal had been fucking and sucking him every day, sometimes twice a day. She had taught him how to fuck the right way, where a woman's G-Spot was, and how to hit it, and how to eat pussy lesbian style. Ken felt like he was a beast in the bedroom now.

"Nigga you know yo corn ball azz ain't fucking or getting yo dick licked by no other bitch, so stop playing games, come get me, and I'mma handle that," she stated matter of factly as the bass to 'Gold Bullion' by Qwel Milez featuring Ray Rizzy could be heard from the car entering the parking lot.

"Check this out, Rudy, you a fuckin' bust down wit ya ratchet azz, I'm still kickin' myself in the azz for fuckin' wit you like that in the first place. Don't no real nigga want a bitch who can't respect herself because if you can't respect yourself, how will you ever respect a relationship? You simply can't, so find another nigga dick to suck on, I'm sure you won't have a problem with that, and since I'm a corn ball, don't call my fuckin phone no more wit yo' buzzard azz, Bitch!" Ken scolded her before ending the call. He repeated some of the things CMoney said to him about Rudy because they made a lot of sense. 'Fuck that bitch,' he added to himself as Dre pulled up, parked, and hopped out his four door '05 Dodge Magnum with the Hemi in it. He had gotten it out of the shop three days

ago, and he couldn't keep it parked. The car was painted metallic gold with Magnum XL going across the doors on both sides in black bubble letters, .26" gold Onyx rims with low profile tires, six TVs, tinted windows, black leather guts with 'Magnum XL' in gold stitching on all four headrests, four 12' Memphis subwoofers, sixteen tweeters throughout the car and two extra batteries in the back to keep his power live and loud. Dre was sitting on every Magnum in the city of Milwaukee, and if you let him tell it, he was in the discussion for the Midwest.

"Dawg, you snapped with this muthafucka," Ken smiled while walking up to the car and lookin through the window like this was his first time seeing the car.

"You got plenty of condoms back there, them muthafuckas bet not be used," he added laughing.

"Hell, naw nigga, I   just   bought   fifteen   boxes
and spreaded 'em all over the backseat because my

theme is Magnum, so why not put the condoms in the
whip," Dre explained.

"I know, I'm just fuckin' wit you," Ken replied while
looking at the screen on his ringing phone. Seeing it was
Rudy, he sent it to voicemail.

"Where Money at?" Dre asked while walking into the spot
with Ken right behind him.

"He went to the movies with Esther, he said he'll be back
later and to call if you need him," Ken said sitting on the
couch.

"Yeah right, he gon' hit something after that movie, fuck
around and fall asleep," Dre said while holding
his stomach, he had to fart bad, so he filled the colostomy
bag up with his gas.

"Probably," Ken co-signed with a smile because he knew
that if he had a girl that was fine as Esther, he'd do
the same thing.

"You wanna ride wit me over these hoes house?" Dre asked placing a fif of Hennessy on the living room table,

then walking towards the bathroom, he had to let the gas out of the bag, otherwise known as 'Burp It'.

"Hell yeah, do I know 'em? Where they live at?" Ken replied excitedly. Dre just laughed at him.

"Calm down   nigga, her   name Tysheba, she lives in Northridge Lakes. She got plenty of sisters and friends too, so you rollin' or what?" Dre asked before closing the door to the bathroom, then he laid his pistol on the sink, raised his shirt up, and popped 'THE SHIT BAG' open to let the gas out. This was part of the requirements that had to be met when wearing the colostomy bag.

"Oh, I'm going," Ken responded knowing that he needed some new hoes on deck. Grabbing his .380 from under the couch cushion, he put it on his waist just as his phone rang. 'This betta not be Rudy, if it is, I'm finna snap,' he thought while pulling his phone out. Seeing it was Crystal, he answered it.

"What's good,   Crystal?" he   answered happily,   then a strange aroma hit his nostrils.

"Ken, I gotta talk   to   you   about   something," she   said coyly.

"Wait, hold on Damn nigga, open a window wit yo stankin' azz, that shit bogus as hell boy, smellin' like the zoo and shit," Ken scolded Dre when the smell from the bag violated his nose.

"Fuck you nigga," Dre laughed.

"I'm back, what's happenin?" Ken asked stepping outside trying to get away from the funk. He thought Crystal was about to tell him to come over and drop his dick off in her panties, but that was not the case. "Ken, I'm pregnant," she replied while crying.

"You what?" Ken retorted puzzled. 'Oh shit,' he thought.

∞

Chante pulled up in front of Legacy's house in her Camaro beating 'I Know' by Launde featuring B Justice out of her speakers. Legacy had complained of being tired and had asked her to run a couple of errands

for her. Chante quickly obliged; Legacy was her little sister as well as her best friend, so she'd be there for her anyway she could. Getting out of the car, she hit the alarm, and went into the house using Legacy's key. Putting the bags onto the counter, she abruptly turned her head to the direction of what sounded like moaning. 'I know she ain't fucking no nigga in this house,' Chante thought as she made her way to Legacy's closed bedroom door. Putting her ear to the door, there was definitely a lot of moaning taking place behind the door. Curiosity had indeed killed the cat as Chante nosily turned the knob slowly and opened the door.

"Damn bitch!" Legacy screamed when she saw Chante standing in the opened door way. The moans that Chante was hearing definitely came from a sexual act, but it wasn't with a man or a woman for that matter, not that Legacy was a lesbian or anything. But after seeing what

Legacy was doing, Chante put her hand over her mouth, and ran in the opposite direction.

"My bad!" she yelled while running as Legacy got up and slammed the door. Chante saw Legacy sitting the reverse way in a chair butt naked, one arm in a sling with a dildo in between her legs that was suction cupped to the chair while she rode it putting a deep arch in her back. Legacy wasn't embarrassed though, shit, that was her house, but she'd be lying if she said she didn't feel some type of way about her sister seeing her pleasing herself.

'Damn, right when I was about to get off, how am I supposed to finish now with images of Tay standing there fresh in my head,' was her first thought. 'Fuck that, I don got too wet and turned on, I gotta get this bad boy out,' was Legacy's second thought, referring to the orgasm that she was working for. She then mounted the plastic male organ that was still stuck to the chair and pushed the images of Tay to the back of her head almost as fast as they came while sliding down on the dildo and finishing what she started.

After handling her business, she cleaned up, hopped in the shower, then oiled her body down before dressing in a pink couture terry-cloth spaghetti-strapped baby shirt that showed off her mid-section with matching booty shorts. She combed her wrap out and slid into her Mickey Mouse house shoes.

Walking into the kitchen, Legacy saw Chante sitting at the table eating a Cousin's sub. She got a glass of water, then walked to the counter and took a pain pill from the prescription that Chante had just picked up from Wal-greens for her.

"Food in the bag, soda in the fridge, and that money in the book bag," Chante said after wiping her mouth with a napkin.

"Alright, thank you," Legacy said grabbing the bag and her soda, the two of them acted like nothing had happened as Legacy went back to her room.

"Yep," Chante replied.   'I know   she   hungry, she got to be, the way she was bouncin' her ass on that dildo, shit, I gotta buy me one of those because how

intense   she was,   it had   to   be   good, no homo,'
Chante thought with a giggle .'Naw fuck that, I gotta get
me the real thang and I know just who's gonna give it
to me,' was her second thought before biting into her sub.

∞

Boss had just gotten into his cell after getting his mail. He
got two letters, one from Legacy and the other was from
Big Ball's baby mama, Nicole. After seeing the picture of
Dre wearing Big Ball's chain, Boss grew very suspicious
of the two. He didn't have any solid proof of anything, for
all he knew, they could've bought the chain from
somebody   else, so   he   did a   little   investigation
himself. Hopping on the phone, he called his mother
because he didn't want Legacy to know anything about the
situation at hand. After playing phone tag for a few
calls, they were able to reach Nicole. Once he talked to
her, he asked to write her about something important, she
said it was cool and gave him

the address, she said that she had been staying with her
mother since Brandon's death.

That night, Boss wrote her a long letter, he started by sending his condolences for her loss, asked how she was holding up, and if she or Brandon Jr. needed anything, just let him know, and he'd take care of it. Then he eased his way into asking her about the night Brandon was killed. He told her that he would respect her wishes if it was unbearable to relive, but she wrote him back ASAP.

Boss sat on the bed and read Nicole's letter first.

Dear Boss,

I received your letter today, thanks. I am doing better coping with our loss. I won't ever get over this ordeal, but I will get through it one day at a time. As far as Brandon Jr. goes, he just got the staples out of his head, but unfortunately, he lost fifty percent visibility in his left eye. He's just a kid and didn't deserve what they did to him. As for your questions, I will try my best to describe to you the night in question...

Nicole went on and explained in vivid detail about the horrific night. Boss had not known any details up until this point. He was outraged to find out how Brandon Jr.

lost some of his vision, but what stuck out the most to him is when she said it was two masked men who entered her home, who couldn't have been no older than twenty. She came to that conclusion from the way they talked. Boss sat the letter down and put his head in his hands.

'They did that shit, it gotta be them,' he thought as he slid his shower shoes on, grabbed the letter, and left the room. Wayne had just hung up the phone, when Boss called him over to the table to sit down.

"Cuzzo, come holla at me," he yelled as Wayne made his way over to the table, sat down, picked up the letter that Boss slid to him, and started reading it. His eyes seemed to turn dark as he read the letter.

"Them bitch   azz   niggas   did   that   shit cuz, and I ain't acceptin' it," he said loud enough for only Boss to

hear as he passed the letter back. This was also his first time hearing the details.

"I was thinking the same shit," Boss replied while deep in thought.

"When I get out, I'mma take a look at 'em, and that's on er' thang," Wayne spat with murder on his mind.

"You already know," Boss stated giving him some dap. 'Chris and Dre definitely gotta die for what they did to my family, but how am I ever going to be able to fuck with Legacy like that if I kill her brother and she catch wind of it? fuck it, death
before dishonor, them lil niggas gotta go,' Boss thought.

∞

"Tyler Perry azz a fool for that movie, did you enjoy it?" CMoney asked while walking out of the movie theatre sipping his soda before tossing it in the garbage can that they were passing.

"Yeah, it was funny as hell, thank you," Esther smiled while interlocking her fingers into his.

CMoney wasn't with that public display of affection shit, but he knew that women loved that type of stuff, and Esther was no different. It would take some getting used to, but he was open-minded to it, and willing to do that for her. Besides, every nigga that they passed stared her down wishing they were the one that was holding her hand, she was so damn fine which made it that much easier to get used to.

"You ain't gotta thank   me, I'm yo man, and   it's my obligation to assure that you're happy, we on the same team, so I always got your back, believe that. Now, where you wanna eat   at?" CMoney asked   while   they walked out of the mall on their way to the car.

Esther loved the way he treated her, no man had ever made her feel the way he did. He put her first and she felt completely secure and protected with him, and she would never take that for granted.

"We can get something on the way home, then I can give you dessert right after that," Esther said seductively while batting her eyes.

"You ain't got to tell me twice, come on," he laughed and without warning he picked her up and speed walked towards the car in a hurry to get home to that dessert she was talking about.

"Ah! Put me down," Esther smiled elated as he put her down by the passenger's door.

"We can do that, I just gotta stop over my sister's house first," he said opening the car door for her.

"Okay, but you better hurry up," she teased then kissed his lips before she got in.

'I'mma go bananas in that rump shaker tonight,' he thought while walking to the driver's side and getting in. He put his mixed CD in the deck with nothing but slow jams on it. 'Say Yes' by Fourtune blasted out of the speakers as he pulled off. Pulling up on 68th and Brentwood with 'Ah Yeah' by Jacob Latimore featuring

Rico Love blasting out of the speakers, they parked behind Tay's Camaro, got out of the car, and rang the doorbell.

"Who is it?" Chante asked.

"Whoever you want it to be, now open this damn door," CMoney demanded smiling as the door swung open.

"Yo azz betta call next time, because the next time you show up over here unannounced, I ain't letting you in," Chante stated like it was her house.

"You ain't gotta let me in, I'mma kick this muthafucka in, therefore letting myself in, and I did call, but y'all ain't answer," he said matter-of-factly.

"Play wit it if you want to, you lucky Esther wit you or I would've left yo azz out there, how you doing, Esther," Chante said with a smile.

"Hey Tay, I'm good girl," Esther responded pleasantly.

CMoney shook his head at his sister, she was talking crazy one second and nice the next second. Now he knew why his grandmother called her Ms. Nice nasty.

"Whatever, where Legacy at?" he asked.

"She in her room, but you better knock before you go in," Chante said remembering the situation that happened earlier that day. CMoney told Esther that he'd be right back before he made his way to Legacy's room door and knocked.

"Come in," she said casually.

"What's up, sis?" he said having a seat in the chair by the door. If he knew what went on in that chair earlier, he surely wouldn't have sat there. Legacy had cleaned up everything good anyway.

"Shit, where you coming from all Louie V'd down?" she asked speaking of the Louis Vuitton attire that he wore while she removed polish from her toenails.

"The movies wit Esther, we saw that new Tyler Perry joint," he said nonchalantly.

"Madea's witness protection," she said as he shook his head up and down,

"That's good that y'all go on dates because that's important, you gotta spend time with that girl if you wanna keep her. Don't get trapped in them streets and forget the people who are really down for you because in many ways them streets is like them hoes, no matter how much time you spend up in 'em, it still ain't no love, you hear me?" Legacy said now removing the polish from her fingernails.

"Yeah, I feel you," he said casually. He always listened to his sister's advice about relationships because a woman knows what a woman wants and needs best. Legacy and Chante had been lacing him with game since he could remember. Men truly got there from woman whether they knew it or not.

"Great, now how was the movie?" she asked coldly.

"I liked it, but I wanted to ask you, when the next time you goin to see yo plug?" he inquired.

"Maybe like a week or two, why what up?" she retorted.

"That's enough time, I been doin' good out here, but I feel like I need to step it up a tad more, so next time mark me down for ten of 'em and I'm sure Dre wanna cop something too," he said seriously.

Legacy looked up from what she was doing and smiled at her little brother, he had put in hard work to become the man he was today, because anybody could be a bum, but it takes dedication to become something in all aspects of life.

"Alright I got you but be careful. You know these niggas out here workin' for these people, telling and shit. The more money you get, the more problems will arise. Do not follow where a path may lead, instead go where there is no path and leave a trail, you hear me?" she stated, dropping some jewels on him.

"No doubt," he replied while soaking up what she had just told him.

"Ay, I gotta ask you one question that's been fuckin' my head up. Was that heat I got from you in Atlanta in yo name?" he asked puzzled. He knew that if it was, they were coming for them, so they might as well hit the highway now.

"Boy hell naw, you think I was gon' give you and Dre's trigger-happy azzes a gun that's in my name? Boy stop, that was a throw away that I brought to Atlanta specifically for y'all because y'all too damn flashy and I knew y'all was gon' need it," she said seriously.

"You always thinking ahead, huh?" he smiled at her cleverness.

"Got to, it could be the difference between living and dying," she stated seriously as her phone rang. "Oh, this Boss," she added while accepting the call.

"Tell him I said what up," CMoney said getting up to leave the room, so she could talk privately.

"Money!" Legacy yelled, and he came back into the room. "He wants to talk to you," she added passing him the phone. "I gotta use the bathroom and speak to Esther, so just talk until I get back," she continued then left the room.

"What's good Boss Baaabbby?" CMoney asked smiling.

"Lil Chris, I see yo doin your thang out there," Boss spat.

"It's CMoney now my nigga, and yeah, my name like honey got a lot a chicks buzzin," he said jackin' hard.

"Lil Chris, I ain't yo nigga and I ain't talkin' about none of that mediocre azz shit you on either, just know that I'm on to you," Boss stated coldly.

CMoney was taken aback at the tone in his voice and the shit he was saying. 'I just told this nigga my name, fuck he on. I ain't gotta be his nigga,' he thought while becoming agitated.

"Listen, I quit school because of recess, I don't play no muthafuckin' games nigga, say what the fuck you mean or miss me wit that hoe shit," CMoney scolded him while cutting right down to business.

"What lil nigga, you must've forget who yo mog azz talkin' to," Boss said matching his aggression.

"I'm talkin' to yo bitch azz nigga," CMoney said pissed off that Boss called him a mog.

"What up wit that platinum number 8 pool ball piece that you got?" Boss asked. CMoney thought for a minute, then he remembered exactly what he was talking about.

"I don't know what you talkin' about," he replied faking ignorance, but he was not going to say shit over the phone, he knew better than that. Boss now knew for sure that CMoney had indeed committed the crime.

"Bitch azz nigga stop playin' wit me, that was my cousin shit, so we gotta holla," Boss stated

firmly. CMoney was completely unfazed to find out that Big Ball and Boss were cousins, what was done was done.

"Maybe he'll find it then," CMoney chuckled into the phone. "Nigga I'm out here and I ain't worried about nothin," he said menacingly.

"You jackin, oh yeah, you gon' have to see me later," Boss replied.

CMoney wanted to tell his azz that he could get the same fate his cousin was dealt, but no way was he going to incriminate himself on recorded call. He then saw Legacy coming down the hallway towards the room, so he turned his back to where she was coming from and said what he had to say.

"Don't drop the soap bitch," he whispered, passed the phone to Legacy and left out of the room after saying goodbye and giving her a hug. And just like that, the beef was on.

CHAPTER THIRTEEN

The next day…

"Chris," Esther said shaking him awake while sitting on the king-sized bed beside him. His mother, sisters, and Esther were the only people who he didn't mind calling him Chris.

"Huh," he said removing the pillow from over his head and rubbing his eyes. It had been a long time since he had a good night's sleep, but thanks to the sex session he had with Esther last night, he had gotten some much-needed rest.

"I'm about to go down to the school and get my books. You know school starts next week for me, so I gotta be ready. Then, I'mma go to Columbia St. Mary's to see about my internship that this lady at school is trying to help me get. So I'mma call you as soon as I leave there, okay bae?' 'Esther said leaning in to peck him on the lips with his morning breath and all, that notion had to mean that she loved him dearly. Then she got up, grabbed her keys, and her purse.

"Aight, what car you taking?" he asked while stretching before sitting up in bed.

"I'm driving my truck," she stated.

"I'll see you later, I love you and be careful," she added.

"I love you too," he said as she left. CMoney grabbed the remote to the 55inch TV that hung from their bedroom wall, turned it on, and flipped through the channels. Stopping on a news station that was covering the story of a seventeen-year-old boy from Florida named Trayvon Martin who was shot in cold blood, CMoney turned the volume up. After seeing what was going on, CMoney got pissed, and turned the TV off. 'If that ain't racial oppression, I don't know what is. It took these rnuthafuckas seventy something days to lock the dude up, let his azz would've been black, they would've booked his azz the night before. That shit crazy as hell, you got a grown azz man with a gun following an unarmed kid, then he shoots him for no reason, it seems to me the dude was looking for trouble after the police operator told him to stop following Trayvon, then they take forever to lock his azz up, I don't understand that. but rest in peace, Trayvon' CMoney thought while on his way to get in the shower.

After showering, handling his hygiene, and sending a few texts, he got dressed. Putting on a pair of black cargo shorts, a white Polo V-neck t-shirt that showed off his muscular chest and arms, he then put on his black, university blue, and white retro #5 Air Jordan's. Putting a stack in his pocket, Brietling on his wrist, and his chain on his neck, he looked in the mirror and brushed his waves and decided that he'd stop by the barbershop to get cut up.

After arming himself with his P99, he grabbed both phones, put a kilo in his book bag, and left the house. Getting in the MC, he put the book bag in the stash spot. He had taken the car the day after Esther bought it to get a much-needed stash spot. Sliding his CD in the deck "Next man up" by Will Gates came out of the speakers as he pulled off heading to Excell's barbershop on 5th and Center, then he was off to the Meadows to get money.

∞

Ken was riding in his truck with Crystal in the passenger's seat looking out of the window and her eight-year-old son, Emmanuel, in the backseat enjoying his kid's meal from McDonald's.

"Huh ma," Emmanuel said holding out two French fries for Crystal. She looked to the backseat, smiled, and accepted the fries. Ken watched closely, he couldn't deny that even with the skeletons in her closet, she was still a good mother, and the little boy loved her very much.

"Thank you, baby," she smiled while eating the fries.

"You welcome," Emmanuel responded while stuffing fries into his own mouth.

Ken had spent all night at Crystal's house talking to her about several things, and one of them was about her being pregnant. She told him that she was against abortions, so therefore she wanted to keep the baby. Ken was skeptical about this because he didn't know for sure if he was the father, but Crystal assured him that he was the only person that she had sex with since her last period. Ken knew it was a possibility, so he coped with the idea of having a Ken Jr. or Kendra running around. He'd get a DNA test as soon as the baby was born to satisfy his curiosity.

However, they still had the biggest problem of them all on their hands, and that was Crystal's habit. Ken told her that he'd help her out in any way that he could, and he meant that, so they came to the conclusion that she'd check into a rehab facility for ninety days to try and shake her addiction. There was no way that Ken would allow his first born or any child he may have to be born with drugs in his/her system, so this was best for all parties involved. Ken was now taking her to her mother's

house because she had agreed to look after Emmanuel since his father was absent in his life, but she was only going to do it if Crystal was serious about cleaning herself up. Crystal promised her that she was dedicated to a new life, so she was given the blessing of dropping her son off at his grandmother's home.

Pulling up on 63rd and Sheridan in the Westlawn housing projects, Ken pulled up in front of Crystal's mama's house as Crystal sat there for a moment. She was scared to get out of the car because she hadn't ever been without her son before, and she didn't want to be without him now, but she knew she had to take the initiative to get the monkey off her back, so that she could live a better life, and be a better mother to her son and her unborn child as well.

"You making the right choice," Ken assured her. She turned to meet his stare with one hand on her stomach, the sincerity in his eyes gave her all the courage she needed to get out of the truck.

Opening the back door for Emmanuel, she helped him out, then they walked hand in hand to her mom's front door, and rang the loud buzz sounding doorbell while he looked on.

"Who is it?" came from behind the door moments later. "Crystal," she retorted then the door swung open. "Grandma," Emmanuel said excitedly.

"Come in," Cheryl said smiling while opening the screen door and hugging her grandson.

"I can't come in ma because I gotta go, but I want you to know that I appreciate what you're doing for me, and Emmanuel, thank you. I'm going to get myself together and I'll call you when I can," Crystal said holding back tears as Cheryl wrapped her arms around her daughter and hugged her tightly.

"I'll always be here for you baby, now you go do what you gotta do and remember that we love you, okay?" Cheryl said after breaking their embrace.

"I love y'all too," Crystal said as tears started to fall while she passed her mother the five hundred dollars that

Ken gave her to help take care of her son. "I'll have more for you soon," she added.

"Don't worry about that, I got him," Cheryl said while tucking the money away in her bra, then she hugged Crystal once more. Crystal called her son to the door, hugged him, kissed him, and told him that she loved him, then she left.

"Ma, where you goin'?" Emmanuel asked puzzled. Crystal wiped her tears away and kept on walking. She knew that she couldn't turn around because it would've made it just that much harder. She had to get herself together, so that she could raise her kids in a stable home the right way.

"Mama, mama mama, I wanna go," Emmanuel cried after her as Crystal hopped in the truck with tears

running rapidly now. Ken pulled off while trying to console her at the same time. They were now headed to the rehab center on 4th and Locust in the enterprise building to get Crystal emitted. She knew that after this was over, better days would follow ahead for her family.

∞

Chante sat on the bed watching TV while sipping Patron out of a champagne glass in room 112 at the Excel Inn hotel in Bayshore on Port Washington Road with her robe on.

She contemplated leaving several times being that she had already been there for a half hour, but she knew that the person she was waiting on would be there any minute now. She had secretly been talking to the person for a couple of months now, and now it was time to do what they both had been waiting for. She wanted it, needed it, and she was sure the person she was waiting on felt the same way.

Her thoughts were interrupted by a knock at the door. She got up, sat her drink on the dresser, walked to

the door and looked through the peep hole. A smile crept across her face because her guest had finally arrived.

"What's good, Tay?" Ant asked as he stepped into the room smiling. The diamonds in his mouth and chain caught the gleam of the lights and Chante estimated him to be wearing at least 100K in jewelry if not more. Ant was the plug that she and Legacy had been buying their work from.

"You big daddy," she smiled while closing the door and walking behind him. Once they were in front of the bed, Chante pushed him onto it.

"Okay shawty, that aggressive shit get a nigga ready, don't start no shit you can't finish," he said liking the game she was playing.

Chante didn't say anything, she just raised her leg up and placed her red 3-inch Manalo stiletto on the bed right next to his leg. Doing this, her leg and thick thigh were exposed, then she ran her index finger from her ankle all

the way to the top of her thigh seductively while Ant watched. When he reached out and tried to touch her thigh, she knocked his hand down.

"Uh uh," she said waving her finger from side to side. Ant was going to play her game because he ultimately knew that he'd be in between those thick thighs before they left the hotel.

Chante then undid the strap on her robe and let it fall off of her shoulders revealing her naked all natural, oiled down 36C-26-45 curvaceous frame. She had gotten a little thicker due to the ten pounds of good weight that she gained   from eating good. Nevertheless, she   looked absolutely great. She could tell Ant liked what he was seeing   because   of   two   sizes, the   size   of   his eyes, and the size of the bulge in his pants, so she gave him something to remember.

"If my pussy was a fruit, it would be
a cantaloupe because cantaloupes are sweet, very
juicy, and fat. So, do you know why I said

a cantaloupe?" Chante smiled, then opened her legs to
show him her hairy, but well-manicured pussy.

"Ummm, yummy yummy," she added. Being a former stripper, she knew all about the art of seduction, and when she was with a man, she aimed to please in great fashion.

Pleased with her tease, she turned around, downed the rest of her drink, told Ant to scoot up, then she

unfastened his belt and pants after putting his pistol on the dresser. Once she pulled his fully erect thick veined shaft out of his boxers, she was pleased with his length and girth. Getting between his legs, she wrapped her lips around the head of his large member and blessed him with her best head game.

Ant happily laid back, put his hand on her head, and guided her while he watched her deep throat him, she was doing her thing to say the least, and Ant had to admit that she sucked a mean dick as she gripped him tightly in her mouth, he even tried to pull his dick away from her to no avail, she was not letting that thing go

until she was done with it and knew that he was pleased from the oral pleasure that she was giving him. Noticing the change in his breathing pattern, she abruptly stopped making him lose his nut while she licked her lips, loving the taste of his pre-cum.

Chante then got in the bed with her heels on and stood over Ant. He knew what she wanted, he had only ate two girls out in his life at this point, but here he had a bad

thick ass red bone standing over him wanting his services.

She did just do a number on him, he reasoned with himself.

'Fuck it, here goes number three,' he thought while welcoming Chante as she squatted down over his face while holding the bed post until she introduced his lips to her lower lips. Ant flicked his tongue expertly over her clit while sliding two fingers into her slit.

"Ah shit," Chante moaned as she moved back and forth on his tongue while holding his head in her hands.

Feeling that she was nice and wet, Ant flipped her over onto her back, and got up to take the rest of his clothes off. It was time for him to take over now, she had her time, besides. 'Dick drive this car, not pussy,' he thought as he got between her legs and slid into her warm, tight, and wet pussy.

"Ummm," Chante moaned as she squeezed her pussy muscles tightly around him. As soon as Ant got in some

pussy, he could tell if it was going to be good or not within the first stroke, and Chante definitely had a mean wet shot on her.

Ant pumped into her for 10 minutes, then they switched positions, and he slid into her from the back. Chante was throwing that big ass of hers back on him while looking over her shoulder watching him, so Ant being experienced himself grabbed her waist and as she pushed back on him, she was met with a powerful inward thrust. Although this was their first time fucking each other, they shared a great sexual chemistry.

"Oh, shit nigga ah...ah oh, I... I'm finna cum!" Chante yelled still popping her ass on him until her juices coated his member. Once she came, Ant noticed the pussy became even wetter if that was possible. Wanting to be back in control, she bounced her ass one more time into him before telling him to lay down because she wanted to ride him. Chante straddled him and rode him reverse cowgirl style while he palmed her phat ass in his hands. She bounced her ass up and down round and round professionally without slamming her ass onto him, Ant hated when girls did that.

She came down only far enough to let his pubic hairs tickle her ass before she went back up and did it again. Chante was pulling out all the tricks to show him what he could have on a nightly basis if he was her man because she was never a lazy lover. Chante could tell that he was close to cumming because the grip he had on her ass got even tighter, so she got up abruptly making him lose his nut again, she wasn't ready for him to nut just yet. Laying back down in the missionary position, he got between her legs and slid his pussy

juice-soaked dick back into her. Chante put her legs on his shoulders and allowed him to pound away at her sweet pussy. Every time he was getting close to a nut, Chante would stop what she was doing, making him lose his nut in the process, but now he was in control and pumping vigorously into her to reach his peak. He was hitting her with strokes the way a serial killer would stab their victims.

"Ah umm...umm oh, get it get it, ah shit!" she moaned, encouraging him to blast away. Ant just kept right on

pumping at her tight wet box. She could tell that he was about to cum because his strokes became more forceful. Sensing he was about to pull out because he raised up slightly, Chante coached him into what she wanted him to do.

"Oh baby, please don't take it out, ah, don't stop, ummm you so big I'm finna cum wit you, oh ah...ah... ahhh," she yelled in his ear while pulling him back on top of her. Then she took her legs down and wrapped them around his waist tightly. Caught up in the

good pussy and what she was saying, he came deep inside of her and once again she coated him with the juices from her orgasm.

"Shit," Ant said after he shot his load into her. He could not deny that she had some bomb azz pussy as he pumped a few more times before he pulled out.

"I see you know how to keep a nigga happy, huh?" he added while laying next to her. Chante smiled in satisfaction that they both had gotten what they wanted.

"You think that was something, I ain't done with you yet," she smiled before she took the sex session to the

next level. Leaning over him, she sucked all of their juices off his shaft much to his pleasure. Ant loved it when women got nasty with it. Chante sucked him until he came for round two, round three he came in her from the back while she laid on her stomach, and then for round four, she rode a nut out of him.

Ant was spent and very satisfied to say the least as he laid back. Chante was feeling Ant in a major way since

they had been talking a lot, so she put that pussy on him in every way possible, she knew he loved being inside of her already by the faces he was making while he fucked her. If things worked out right between them, she was going to be his woman.

∞

CMoney pulled into the alley behind Quick Pantry on 91st and Brown Deer, drove halfway through it, and parked behind one of the apartment buildings as his text alert went off. Seeing that it was from Esther, he read it. She was letting him know that she was leaving school

heading to her possible internship site at the hospital, and she'd see him later. He texted her back, got his book bag out of the stash spot, put his pistol in his waistband, got out of the car and hit the alarm. Putting the bag on his shoulder, he ran his hand over his freshly cut one and a half with a taper fade that had his waves spinning hard. Then he started his walk to the spot through the back path. The reason he packed there was because he didn't want anybody to know when he was in the hood

or when he wasn't. He also didn't want people to recognize the car he was in because Esther drove it too, and he was still on high alert about killing Big Ball since Boss now

293

knew. He had to be prepared for anything that came his way and he certainly was.

"Lil Chris!" a female voice yelled to him getting his attention. He turned around and smiled as she walked towards him.

"What's happenin Lou Lou?" he smiled. Lou Lou was a pretty light-skinned chick with freckles and black

shoulder length hair with burgundy highlights that he used to fuck on from time to time, but he had not seen

her since he had been back. She was a hustler who used to sell fake designer bags, shoes and clothes.

"Nothin' damn! I see you shinin' with that new money glow, Chris," she complemented with a smile.

"Well you know, you lay somethin' small, turn it tall, and ball to you fall, but I ain't tryna fall, ya feel

me?" he said making her blush. "And the name is CMoney now baby," he added.

"CMoney huh, where you get that from?" she asked loving his new and improved swag.

"When you look at me, what you see? Stevie Wonder could see I got money," he jacked it down on her.

Lou Lou looked him up and down and she could definitely tell that he was shining like a pair of high beams on a new Benz at midnight, and like Brandy sang, she wanted to be down.

"I see you nigga, you know I got that bag now, right?" she smiled.

"What happened to the purses, shoes, and shit?" he asked.

"They still on deck, but a bitch tryna expand her hustle, you near me?" she laughed as CMoney joined in.

"I feel you, let me see that bag thou," he said wanting to see the quality of her weed.

"Man, if you don't get that bobby out my face," he teased her.

"Nigga   please, this   shit smoking', on er' thang," she assured.

"How long you been hustlin' and how much the pounds going for?" he inquired while thinking.

"About a month and I think my brother sell pounds for like twelve hunnid apiece,"   she   said skeptically. CMoney knew with those numbers that he was not

selling kush which was the hottest thing out. He knew her brother Vance, and he decided to holla at him later

about a business proposition. "Man, Vance trippin', is you tryna eat steak or peanuts?" he asked.

"Steak nigga, of course," she stated. CMoney looked her over for a minute for a sign to say that he shouldn't say what he was about to say, seeing none he spoke up.

"Take this number down and call me tomorrow and if you wanna fuck wit me on this money side, we gon' eat," he said seriously.

"What's the number?" she retorted while pulling out her phone and pressing the numbers in it as he said them.

"Get at me in the mornin', aight," he said then turned to walk away. He would run her through several tests before he put her on his team.

"Okay, wait thou," she said stopping him in his tracks. "What up wit us tonight?" she added with lust in her tone. CMoney smiled before he turned around

because he knew that question was coming at some point.

"'We'll talk about that when you call," CMoney said then walked away. That was the first thing that came to his mind after she   asked   him   that question. Sure, he had fucked her before, but that was before Esther came into his life. If he was gon' cheat, he was gon' cheat up. Although Lou Lou was pretty,

had some 'G' about herself, and had a wet shot, she did not possess half the qualities that Esther did, so fucking her was out of the question.

Walking through the cut to the parking lot where the spot was, he observed everything that was going on before he went inside of the house.

"What up fool?" Dre said while sitting down on the couch smoking a blunt and watching TV with the AR-15 right beside him.

"Shit, where Ken azz at?" he asked closing the door.

"I don't even know," Dre replied as CMoney took his book bag off, sat on the couch, and opened it.

"Fam, what the fuck nigga say when you talked to him, you ain't finish tellin' me," Dre said seriously cutting right down to business.

"Oh yeah, the nigga asked about the platinum #8 pool ball piece, talkin' bout it's his cousin shit, so I tell him I don't know what the fuck he talkin' about and shit, you know, playin' the role, ya feel me? Then this hoe azz nigga got the nerve to get hostile wit me over the phone, I was so heated, I would've fucked him up if I could've got to him," CMoney said getting upset about

298

the situation all over again as he went in the kitchen and grabbed the digital scale, a rubber mallet, some plastic wrap, Zip Lock bags, latex gloves, a surgical mask, and a big spoon.

"So, the nigga Big Ball his cousin, huh?" Dre asked. He didn't really give a fuck, but he was just thinking how small Milwaukee was.

"Yep, and the nigga gon' say he comin' for me," he said sitting in a chair and putting everything on the table.

"That shit laughable, he and I both know that he don't wanna see me in dem streets, I aint playin' games wit no nigga, on my mama. Anyways, he fuck around and don't make it back from that situation he in now, wit his stupid azz," CMoney continued while putting the gloves and mask on before breaking down the kilo.

"I know right, the nigga gon' be seventy eighty years old tryna look for a nigga, he gon' have a cane and all type a shit," Dre laughed.

"Fuck that hoe nigga thou, but I'm still tryna find out how the fuck he know about that muthafuckin chain," Dre said puzzled.

"I asked myself the same shit, and the only thing I could come up with was when we was in the 'A', Legacy must've snapped a picture of you wearing the chain unaware of the situation and sent it to the nigga.

That's what   it gotta be,   because I ain't wear the chain at all, and the only time you wore it was the day we went

to Stunt fest," CMoney said logically while he weighed up a half brick, two-four and a splits, and nine ounces. Dre shook his head up and down knowing that was likely the scenario of how things must've played out.

"Ay, I think the nigga Ken got a baby on the way too. I heard the   nigga tryna whisper   when   I   was   in the bathroom yesterday about what the chick can't do

because she pregnant," Dre said smiling because he thought that Ken got Big Booty Rudy pregnant, and CMoney was thinking the same thing.

"I know this nigga ain't get Rudy pregnant," he said in disappointment while shaking his head from side to side in disbelief as he finished wrapping and cleaning everything up.

"I was thinking the same shit," Dre retorted while laughing.

"This nigga really trippin'," CMoney said as his cell phone rang... "Hello," he answered.

"Money what's good?" the voice asked.

"Who dis?' he replied.

"Big Head nigga," he responded.

"Oh, what's good fool?" Money smiled.

"I need a ning ding," Big Head said meaning he needed a quarter kilo which was nine ounces of dope.

"You down the hill?" CMoney asked.

"Yeah, by Mark crib," he replied.

"Aight, meet me at the basketball courts on the hill," CMoney said then ended the call just as some loud music could be heard. CMoney looked at the small TV that sat atop of an end table next to the big screened TV that they watched with a four-way split screen to see the Audi pull up. They had two cameras strategically placed at the front and back doors, so they'd have a heads up on any activities that was going on out there,

regardless of what or who it was. CMoney then

answered his ringing phone. "I'll be out there in a minute homie," he said then hung it right back up.

"My nigga, I gotta handle this right fast, I need you to take these nine pieces to the nigga Big Head for me, he gon' meet you at the basketball courts on the hill," CMoney said while putting the half kilo in the book bag.

"I gotcha," Dre said getting up from his seat and grabbing the dope.

CMoney put the book bag on his shoulder, went outside, and walked towards the Audi which was pearl black with tinted windows sitting on 24" Diablo Spider black rims with a 7" chrome lip. It looked just like the white one that Shawn had, but it was not the same car.

"What's good, Shawn?" CMoney asked getting in the passenger's seat.

"Chillin, what up wit you?" Shawn replied before he hit his blunt one more time and flicked the duct out of the sunroof.

"I see you got this muthafucka right," CMoney said while running his hand over the black plush leather seats while thinking that he needed to flip something foreign too.

"It's aight," Shawn said modestly with a smile. CMoney nodded his head liking Shawn's style and The Marquette Golden Eagles piece with the blue and yellow diamonds that hung from the white gold chain around his neck.

"That was some real shit you did for us in the 'A' my man, words can't express my gratitude, but here's a little something to show it," CMoney said passing him the book bag.

"You know yo sister already gave me a slab, right?" Shawn asked puzzled.

"Yeah, but that's from me, real recognize real and you look real familiar,   know what   I'm talkin' bout," CMoney stated, then the two chopped it up for a little while and promised to kick it in the near future.

CMoney gave him some slap and Shawn pulled off beating that song about getting off the wall.

"I gotta ask that nigga who rap that shit because that shit weak azz a bitch," he said to himself as he went back in the house.

"Dre! you stankin' azz nigga," he yelled. Dre was in the bathroom emptying the contents out of his colostomy bag and he had the whole house smelling like baby shit.

∞

"Ay big homie, come check this hit out on the news about this dope dealing MPD cop," Larry said standing in Wayne's doorway. They had gotten cool since the incident that happened the first day Wayne made it to the pod. Aside from Boss, Larry was the only person Wayne rocked with.

"Boss back from court yet?" Wayne asked getting up and removing the du-rag made out of a state T-shirt from his draw Boss started trial today and Wayne wanted to see how things were looking.

"Hell naw," Larry replied nonchalantly as Wayne came out of his room and walked down the stairs with him. Wayne and Larry kept walking until they got into the TV area. Being that it was a little loud, they cupped their hand around their ears in efforts to hear better.

'BREAKING NEWS' flashed across the screen before a reporter appeared and started talking. Apparently, there was a six-year veteran Milwaukee police department officer that had been arrested and named in a Federal indictment along with a few black and Spanish dudes on the soutside of Milwaukee who said the officer was supplying them upfront with drugs for the past two years and getting his cut on the back end.

The news reporter went on to say that one of the alleged suspects the officer was supplying apparently sold to an undercover cop about a year ago and was arrested. During interrogation, the suspect volunteered information that a Milwaukee police officer was indeed the one supplying him with drugs and allegedly threatened and made him sell the drugs against his will.

In fear that the officer would frame him with drugs and arrest him if he didn't cooperate, he did as he was told knowing that he was on parole, so any police contact involving drugs would surely violate the conditions of his parole, meaning he would go back to prison. The alleged suspect turned alleged victim agreed to wear a wire in exchange for his immunity from any charges if he could prove what he was saying to be true, so with a strong allegation of that sort, an investigation ensued by the High Intensity Drug Trafficking Area. H.I.D.T.A was able to obtain several hours of audio and footage of said officer making several drug transitions over the last year or so. Having enough evidence, the Wisconsin State Department of Justice and the D.E.A (Drug Enforcement Administration) gave the go ahead and federal agents moved in and apprehended the officer from his lavish home.

"What the fuck happened?" Boss said walking up as soon as he came through the pod's door while looking at the TV trying to see what everybody was so geeked up about. Wayne brought Boss up to speed on what

was transpiring, but he was unable to finish as seven wallet-sized pictures appeared on the screen. One was an all black John Doe frame which Boss, Wayne, and Larry presumed to be the one that was snitching. Wayne scrolled through the pictures with his eyes, and stopped on the last one, which was the picture of the MPD officer whose name was Jerome Herman.

Cuz, that's the muthafuckin' faggot azz cop who pulled me over on this case," Wayne said seriously.

"On what?" Boss and Larry asked in unison. It was more out of shock than disbelief.

"On er'thang" Wayne said, still looking at the picture.

"Hastings can prolly beat that shit for you how," Boss smiled speaking of his lawyer who was now representing Wayne too. Wayne knew that the situation was likely to end in his favor and warrant his freedom, if no one knew that he'd have a good chance to get back on appeal.

"I hope so, I'm finna call mom's and have her call his azz now," Wayne said seriously while heading towards the phones.

'I get out, I'll be to see you CMoney, all that barkin you been doin' ain't gon' mean shit
when dem choppa bullets spittin' at ya azz,'
Wayne thought as he picked up the phone and started dialing.

CHAPTER FOURTEEN

Three weeks later, Esther sat in front of the computer screen in the living room of the plush apartment that she and CMoney shared. She was on the internet browsing through homes on a realtor company's website.

CMoney had told her when they were on their way to Milwaukee to start looking for a home for them, but she had taken it a step further, and was looking for properties to buy, invest in and rent out.

She had already found one potential home on Port Washington Road that was in between Vienna and Keefe. It was a duplex with two bedrooms and one bathroom on each floor, a spacious basement, and a two-car garage. Being that the house was boarded up, they only wanted $4,700 so she wrote the information down in her notebook. Continuing her browse, she spotted another home on 62nd and Bobolink. It was a duplex with two bedrooms, one bathroom on each floor, a nice-sized kitchen, but instead of there being a garage, it was a gravel parking space in the back of the house. Since it was boarded up also, the asking price was

$5,000 so she wrote that down as well. Esther purposely only searched for duplexes because two rents were better than one.

"Baby!" she yelled.

"What up?" CMoney replied. He was upstairs and had just finished counting out the rest of the money for his tab at the car shop. He didn't keep more than $30,000 in the apartment at a time in a small safe in the back of the closet, and that was primarily emergency money. He just didn't feel like riding all the way across town to his mother's house to get the tab money, so he used the money in the safe and would replace it later.

Counting out 6 gees that he owed for his tab because he had been dropping money off over the weeks to shorten his bill, he stuffed that in his pocket. All the

money that didn't occupy the safe went in to the safe of the basement at his mother's house.

"Come here once," she said while still browsing through more as CMoney walked up and stood next to her.

"You rang," he said sarcastically like the guy off 'THE ADAMS FAMILY' making her laugh.

"You so silly, but I wanted to talk to you about this...," Esther said and went on to explain to him her thought process.   As she talked,   he soaked everything up, and when she finished, he spoke.

"To keep it a hunnid, when I first started seeing some real money, this was my plan, but you can say I sorta got side tracked, but I think it's a great idea because the economy will rise again and so will property value, I'm wit that," CMoney said leaning down to kiss her lips.

"So, you think we should get them even though they boarded up?" she asked skeptically.

"Hell yeah, I know somebody who can do all the work we need to get done, so how much you gon' need?" he inquired as she scrunched up her face at him.

"What?" he asked puzzled by her expression.

"Are we together?" she asked slightly offended.

"Absolutely, why?" he replied wondering what she was on.

"Well stop coming at me like I'm broke then. I know you got money, but that's not why I'm with you, I'm with you because I love you and you're the best choice for me, okay. Now, you buy the one for the forty-seven hundred, and I'll buy the other one, and we gon' do this together," she stated firmly as CMoney pulled her up out of her seat and kissed her passionately. He knew men or women didn't like to feel overshadowed if their significant other was the breadwinner, so he definitely didn't want her to feel that way.

"My bad baby, I love you too, it's just that I wanna take care of home and make sure you good. After all, I did

bring you all the way up here, so I gotta do right by you," he said meaning every word.

"Don't worry baby, I just want you to know I got my own and believe me when I say that I feel the love every day, okay?" she said while looking directly into his eyes

before pecking his lips, then she checked the time on her watch.

"That's all I needed to know," he said.

"You ready because I gotta go back to school and then to the hospital," she stated. Esther had gotten the internship at the hospital two weeks ago, so she was ecstatic about that, and school had been going great as well.

"Yeah, I m ready," he said putting his all white New England Patriots fitted hat on his head while Esther gathered her things to leave.

Getting into her truck, Esther turned the AC on, and pushed her CD in. 'So Fly' by Essential thumped out

of the Cadillac's factory speakers as she pulled off. Pulling up in front of Auto Customizations on South 27th Street,

Esther double parked and turned her hazard lights on. "You want me to wait fo you to come out?" she asked.

"Naw, get to school before you be late and call me when you get out, aight?" CMoney said before grabbing his CD and kissing her.

"You sure?" she asked skeptically.

"Positive, I'mma get wit you later," he said while getting out of the truck.

"Okay bye," she said turning her hazards off before pulling back into traffic as he went into the shop.

CMoney walked to the counter, told them who he was, and asked to see Javier. The dude behind the front desk picked up the phone, called Javier, and told CMoney that he would be out in a minute.

"CMoney!" Javier smiled as soon as he entered the room a few minutes later.

"What's goin' on, Javier?" CMoney smiled.

"I don't know, you trying to blind me? Close your mouth my friend," Javier teased, making him laugh.

"Follow me," he added, then CMoney followed him into the garage area. CMoney smiled when he saw one of the hydraulic spray painters painting Ken's truck.

"Your gonna like this my friend," Javier continued then pulled the car cover back.

CMoney blinked his eyes a couple of times because the glossy paint job looked like the early morning sun rays peaked through a window. A smile crept across his face as he ran his hand over the top of the car. Javier had definitely done a fantastic job on his car.

Javier then opened the passenger's side door using the remote in his hand bringing the 90-degree vertical door straight up. Javier had mounted a small hydraulic pump in the trunk to spring the lambo doors up automatically at the press of a button. Then he popped the trunk using

the same remote while CMoney stepped back, smiled, and took in everything he was seeing.

The 1973 Buick Riviera Boattail was candy painted forest green with a full purple soft top. Shaved door handles and trunk, purple leather seats with forest

green piping, and 'MILWAUKEE BUCKS' in the front of both headrests.

Forest green fiber glass dash board, door panels, and rear deck lid. Hardwood floor on the driver and passenger's side with the Milwaukee Bucks decal emblem embedded in the middle. Two 15" flip down TVs hanging from the ceiling, 7" TVs in the headrests, and on the visors. Nardi steering wheel and gearshift, Xbox 360 mounted under the dashboard, the new Pioneer Premier radio, three 12 Kicker L7 subwoofers with three Rockford Fosgate 1,000-watt amps, and an epic center. Four Pioneer four-way 6x9 speakers going across the back, seventeen tweeters throughout the car, custom 4" Flow Masters dual exhaust pipes hanging from under the bumper, and a 5" Gorilla

lift kit to squat perfectly over the 28" chrome DUB Showtime spinning rims with the purple background.

The car already had a 429 cubic engine with a four-barrel carburetor, so CMoney had Javier's mechanic

Carlos tweak a few things to his liking and add an extra car battery.

"Let's do the paperwork," CMoney said ready to get in traffic after Javier showed him where the stash spot was and how to open it.

"Let's go," Javier replied walking towards his office with CMoney right behind him.

∞

"I don't know where the nigga at, I ain't seen him in a couple of weeks," Curt said. He was one of the dudes that Legacy fronted work to.

"If you see that nigga, tell him to call me ASAP," Legacy stated firmly.

"Aight Lady, I got you," Curt assured her. Lady was the alias that Legacy hustled under.

"Good lookin'," she said ending the call. 'This nigga gon' make a bitch have to pop him,' She thought. She was referring to Ben, another nigga

that she fronted work to. They both worked for Boss when he was out, and they seemed to be loyal, so she

kept dealing with them after Boss got knocked. But after the last transaction, Ben stopped answering his phone, and was nowhere to be found.

Legacy was pissed because she knew that he was trying to run off with her work and money. She called Curt to see if he'd seen him and he hadn't. Legacy didn't think he had any reason to lie because he was not ducking her being that he paid her what he owed.

Legacy was supposed to go see Ant a week ago to get fresh, but she was delayed while waiting to collect her funds from Ben, not to mention that she'd been going to Boss's trial and stressing over it. She could've went to

see Ant anyway, but she didn't want to dip into her profits or her weekly shopping money. But from the look of things, that's just what she might have to do. She contemplated calling CMoney and having him fuck Ben up, but she thought better of it because knowing her little brother, he would've

killed Ben. Her next thought was to just say fuck it, take the hit, and stop fucking with him, but she couldn't bring herself to let anybody treat her like that. If she was going to play the game, she knew she had to be versatile on both ends, and from now on, that's how she was going to play.

"Tay!" Legacy said walking down the hallway towards the living room.

"Bae, call me back in twenty minutes," Chante whispered before hanging up the phone as Legacy walked in. Unbeknowingly to Legacy, Chante was just talking to Ant. "What up?" she asked.

"I need you to drive me to go holla at Ben," Legacy said firmly. Chante knew something was up by the tone in her voice and the fact that she wasn't wearing her sling when she was scheduled to have it on for at least another week, but Chante didn't know the extent of what was going on.

"Alright, let me use the bathroom first," Chante replied before walking off towards the bathroom.

Legacy went to retrieve the throw away .38 from her safe, and put it in her waistband, then she turned and looked in the mirror at herself. 'First this bitch azz nigga in Atlanta shot me, then this hoe azz nigga ran off with my money, my man locked up, and I don't know when he coming back. Fuck that, ain't nobody gon' play me like I'mma weak azz bitch, I got something for his azz,' she thought as she turned to leave the room.

Getting into the Jeep with Chante behind the wheel, they pulled off. About twenty minutes later, they were making a right turn on the corner of 11th and Keefe, Chante made a right, drove down, and stopped at the red light by the corner store. Legacy sat up and squinted her eyes as the light turned green.

"Pull up right here on the right Tay, and keep the car running," Legacy said calmly. Chante pulled up to where Legacy instructed her as her phone rung. Seeing it was Ant, she answered it. "I'll be right back," Legacy added getting out of the truck and running across the street.

"Hello," Chante smiled.

"What's happenin, shawty?" he asked.

"Chillin wit my   sister now,   but I'm tryna chill   with you tonight," she stated seductively.

"I think I can do that," he laughed.

"Oh, you think, huh? I got something to change yo mind then," she smiled.

"Oh yeah," he said as they both laughed.

"What time you want me to come through?" he added, but Chante couldn't respond, she suddenly lost her train of thought by the loud ring of a single shot Boc. She dropped the phone, looked to her left and see

Legacy pointing a gun at some nigga while yelling at him to lay on the ground. Then she saw Legacy kick whoever it was laying in front of her as the person clenched their chest. Chante knew Legacy had just shot the person before she bent down and went in his pockets.

"Oh shit!" Chante yelled, then she threw the truck in drive, busted a U-turn, let Legacy hop in, and smashed off.

'Bitch azz nigga think he gon' play me, he got another thing comin' Legacy thought as she shuffled through the large wad of bills while Chante sped away.

∞

Ken had just come from catching a few serves from some of his hypes. He had been doing good in the streets, but two things weighed heavy on his mind. One was Crystal and his unborn child, he'd be lying if he said he hadn't been thinking about them. It had been three weeks since he dropped her off at the rehab center, it was procedure that for the first thirty days, she wasn't allowed visits, mail, or phone calls, so he had no idea how she was holding up in there, but he hoped she was good.

The second thing that plagued his thoughts was pussy, he had not had any since Crystal went to rehab. He had been talking to Tori, she was Dre's

chick Tysheba's younger sister who he met the day they went to the apartment building in Northridge Lakes.

Tori was 20 years old, bad, and thick in all the right places, but Ken couldn't get her to come off none of that pussy yet. Big Booty Rudy had still been blowing up his phone but fucking her was out of the question. 'Hopefully my luck will change soon,' he thought as he made a left into the parking lot in the Meadows. Although he was in need of some sexual healing, his pockets weren't hurting for nothing. He had put his truck in the snap two weeks ago to get some paint, rims, and a few other things before school started next week.

He was almost on his third shoe box since grinding became a full-time thing for him.

Parking in front of the spot, he saw Dre standing out front with two chicks, and he hoped his prayers had been answered as he hopped out of CMoney's Impala, which had turned into the spot's car whenever somebody had to bust a move and walked up on the porch.

"What's good fam?" Ken greeted Dre with a handshake.

"Shit just chillin wit a couple of my lady friends. This Jasmine and that's her friend Keisha. Y'all this my cousin Ken," Dre said introducing everybody.

"Hey Ken," the girls said in unison.

"How y'all doin? Especially you wit yo cute self," Ken said sliding up on Keisha. Keisha was decent in the face with shoulder length hair, and some tig-ol-biddies. Ken stole a look at her ass and it was flat as a TV screen 'It'll work thou,' he thought while they chopped it up and got better acquainted.

"Oh Ken, you so funny," Keisha laughed while she touched his chest. Then she put what little butt she had on his lap as they leaned against the Impala.

Ken wrapped his arms around her and knew she was feeling him. 'I'm hittin this tonight,' he thought with a smile.

Suddenly they all heard 'Winnin' by Mr. Competition and Erl Will from afar. Everybody turned and looked towards the parking lot entrance, but nobody had arrived yet. About twenty seconds later, a car turned

into the parking lot with the music so loud, it was as if it had a live marching band in it as it came to a halt. CMoney pulled up with both doors ajar and hopped out with his rims still spinning.

"You see me my niggas, then you see money, if you ain't spinnin' you can't be winnin', and niggas definitely ain't winnin' if they ain't fuckin wit us, ya hear me?" CMoney said, turned all the way up with his arms folded across his chest and his head cocked to the side.

"Who is that?" Keisha turned to ask Ken. 'Damn, just when I thought I was about to get some,' Ken thought.

"I see you lookin like money, smellin' like a check," Dre smiled quoting Yo Gotti as he walked down the steps to go greet his boy.

"You like this muthafucka?" CMoney asked smiling while he shook up with Dre.

"Hell yeah," Dre said enthusiastically while looking in the car. CMoney had told him a little about what he was doing with the car, but to see the finished product was a sight to see.

"My nigga, you got the hardwood floor in this muthafucka with the 'BUCKS' sign on it, you went stupid hard wit that," he added gleefully as Ken walked up.

"Wanna take it for a spin?" CMoney asked nonchalantly. He didn't have to ask Dre twice as he hopped behind the wheel and pulled off with the doors still up.

"You did that cuz," Ken acknowledged with a handshake.

"I'm tryin' my nigga, I seen them sprayin' yo shit down when I was there too," C Money said.

326

"On what?'" Ken smiled more out of happiness than disbelief.

"On er' thang, that muthafucka wet too," CMoney said as Dre pulled back up, parked next to his Magnum, and hopped out smiling.

"Bro, that muthafucka snot," Dre said letting the door down on the driver's side.

"I already know," CMoney smiled as he let the passenger's door down before catching his keys that Dre tossed. After activating his alarm, they all went inside the house with the girls in tow. Dre sat on the love seat with Jasmine next to him while CMoney sat on the long couch with Keisha right next to him and Ken next to her. CMoney pulled out his phone after his text alert went off. It was Lou Lou letting him know that she had his money ready. CMoney had been fronting her kush and she was getting it off at a rapid pace,

putting her on his team was proving to be quite profitable.

Over the last three weeks, he had given her a total of 4 pounds of kush and she showed true characteristics of a hustler and getting money. CMoney was going to cop

his next batch of weed tomorrow, so he was gon' throw her something nice because if he was eating, his whole team had to be eating.

After reading the text, he replied, put his phone away, and noticed Keisha staring him down admiringly.

"What up lil mama?" he asked.

"Nothin, I was wondering how old you are?" she smiled with lust in her tone.

'Here we go wit that question again,' CMoney thought. "Seventeen, why?" he asked, wanting to confirm what he already knew.

"You for real? Did you know you fine as hell?" she giggled while scooting closer to him.

"That's what they tell me," he smiled.

"Hold on lil mama, I'll be right back," he added before heading to the basement. He noticed Ken's demeanor and the look of disappointment all over his face because when he pulled up, he saw Keisha damn near glued to

Ken's lap, but she seemed to be more into him since he got on the scene, but you know CMoney wouldn't dare because she wasn't even in the same equation as Esther, she wasn't even fucking with Lou Lou. But you couldn't be mad at her for hopping from one nigga to the next because that's what hoes do. Many of them would start at the bottom and fuck their way to the H.N.I.C (Head Nigga in Charge) just to say they fucked some niggas with long paper, which CMoney could never understand because at the end of the night, they were going home broke, hungry, self respect down the drain, a sore mouth, a sore pussy, and possibly a sore asshole. However, CMoney had a trick up his sleeve to get Ken what he wanted. Getting in the basement, he got the 15 gees he had stashed in the ceiling because he neglected to take it to his mother's basement last night when he left the spot. Going back upstairs, he noticed Dre and Jasmine were gone as he walked up next to the couch where Ken sat and counted out the money.

"My nigga here go 15 of that 20 bandz that you let me borrow, I'll have the rest for you next week," CMoney said holding out the money.

Ken looked at him clueless about what the fuck he was talking about. Sensing he was about to fuck up his plan, CMoney quickly looked at Keisha who had her eyes fixated on the large wad of money in his hands, so he quickly winked his eye three times at Ken to get him on the same page. 'This nigga will fuck up a wet dream, he still got a lot to learn,' CMoney thought as the light bulb finally came on in Ken's head about what he was trying to do.

"Just hold it down my nigga, I ain't trippin' about no 20 gees, you know we havin' money baby, just get it to me when you get it all, ya feel me?" Ken said extending his hand for some love.

"Aight, good lookin' boss man," CMoney said trying to hold back his laughter at his crazy cousin as he tucked the money away.

Seeing what had just transpired, in true jumpdown form, Keisha focused her attention right back on Ken as quickly as one could snap their fingers.

"Ken, you got somewhere more comfortable we can go," Keisha smiled with her hand sliding up and down his leg while getting closer to his member every time she slid her hand back up.

"Yeah, come on," he smiled and hopped to his feet, then he helped her off the couch, and walked towards the stairs. Ken looked over his shoulder and mouthed 'Good looking'. CMoney nodded his head and mouthed back 'Strap up then' before leaving to go meet Lou Lou.

Ken took Keisha upstairs where they undressed themselves, then he laid back on the mattress that was on the floor and got some head from Keisha. After that, he put his condom on, fingered her til she was wet, then he fell in that pussy like it was quick sand. As Ken

331

pumped into her, he noticed that her vaginal muscle tone was loose as hell, but he kept right on fucking her like Crystal had showed him how to. When he busted,

he pulled out, laid next to her, and smiled because he had just got #5 under his belt. Keisha rolled over and asked could they do it again, so he strapped on another rubber and went for round two.

∞

I'm looking for a Mr. Dwayne Paul!" the sheriff's deputy yelled through the crowded and loud dayroom of the 5-C pod in the Milwaukee County jail.

"Cuz, they calling for you," Boss said to Wayne. They were chopping it up while playing a card game called deuces wild.

"I hear 'em, let me go see what the fuck they want," Wayne said while getting up from his chair and walking towards the officer's station.

"Are you Mr. Paul?" the deputy asked once he got there.

"Yeah, what up?" Wayne replied skeptically.

"Come with me, you have an attorney visit," the deputy stated which was music to Wayne's ears, this was his

second time seeing Mr. Hastings in the last three weeks. The last time he saw Mr. Hastings, he told Wayne that he believed they had a solid case to argue, and that he'd file the motion to dismiss all charges immediately, highlighting the latest events surrounding the arresting officer on his case. The deputy led Wayne through the secured doors, then to the elevator, where he pressed the button to go to the sixth floor. When the doors opened up, to Wayne's surprise, there were three female inmates on the elevator escorted by a female deputy. Wayne smiled as he stepped in the elevator and surveyed them. Only one looked decent in the face but being that it felt like he hadn't been in the presence of a woman in years, even though he had not been down that long, but with the time he had been down, they looked like Rihanna, Nicki Minaj, and Meagan Good to him, which were some of his favorite women in the industry, so he could've took all three of the female inmates down at that time, ugly or not. The girls smiled back, and Wayne knew that more than likely, they

were thinking along the same lines as him, so he winked at the cute one.

The deputy that escorted him was flirting and indulged in a deep conversation with the deputy that escorted the girls, so when the elevator stopped and the doors opened to their stop, the two talkative deputies walked off first which they usually didn't do then the girls filed out with the cute one last, so Wayne being the cocky guy that he was, reached out quickly and squeezed a handful of her plump ass, told her his name, and that she should write him as he got off the elevator. She smiled and nodded her head before they were escorted in opposite directions.

'I still got it,' Wayne thought as the deputy led him to a small conference room on the 6th floor.

"Mr. Paul, how are you?" Mr. Hastings asked as soon as Wayne entered the room while standing from his seat to shake Wayne's hand.   Mr.   Hastings was   a tall balding white man with Versace glasses who

exuded confidence. He was dressed sharply as usual in a grey tailored Versace suit with grey alligator loafer shoes and a Rolex watch on his wrist. Wayne came to the conclusion that he was either married to a black woman or dating one because he had never seen a white man with gators, a Rolex, and Versace glasses on all at once; that had   black   written   all   over   it.   "I'm alright, but hopefully after this meeting, I'll be doing a lot better," Wayne said seriously as they sat down, on opposite sides of the table.

"Hopefully so,"   Mr.   Hastings said   as   he popped the latches on his briefcase that laid on the table and slid a thick packet of papers towards Wayne.

"These papers   are the unsealed   federal   documents concerning Milwaukee Police Department officer Jerome Herman and others. If you continue turning through the pages, you'll find that he was in fact stealing drugs, that being cocaine, marijuana, and heroin from dealers and the evidence room. That man has a lot of skeletons that just fell out of

the closet, and those very papers in your hands, are the reason why I feel so confident that we can get this case thrown out. You didn't make a statement which was vital because to be blunt, that would've fucked you badly. The car is not in your name and that's where they found the drugs, so what if you ran, you were scared. I think we can present our case as he tried to get you to deal drugs for him on several occasions, but you declined, and therefore he planted the drugs on you which ultimately led to your arrest since that's what he's been doing to others. He'd been victimizing them all, what do you think?" Mr. Hastings asked while he put one leg atop the other.

"I think it's a great plan," Wayne smiled.

"Alright prepare for battle, court is in one week. Keep that paperwork and look it over, if you see anything further that can possibly help us, get in contact with me as soon as possible, I'll have you out of here soon," Mr. Hastings stood up and grabbed his briefcase and shook Wayne's hand before turning to leave.

"I'll do that," Wayne said, then sat back down until the deputy came to take him back to the pod. Wayne skimmed through the stack of papers, he smiled because he could taste his freedom and it tasted good.

CHAPTER FIFTEEN

One week later…

"Shit," CMoney said before he pulled out and laid next to Esther with his chest heaving. They had just got done sharing an early morning quickie before starting the day.

"Don't forget what you have at home when them lil hoes be all up in yo face," Esther stated seriously while looking in his eyes. Although she was a beautiful and confident woman, she also knew how conniving a woman could be in pursuit of a man, furthermore, she knew the power a woman's pussy possessed.

"You ain't gotta worry about nothin like that, my main priority is us, and I'm not going to let anything come between that, especially not no hoes," CMoney assured her as his text alert went off. He grabbed his phone from the nightstand and saw it was from Dre, letting him know that he was on his way.

"Okay," Esther smiled satisfied with his response. She felt even more secure with the surprise she was going to get for him today.

"I gotta get ready baby," he said before he kissed her. He knew that even the most beautiful women needed reassurance from time to time, so he would always provide that for her whenever needed. CMoney rolled out of bed and headed to the bathroom to get himself together because today was the first day of school and he was excited.

"I'm sure glad we got those houses," 'Esther said to CMoney before he turned the shower on.

"Me too, keep lookin' for more because as soon as we get these up andrunning, we

gon' get more," CMoney yelled before stepping in the shower. A few days ago, Esther closed the deal on both houses that she found on the internet, now it was about getting them up to code, therefore raising the property value.

After showering and handling his hygiene, he made his way back into the bedroom, put on a pair of boxers, ankle socks, and a beater, then he got dressed. CMoney put on a pair of all white Gucci jean shorts, an all white Gucci

belt with light grey interlocking Gs, a forest green short sleeved Gucci button-up shirt with the interlocking Gs on the right chest pocket, and his white, black, forest green, and light grey retro #14 Air Jordan's. Then he put his chain on his neck, Brietling on his wrist, pinkie rings on both pinkies, 5 gees in his pocket, took off his du-rag, and brushed his freshly cut waves before he wiped his teeth off with the jewelry rag. Grabbing both phones, two ounces of kush, he checked himself in the full-length mirror behind the bathroom's door and was ready to set the school year off the right way as his phone rang.

"What's up'?" he answered.

"We outside," Dre stated.

"Here I come now," CMoney replied then ended the call. "Minor gon' meet us at the house on 62nd after I get out of school. My keys on the dresser, make sure you bring that book bag for me, I'mma see you later baby, aight?" CMoney said before he kissed her. Minor was a family friend who was really good at fixing whatever needed to be fixed, so CMoney was going to pay him to bring both

houses up to code so they meet the requirements for living.

"Alright baby, I'm off to school today and I don't have to be at the hospital until later, so I'mma go get my hair done, and take care of a few other things," she said before laying back down to get some rest before going to handle her business.

"Aight sexy," he said turning to leave.

"Wait baby, let me take a picture of you first," 'she said sitting up and letting the sheet fall, exposing her bare ample breasts as she reached for her phone. CMoney posed, let her take a couple of pictures, then he left the house. Once outside the apartment building, he saw Dre smoking a blunt while he and Ken leaned against his Magnum.

"What's happenin?" CMoney said walking up and shakin both of their hands.

"Shit, chillin,'" Dre said puffing his blunt. He was dressed in an orange and white True Religion outfit,

orange and white AFls, and an orange and a white New York Knicks fitted hat. He also had on his chain, earrings, and watch.

"Coolin," Ken replied. He was dressed in a blue, yellow, and white Parish Nation outfit. White, blue, and yellow Air Max 97s, crispy braids with designs, a pair of Cartier glasses and a Cartier watch. The three of them were sure to turn heads at school.

"Let's get up outta here," CMoney said getting into the passenger's seat of Dre's Magnum while Ken got behind the wheel of his Envoy truck which was now candy painted his favorite shade of yellow and sitting on chrome 24" D'Vinci rims. The truck had black leather guts, four TVs, four twelve-inch subwoofers, a stash spot, and tinted windows. Dre turned up 'Medicine' by Big Bando featuring Looney, then he pulled off heading to school.

342

Arriving to Harold Vincent High School, they swerved a little as they passed the front of the school doing 5mph, so everybody saw them on their way to the parking lot.

After parking, they hopped out, and walked towards the school.

"Chris!" a female voice yelled out, getting his attention. He turned around to see Toya's fine azz.

"What's good?" he smiled. Toya was one of, if not the, baddest chick in school that CMoney used to flirt with, but he never hit that because she was involved with some nigga who played on the football team in an on-again-off-again relationship. Not wanting to have a label on her name as a hoe, she played hard to get, but she was cool peoples. "I thought that was you, you look real good, all bling blinging and stuff," she smiled while holding the gold coin on his chain.

"Thanks, you looking good yourself, and the name is CMoney now," he replied.

"Um, okay CMoney, I'mma see you at lunch period," she smiled, but her eyes said so much more before she walked away.

On the way into the school, all three flashy young men were stopped by several different chicks. CMoney sold a few niggas and chicks some kush and kept correcting them on his name. Then, the bell rang signaling that it was almost time for first hour, so they made their way to the lockers, and then to class to start their senior year.

∞

It had been a week since Legacy caught up with Ben, shot him, and took the money from his pockets. Although he only had a little over 3 gees, which was a far drop from what he owed, she was content with that since he tried to play her. CMoney was furious when he learned about the situation Legacy had gotten herself into because she didn't call him, but she explained why she didn't, and after hearing her reasoning, he knew she was right. He knew that in order to survive in the game, one would have to stand two feet and ten toes down on their morals, and if somebody violated those beliefs, you had to set an example to make the next person think twice about bringing any bullshit your way. CMoney

fully understood that and hoped that she did set that example, but he was still mad about the whole ordeal.

Ben tried calling Legacy after she shot him to correct his wrong because he was in fear of losing his life because Boss was plugged with a lot of people, something he had not thought about before, but Legacy had already switched phones and dumped her old one. She called everybody who needed to have the number and supplied them with it. Anyways, she felt like he should've paid her in the first place and saved himself some pain since she had always kept it one hunnid with him. However, she'd have to learn that in this game, there is no such thing as playing fair because somebody is always trying to get over on somebody else to benefit themselves and get further along in the game. They say it's a dirty game, but it's fair, and from now on, she would always stay alert to the cross move because to be aware is to be alive.

Legacy rode through the streets with her pistol on her lap and Destinee Lynn's 'Tatted up' bumping out of the speakers while behind the wheel of her new '08 Ford

Explorer truck that she bought the very next day after the shooting. Being that she just saw Ant four days ago, she was in full time grind mode. Boss had told her to fall back after she got shot, but she was already knee-deep in the game and couldn't bring herself to just suddenly stop like that, so she wasn't trying to hear that. She still didn't tell him about shooting Ben because he would've pressed her even more to stop, so she kept it to herself. Legacy made a left on 26th and Burleigh and pulled out her phone. "Vic, I'm outside," she said then hung up. 'Niggas out here spending too much money for this work, I can't stop now,' she thought to herself as she did what she had to do to open the stash box.

∞

"Fuck," Dre said after he crapped out trying to hit a #4 point as everybody's hand swarmed in to pick up their cash. Dre and a few other dudes were skipping fourth period in the bathroom shooting dice.

"My dice, shoot five hit five, point seen money gone, catch what you don't like, who got me," Isaac said as

he picked up the dice, blew on them, then shook them in his hand.

"I got him, shoot ten hit ten," Dre countered, dropping his money.

"Money down," Isaac said dropping a ten-dollar bill on the floor before he rolled.

"Naturals," he added rolling the dice before he snapped his fingers. Seeing one of the dice land on the #5, Dre stuck his hand out and slapped the dice away.

"Let me get dem," Dre said.

"Good catch," Isaac said sitting one dice atop of the other before he picked them up and shook them...

"Naturals," he added with the snap. The dice rolled and stopped on #5 and #6, Isaac quickly scooped up his money.

"Bet back lucky azz nigga," Dre said putting his money down.

"Luck? luck is for leprechauns, this skill my man," Isaac boasted.

"I bet he hit for the dub, Dre," Nell said holding a twenty dollar bill out.

"Drop it," Dre replied then dropped his money.

"Naturals," Isaac said rolling the dice. One landed on the #2 while the other one spinned.

"Told you that shit was luc...," Dre said but the words got caught in his throat when he saw the other dice land on the #5 after spinning six times. Isaac and Nell scooped up their money as Dre looked on puzzled. He saw the #1 winking before it landed on #5, so he surely thought Isaac was going to crap out. 'This nigga can't be that good,' Dre thought. He used to sting Isaac and Nell all last year, but Isaac worked hard over the summer to

perfect his craft with the dice, and now he was a force to be reckoned with.

"Let me see dem dice," Dre said snatching the dice out of Isaac's hand because he thought they had snuck a pair of trick dice in the gamble the way he was rolling. After seeing the dice were valid, he rolled them on the floor.

"I'm insulted that you think I would cheat you, this what I do my nigga," Isaac said picking up the dice.

"You don't do shit, and I aint yo nigga, shoot fifty hit fifty," Dre said dropping the money.

"Bet," Isaac said dropping hismoney before he rolled. He rolled #4 and #2, and two rolls later, he hit that point. Isaac kept hitting point after point, he was blazing hot, and ended up hitting Dre for a little over $1,400.

"He passin' on yo azz," Nell laughed while collecting his money, he had won a few hundred on nothing but side bets.

"On his thang," Jay smiled, he was cool with Isaac and Nell, but he was spectating only.

"Shut y'all bum azz up and hold ya own nuts," Dre said going in his pocket. "Since you think shit funny, shoot five gees Nell," he added holding the money out.

"I ain't got it," Nell said plainly.

"I know you don't bum azz nigga wit dem Mega Fashion azz Jordan's, the number three's ain't even come out in that color," Dre said pissed that they hit him for the little money as CMoney came crashing in the door.

"Here comes security hoe azz," CMoney said walking into the stall and locking the door, everybody but Nell followed suit. He used the urinal because he really had to piss.

"Y'all betta clean this up in here and get to class, I know all y'all ain't using the bathroom," the security guard said before he left out of the bathroom. Everybody came out of the stalls and Dre being the sore loser that he was, was still a little salty, so when he saw Nell pissing, he wanted to embarrass him for holding another nigga's nuts. After hollering at CMoney about what he wanted

to do, he walked up behind Nell as CMoney pulled out his phone and turned the video camera on.

"Weak azz nigga!' Dre said while pulling Nell's pants the rest of the way down to his ankles. Everybody in the bathroom bursted into laughter at what they were seeing. They weren't just laughing at the fact that Dre pulled his pants down, they were laughin because there Nell stood in a pair of white tight draws with a shit stain in the back of them and what appeared to be a folded-up paper towel to separate the shit stain from his bare ass. "Look at this nigga, draws bogus as a bitch, then he got the nerve to have a fuckin' paper towel in there," Dre laughed with everybody.

"How you know it was a paper towel my nigga?" CMoney laughed.

"Cause I see the design on that muthafucka, shitty booty ass lil boy," Dre laughed while holding his stomach. "That quicker picker upper forgot to pick that shit up out yo draws," he added, making everybody laugh even harder than before as Nell finished pissing, then pulled

up his pants. He was furious and embarrassed all at the same time as he turned to face Dre.

"Why the fuck you do that weak azz shit nigga," Nell spat walking up on Dre with his face scrunched up.

"First of all, you betta get the fuck up out my face before I put stupid hands on yo fool azz," Dre said pushing him backwards as CMoney put his phone away, tucked his chain in, and took his watch off preparing for battle. He didn't know why Dre pulled that stunt on Nell, but it wasn't the time or place to ask questions. Dre was his nigga and if he was getting down, CMoney was getting down with him whether he was in the wrong or not.

"Man leave that shit alone y'all," Isaac said stepping in between the two.

"You better listen to yo boy before I hurt you," Dre stated as the bell rang.

"Come on we outta here, they ain't on shit," CMoney laughed as Dre mugged all three young men before they walked out of the bathroom.

∞

Ken left school early because he had some business to take care of. After making his serves, he drove down Locust and made a right on 4th street and parked in between Locust and Hadley. He tucked his 9mm Ruger under the driver's seat, surveyed the block, then hopped out of his truck, and went inside the rehab center. It had been thirty days, so he was going to see Crystal for the first time. He had just turned 18 three days ago, so he wouldn't have any problems getting in to see her.

Ken walked up to the counter, told them he was there to see Crystal Reed, showed his ID, and was asked to wait in the visiting room. About 10 minutes later, Crystal walked into the room glowing. She searched the room with her eyes not knowing who came to see her, then met Ken's eyes, she stood up and let him know with a huge smile that she was happy to see him. As she walked over she put her lips to his, wrapped her arms around his neck, and pecked. "I'm glad to see you," she said gleefully.

"Me too, you look good," Ken said squeezing two handfuls of her plump ass. He didn't know if it was the

fact that she was off the drugs or that she was pregnant, but she had definitely gotten thicker in the breast and ass areas.

"You too, with yo nasty self," she smiled after they broke their embrace and sat down at the table.

"Can you blame me? Y'all gettin' thick as a muthafucka," he said shaking his head from side to side.

"That's the baby," she stated putting her hand on her stomach.

"How far along are you now?" he inquired.

"Five weeks and counting," she said happily.

"So, you gon' get even thicker, huh?" he smiled. She shook her head and rolled her eyes making Ken chuckle

"On a serious side, how you been holding up in here?" he asked.

"I'm not gonna lie it's hard as hell in here. I'm pregnant, I feel like I'm alone, I'm missing Emmanuel like a muthafucka, and you," she stated holding back tears.

Ken reached out, grabbed her hands, and looked into her eyes.

"Listen, I miss you too, but this is for the best right now, so you can do what you need to do to better yourself as a woman, a mother, and overall be a better person. You needed to take this step, I commend you for it, and I'm gon' support you through it the best way I can," Ken stated firmly. Crystal knew that he was right and with his support, she knew she could make it.

"Thank you very much, I really need your support," she said seriously.

"Oh, and happy belated birthday, you thought I forgot didn't you," she added.

"Nope, thanks thou, it feels good to be grown," he said as they shared a laugh.

"How did you celebrate? You betta not been passin' out none of that," she said pointing at his crotch area.

"You trippin'," Ken said and smiled, and that notion let her know that he had been having sex with other girls.

She wasn't mad, but she did feel some type of way about it because she was carrying his baby. However, they weren't

355

in a committed relationship at that time, so she'd look over that for now, but she'd ask him later if he'd been protecting himself.

Ken noticed her mood change, so he gave her the good news that he knew would cheer her up. "Ay, I went over yo mama's house yesterday to see Emmanuel, that lil boy a mess, he's a good lil dude though, he asked about you too," Ken said getting Crystal's full attention when he mentioned her son.

"What you tell him?" she asked.

"I told him that you love and miss him and that you'll be back to get him soon," Ken said as Crystal smiled. "I took him to McDonald's and he asked me was I his new daddy," he added, then they shared a laugh. "I told him that you only get one daddy and that me and him are good friends, so he was cool with that. He had fries all over my truck, he gon' be a little player too. I left yo

mama a few hundred for him too, so he aigh't," he continued with a smile.

Crystal was all smiles after hearing about her son, she couldn't wait to see him, she thanked Ken for all that he had done for her and Emmanuel, and for the rest of the visit they talked and ate vending machine food. Crystal told him that she'd get a five hour pass next week and promised to put it on him after she spent some time with her son. Ken gave her a few hundred bucks to buy whatever she needed and told her that his line would be unblocked to accept collect calls later on that night.

She promised to call him that night, they hugged each other tightly while kissing passionately, he squeezed that ass, rubbed her stomach, and then he left.

Ken hopped back in his truck, retrieved his pistol, sat it on his lap, and started the engine. He sat there for a few minutes weighing the pros and cons on whether or not he should wife Crystal. He didn't grow up with his biological dad in the picture and he didn't want his child to grow up the same way. He hadn't told his mother or

CMoney that he had a child on the way, however, he planned to tell his mother after Crystal got out of rehab because he didn't want to tell his mother about the personal battle that Crystal was fighting. He was skeptical about telling CMoney because of how him and Dre treated him with the Rudy situation.

'Fuck it, I just turned 18, I'mma grown azz man. I'mma see how things play out with Crystal before I decide anything, but in the meantime, I'mma holla at cuz face to face about what I got going on,' he thought as he turned up the volume to 'OMW' by Reace Bishop featuring Caseload Drell G. Ken rapped word for word with Caseload Drell G as he pulled off.

∞

"Check this out my nigga, in the event that you slide from under that situation you in, I'mma have you get up with my nigga Train, and I'mma get you on yo feet. Now, this my nigga for real or you know I wouldn't even send you his way if he wasn't thorough. I mean this nigga kept it a hunnid when I was out and since I been in here, so

everything straight, you feel me?" Boss said letting Wayne
know that he wouldn't send him into a hazardous situation
if Train wasn't keeping it real with him.

"I feel you cuz, I just hope this shit work out in court first,
not only for me, but for you too," Wayne said seriously.

"That's one hunnid, just know I'm gon' I fight til the death
of me," Boss said seriously while extending his hand for
some love, even though he wasn't as confident as he
seemed, the D.A. had been presenting a good case against
him, and for the first time since being locked up, he was
worried about losing trial.

"You betta nigga," Wayne smiled while shaking his hand.

"If I do get out there, as soon as I get situated, I'mma go
holla at Lil Dawg," he added firmly.

"I figured that already, just don't sleep on that lil nigga cuz,
he young and all, but that lil nigga know some shit,"

Boss stated trying to enlighten Wayne that CMoney wasn't
a typical 17-year-old.

"I hear you, but ain't no little 17-year-old punk on earth fuckin' in my business, on my mama, I'm a giant out there with these hands and them thangs, for real," Wayne said. He couldn't wait to make CMoney pay for what he had done to his cousin.

"I know how you get down, I'm just saying don't overlook his get down because you feel you're older and more superior than him because of his age. If you gon' go at him, you gotta go at him with a leveled head. You think Mayweather get in the ring and play wit his opponents? Hell naw, he knock muthafuckas clean out regardless of who they is. Don't underestimate no man cuz, that could be the difference between killing or being killed, real talk," Boss dropped some jewels on him. Wayne sat silently while soaking up what he said. It's not that he didn't know about what he was saying, it's just the rage of Big Ball's death blinded his vision and

clouded his better judgement of how he was supposed to approach any beef he had in the streets.

"You absolutely right cuz, I'm supposed to know better than that," Wayne admitted.

"Don't trip thou, I'm just glad we found the glitch during the planning and not on the battle field," Boss smiled, then the two sat quietly for a few minutes thinking.

"On a different note, look at shawty right here," Wayne said as he pulled two pictures from his shirt pocket.

"Who dis?" Boss asked while looking at both pictures. One was of a chick in the club dressed in a short dress and the other was of the same chick taking a selfie in a full-length mirror while looking over her shoulder wearing only a pair of short shorts.

"That's Ebony, the chick I told you about that I met on the elevator the day Hastings came to see me," Wayne smiled. He had gotten his second letter from her today after he responded to her first one. She sent him the pictures and her home address because she got out last

Friday after doing a 30-day commitment for outstanding traffic tickets.

"She nice and she got a phat ol ass," Boss complimented before handing the pictures back.

"Another thang, I'mma tear that ass up when I get out," Wayne said before they laughed.

Boss noticed the excitement that Wayne spoke with and it made his thoughts drift to Legacy, he was optimistic about beating the case even though he had his doubts, but he couldn't wait to see if he was going to get back out, so he could tear Legacy's ass up too. "Cuz, let me hop on this line real fast," Boss said before getting up, walking towards the phones and dialing the number.

"Hey baby, I was just thinking about you," Legacy said as soon as the call went through.

"Oh yeah, what is it that you was thinking?" Boss smiled.

∞

CMoney looked at the clock in his eight-hour class, it was five minutes before the bell would ring signaling that school was over. He had forgotten how long the days felt when you were at school, not to mention all the money he had on hold while he was there. But he promised his mother and himself that he would graduate high school. Sure, he had a little money, but he had put thirteen years of blood, sweat, and tears into the Milwaukee public school system and it was almost over, so he couldn't bring himself to drop out with only one year left. However, he knew he needed to get a few souljas on his team to handle the clientele that he would miss while he was at school.

"Alright class there will be no homework since it's the first day of school, however, tomorrow is another thing, I'll see you all then," Mrs. Ducksberry said after the bell rang while everybody gathered their things to leave the classroom.

CMoney stepped out into the hallway and untucked his chain from under his shirt. The reason he tucked it in was because he noticed damn near everybody in his classes couldn't keep their eyes off of it including some of the teachers, so from now on whenever he was in class, he'd tuck it in to avoid all the stares while he was doing his work. After putting his notebook in the locker, he headed by the gym where he was supposed to meet Dre and Ken after school.

"What's good g-ball?" Dre greeted him as soon as he walked up.

"Chillin', where that nigga Ken at?" he asked.

"Don't know, but he said he'd be back by the time school let out," Dre stated.

CMoney made a mental note to holla at Ken because he had been acting real strange lately making him wonder if he really did get Big Booty Rudy pregnant.

"Aight, you ready?" CMoney asked.

"Hell yeah, lets blow this muthafucka," Dre responded before they headed out the door.

"Bye CMoney," Toya smiled while waving as she walked by them with a group of her friends.

"Okay now, you be easy," he smiled back. CMoney had to admit that Toya was a bad muthafucka, but he didn't want to take it there with her because he had Esther in his life and he knew that if he did fuck with Toya like that, fine girls like her had a tendency to get crazy if he tried to fuck her with no strings attached because he certainly didn't want to be with her, especially since she didn't give him no play last year. She told him at lunch that she was single and through fucking with the football nigga, so she insisted that he take her number, he took it on the strength of being nice, but he wasn't going to call her, he had Esther, and she was his wifey, and he wasn't going to jeopardize that for a fly by.

When CMoney and Dre made it to the end of the long sidewalk, CMoney searched with his eyes until he saw who he wanted to see. A smile zoomed across his face as he saw Esther standing next to his Riviera waving with one hand while the other hand was over her eyes

like a visor in efforts to prevent the sun from beaming on her face.

"I see the wifey fool," Dre smiled as they shook up, he'd never seen his friend so into a woman before, so he knew she was the one for his boy. "I'mma finna go get my whip and pull up behind you," he added before heading towards the parking lot.

"Aight," CMoney said walking off towards Esther. "Hey sexy," he smiled.

"How was your day love?" she smiled back before hugging him and kissing his lips while he gripped her colossal ass.

"Good, I see you cut yo hair, I like it, yo shit laced," he complimented her after breaking their embrace while thinking that she looked even more like Lauren London with her Rhianna-styled haircut.

"Thank you, I knew you would like it," she stated.

"Of course, I would, you could cut yo shit bald and still be fine as hell, but don't do that," CMoney said making

her laugh. "Let me see how you look," he continued while holding her hand up and spinning her around. Esther wore a sleeveless fuchsia-colored dress by Prada that stopped just before her knees, fuchsia suede peek toe ankle booties with a 3-inch heel by Alexander McQueen that showed off her freshly pedicured toes, and expensive but tasteful jewelry. She looked like she belonged walking down the red carpet at some event. CMoney looked around and saw plenty of chicks and dudes staring at her, some with lust in their eyes. He just smiled because he knew he had found the one woman who captivated his mind, body, and soul, and she was all his.

"Smt," Esther smacked her teeth playfully.

"What?" he asked puzzled.

"You didn't even peep this honey," she said turning her arm towards him. CMoney was at a loss for words at what he was seeing. On Esther's right arm, she had gotten a tattoo of his face with him smiling and the glare of the diamonds and gold that he had in his mouth. Over

his head were the words 'I See' and at the bottom was 'Money'.

"You know I love you right?" he asked after grabbing and kissing her, she had taken their relationship to the next level.

"Yeah, I love you too," she responded firmly as Dre pulled up.

"Man, if y'all don't get that lovey dovey shit outta here and get in the car, I'm gon' muthafuckin snap," Dre laughed as everybody joined in right before Ken pulled up.

"What up cuz?" Ken said coming to a stop.

"Chillin," CMoney said accepting his keys from Esther then he pressed the button on the remote and watched the passenger's door glide up until it was straight up in the air.

"Go ahead and get in baby, let me holla at them real fast," he continued before walking up to Dre's car.

"What we on?" Dre asked.

"Follow me my nig," CMoney said while walking to Kens truck

"I see Lauren London shuttin the parking lot down," Ken laughed.

"Indeed, she the baddest thing out here, but what you finna do?" CMoney asked.

"Shit, I'm wit y'all," Ken said.

"Aight follow me," CMoney stated as the horn went off behind him. He turned around to see Lou Lou sitting in her Chevy Cavalier. She had come to pick up her little sister Shanaya who was also a senior at Vincent. Shanaya was just as pretty as Lou Lou, but much thicker. Lou Lou had graduated from Vincent when CMoney was in his sophomore year.

"What it do nigga?" she asked once he got to the window.

"Finna go take care of some business, what you on?" he replied.

"Nothing, I see you out here wit wifey, I can't stunt thou, she is really pretty," Lou Lou complimented now knowing why he turned down her advances when she tried to give him some about a week ago.

"Thanks," CMoney smiled.

"Hi CMoney," Shanaya smiled.

"What's good girl," he replied after ducking down in the window to see her, Shanaya had a body similar to Serena Williams.

"Everybody gonna hit the lake front, you going?" Lou Lou asked.

"Probably, but if I don't I'mma get up wit you when I get back to the hood," he stated.

"Do that" she said as he walked off pressing the remote, so his door was open by the time he made it to the car.

Hopping in and starting the car, he slid Party Boi's CD 'I Love Haters' in the deck as Lou Lou rolled past and hit her horn. He threw the deuces up to her as she passed.

"That's Lou Lou who I been telling you about...," he volunteered before she could say anything. CMoney had already told Esther about Lou Lou, leaving out the part about their past sexual encounters because he didn't want to worry her over nothing, but Esther understood that his and Lou Lou's relationship was strictly business and she was cool with that even though she told him to keep it that way.

CMoney pulled his visor screens down and turned up 'New Whips' featuring Trae The Truth and Believe after he let his door down. Him, Dre, and Ken jacked a little bit before they went to the spot so CMoney could catch the serves he had on hold. After that, they were going to meet Minor at the house on 62nd and Bobolink, drop Esther off at the hospital, and then hit the lake front.

CHAPTER SIXTEEN

Three weeks later...

"Hello," Wayne answered his ringing cell phone out of breath.

"What up playboy?" Train asked.

"Shit coolin, what's good wit you thou?" Wayne said watching Ebony as she got out of bed butt-ass naked.

"I'mma finna come slide on you, we got some business to take care of," Train replied.

"Aight, gimme thirty minutes," Wayne said ending the call and sitting up in the bed.

"You hungry?" Ebony smiled. She was the chick Wayne met on the elevator when he was in the county jail and had been writing before he got out.

"Yeah, hook something up," he responded while watching her put on a pair of yoga pants and a T-shirt. Wayne had been fucking her since he came home two

weeks ago, she was trying to play the wifey role, and although she had some G.A.P (Good Ass Pussy) and head, the wifey role required a lot more, now he wasn't ruling it out as of yet because he knew that anything was possible in due time.

Ebony left the room to go prepare a meal for them as Wayne went in the bathroom to take a shower, handle his hygiene, and then get dressed. Wayne was ecstatic about beating those charges like Rocky, when he first went to court on the motion that Mr. Hastings had filed on his behalf. Mr. Hastings had destroyed the credibility of the arresting officer, he brought up the fact that there was no finger prints on the packages of drugs, which likely came from it being planted, and he put the court under the impression that Wayne was the unprovoked victim of a lying drug dealing cop who tried to get him to sell drugs and after he didn't, he was set up in an attempt to send him to prison for not cooperating.

The courts listened intently, they knew that was a likely scenario due to the allegation and charges that the

arresting officer was facing. The courts knew that they were fighting a losing battle if they took it to trial and they would waste a lot of tax payers' dollars in doing so, so the charges were dropped, and after serving a few more days for a warrant, Wayne was able to walk away a free man.

Wayne tied up his '94 Barkley Air Max, made his way down the stairs, and sat at the table in front of a plate with steak and sunny side up eggs on it and a big glass of apple juice. He and Ebony talked and laughed as they ate until a car horn went off.

"I'mma get at you later, aight?" Wayne said getting up from the table, walking over and kissing her lips before turning to leave.

"Wait Wayne," she said rising from her seat.

"I gotta work late, so let yourself in when you come tonight, and I'll see you later," she added before handing him a set of keys from her coat pocket.

Wayne was no stranger to having women in his life, he knew that any time a woman got up and cooked for you the next day after a wild night of sex meant that you put it down and she wanted to keep you around. After the notion of her giving him a set of keys, he knew that she wanted to be with him, and he was going to give her a chance to show and prove.

"Okay, I'mma see you tonight," he said hugging her after he put the keys in his pocket.

"Be careful, and if I'm home before you get back, wake me up when you come in," she said sensually while breaking their embrace, and Wayne knew exactly what that meant as he smiled. Ebony really took a liking to Wayne because he was so different from the men that she dated in the past and she felt protected in his big arms, so she was taking the necessary steps to start a relationship with him.

"Aight," he said while grabbing his .45 from under the couch, leaving out of the house and getting in the passenger's side of the Charger.

"What's up my nig?" Train asked while shaking his hand.

"Ain't nothing to it, where we headed?" Wayne inquired.

"We gotta go pick up the work from Legacy and then hit the spot," Train said pulling off.

"Her lil' brother bet not be wit her, cause I'm poppin' his bitch azz when I see him...," Wayne spat pulling out his pistol and chambering a round. Train looked at him like he was crazy because he was oblivious to the beef that was going on.

"Who CMoney?" Train asked skeptically.

"Hell yeah," Wayne said with his face scrunched up while laying the pistol on his lap.

"Lil dawg a player and he out here eatin', what happened wit y'all?" Train asked.

"Fuck that niggar," Wayne simply put it.

"Dig this my nigga, Boss got us together to do what's necessary, so if you got a problem wit a muthafucka, I

got a problem wit a muthafucka, so tell me what the fuck goin on wit you and, that nigga," Train said puzzled.

Wayne looked at him for a second trying to spot a weakness in his demeanor. Seeing none, Wayne went ahead and explained why he wanted to fuck CMoney up. Train was taken aback as he knew bout Big Ball's death but had no idea that CMoney was responsible for it. Loyal to his best friend, Train was ready to ride for his boy in his absence.

"I know where them little niggas be at too, we gon' pay they azz a visit," Train said.

"In due time my nigga, in due time," Wayne said as they pulled into Walgreen's on 76th and Capitol. Wayne thought he had an advantage because CMoney didn't know who he was, so he knew there was a chance that he could sneak right up on him without him knowing what hit him. A devious smile crept across his face because he could almost taste revenge.

CMoney sat in the passenger's side of Esther's Lac truck. He had her pick him up early from school, so they could do some shopping for winter clothes. They hit up Silver Star's, Playmakers, Mid Town, and Bayshore Mall. Now they were on their way home to drop the bags off and go to dinner. Esther pulled up to the lights on Capitol and Appleton and made a right. CMoney being alert to his surroundings spotted the champagne-colored Explorer going in the opposite direction before making a right at the lights.

"Turn left up in McDonald's bae," he directed. He knew that truck anywhere and he wanted to holla at them. CMoney directed Esther through the McDonald's until she made a right up Capitol and caught the light on 76th. He searched for the direction that the truck went and spotted it in the Walgreen's parking lot.

"Right there at Walgreen's," he pointed for Esther to see.

Once the light turned green she pulled off and turned right in the Walgreen's parking lot just as Legacy hopped out of the truck with a duffel bag and put it in the trunk of a white Dodge Charger before she got into the backseat.

"You want me to pull up next to them?" Esther asked.

"Naw, just ride past," he replied. CMoney knew that Legacy was doing business, he just wanted to make sure she was straight. As Esther drove past slowly, CMoney looked intently from behind the tinted windows. He knew the nigga driving the Charger was Train, he was gon' get at him awhile back after the heated phone call that he and Boss had, just to show Boss that shit will get real out here if he fucked around in his business, but he fell back only because Train had the plug on the kush that CMoney was buying from him through Legacy, so he'd let him live for now, plus CMoney didn't think he posed a real threat anyway. CMoney also saw a big black grimy-looking azz nigga with dreads in the passenger's seat who he didn't know, but he wanted to know who he was because as far as he was concerned, any person associated in Boss's circle was a potential problem and CMoney couldn't have that. He assumed the dude was in

Boss's circle due to him riding in the car with the man's best friend.

CMoney then looked in the Explorer and saw Chante paying close attention to what was going on in the Charger, he smiled because he knew she had that thing on her lap and any sign of trouble, she was getting letting shots off.

CMoney had Esther park in one of the spaces where he could see what was going on. He checked to see if his P99 was ready to fire, he knew Train wasn't stupid enough to pull some bullshit with Legacy, but he had to make sure. After Legacy hopped back in the truck and pulled off, he had Esther pull off too. He decided to call Chante later on and pick her brain about who that other nigga was.

∞

Ken had just dropped Crystal off at the rehab center after they spent some time with her son and he hit that. Crystal was really starting to show because she was now 22 weeks and Ken was proud that he would soon be a dad.

He took her to see the new house that he rented for them from CMoney on 62nd and Bobolink, and Crystal was ecstatic about that. Ken finally told CMoney who he really got pregnant and to his surprise, CMoney didn't clown him, he asked him was he positive that the baby was his, Ken told him yeah, and CMoney told him to do what he had to do as a man and take care of his responsibilities. Starting with getting Crystal out of the Meadows and off of drugs.

Ken didn't tell him that he was contemplating being in a relationship with her, but unbeknowingly to Ken, CMoney already figured that out because that was natural, but he just didn't say anything. Ken would have to learn some things for himself in order to grow as a man.

Ken and CMoney turned Crystal's old house in the Meadows into a spot, so now they had two spots in the Meadows.

Ken pulled into the 'Murder Lot', parked, grabbed his pistol, his Playmakers bag, got out of his truck, and went into the spot. "What's up fool?" he said to Al and Dell.

Albert was Ken's cousin on his dad's side and Dell was his cousin's guy. CMoney told Ken to bring them in to run the spots since they didn't go to school anyway. CMoney liked that they were both trigger happy and no non-sense type of guys.

"What up cuz?" the 5'10 brown-skinned Al said while passing the blunt to Dell before continuing to count the stacks of money on the table.

"What's good Ken?" the 5'9 light-skinned chubby Dell said before puffing the blunt.

"Chillin," Ken said accepting the offered blunt. Ken had started smoking weed on the regular now. "Roll this up fam," he added passing Dell two blunts and a zip of kush.

"Tell that nigga CMoney to come pick this bread up," Al said putting a rubber band around every thousand-dollar stack.

"Aight," Ken said while pulling his phone and texting CMoney. Just as he was putting his phone away, his text alert went off. It was Tori the fine chick from Northridge Lakes apartment building. She wanted to know if they were still on for their date tonight. Ken texted her back to let her know it was a go and he'd call her when he was on his way. He was optimistic that he was gon' be in them guts tonight. Once he finished smoking, he went to get in the shower and get dressed.

∞

"What's good bro?" Chante said, answering her cell phone.

"Ain't nothing to it, what you on?" CMoney asked.

"Oh nothing, just sitting around chillin," she responded.

"Where Legacy at?" CMoney asked trying to make sure she wasn't around before he asked what he needed to know.

"She laying' down in the back room depressed as hell over Boss's trial. They subpoenaed his guy Rio to court and this fuck nigga testified against him, this nigga ain't got no honor or balls. So, it's safe to say that she's going through some things right now," she explained.

"He was on that case too?"

"Naw, he was locked up on a separate case, so for him telling, they dropped his initial charges and let him go," she stated while shaking her head.

"Yeah that's fucked up," CMoney said. Although he and Boss were enemies, he hated a rat azz nigga with a passion. It didn't matter who they told on, once a mouse, you turn into rat, and all rats gotta die, even the Chuck'e Cheese rat.

"Tell me about it," Chante said.

"I saw y'all at Walgreen's earlier! I was parked right down the way from y'all trying to make sure y'all was good, who was that y'all met up there?" he inquired.

"Oh, that was Train and Boss cousin Wayne. Matter of fact, he was just locked up wit Boss a little while ago and now he out here tryna get it together from what I see," Chante stated.

'Just as I suspected' CMoney thought. If he was locked up wit Boss, CMoney knew the chances were likely that this Wayne character knew about the Big Ball situation, for all CMoney knew, that could've been his cousin too.

CMoney was sure to stay on point in case the nigga was feeling heroic and tried to come at him on some drama shit. As far as CMoney was concerned, Wayne and Train could go visit Big Ball permanently if they got on some bullshit.

"Ay see if you can find me another plug on that Keisha, cause that shit wasn't right from dude last time," CMoney lied because he didn't have shit for Train but bullets from this point on.

"Aight I got you, I'mma hit you back later," she said ending the call. Chante sat on the edge of the tub in the bathroom with the door locked. After waiting a few minutes, she picked the white stick up and smiled as her suspicions were confirmed. The home pregnancy test that she urinated on showed the positive sign, letting her know that she was expecting.

Chante put her hand over her stomach and wondered what gender her baby was going to be, either way, she'd love her baby to death. Now she had to break the news to Ant that they were going to be parents.

∞

Once CMoney hung up the phone with Chante, he called Ken.

"What up cuz?" Ken asked answering on the second ring.

"Ay, I need you to bring that box I sent you ASAP," he retorted.

"Aight, I got you, but I got my lady friend wit me," Ken said.

"Cool, meet me at the spot in a half hour," he said before hanging up. CMoney had shipped the guns and stuff that he bought in Atlanta to Ken before he left there, and he was glad he did for times like this. CMoney then texted Dre and told him to meet him at the spot, then he left the

house heading straight there to let them know what was
going on.

∞

Boss sat in the courtroom next to his lawyer dressed in a
black Tom Ford suit and black Mauri alligator loafers with
his stomach in knots. He was nervous and anxious all at
the same time. It had been three long days since closing
arguments happened, his trial ended, and the jury went into
deliberations. Now it was time to hear his fate.

"Has the jury reached a verdict?" the judge asked.

"Yes, your honor," one of the jury members stood up and
said as the bailiff went over to grab the paper from her and
gave it to the judge.

The judge put his glasses on before he read the paper
silently. Legacy sat in between Chante and Boss's mother
in the back of the courtroom looking on in a nervous
wreck, but optimistic that things would work out in their
favor. However, her gut feeling told her something else as
the judge spoke.

"On count one of felon in possession of a firearm, the jury finds the defendant not guilty," the judge said. Sighs of relief and 'Thank you Jesus' could be heard throughout the courtroom, but it wasn't over yet. "On count two of accessory to commit murder, the jury finds the defendant guilty," he added. This time 'Oh God' and sobs could be heard throughout the courtroom.

Wayne and Train got up to leave, they were very saddened by the verdict. Legacy broke down to her knees crying, Chante tried to console her, Boss's mother, and his aunt.

"Was the decision made unanimously?" the Judge asked while removing his glasses and looking towards the jury.

"Yes, your honor, we all made the same decision," the female jury member said still standing up.

"Alright, sentencing will be in one week," the judge said before banging his gavel.

"Mr. Paul, the worst thing you could do is snap out. We'll appeal this Goddamn decision and get you out of here. Call me as soon as you get to a phone," Mr. Hastings whispered to him before the sheriff's deputies escorted Boss away. A million things ran through his head about what had just taken place while he was leaving the courtroom. He heard Legacy yell that she loved him, but he couldn't respond because his words were trapped in his throat as he was at a loss for words. This wasn't part of the plan and he hoped that this wasn't the end of him as he was cuffed and lead back to hell.

CHAPTER SEVENTEEN

A week later...

CMoney and Esther walked through Mayfair Mall with several bags in their hands. CMoney couldn't believe his eyes when he saw Big Booty Rudy there hugged up with some nigga and pregnant as nee. He smirked at her as she walked past, he had to give her credit because no matter how bad her reputation was, she always found a sucka nigga to lock up. CMoney couldn't wait to tell Ken and see the expression on his face.

CMoney and Esther were about to leave, but he wanted to go to Finish Line shoe store to see what new shoes they had out. After buying two pairs of the latest Air Jordan's, they left the store and as they were passing the Cinnabon shop he heard somebody call his name. Turning in the direction he heard it from he smiled when he saw Chante standing up and waving him over.

"Let's go see what she on," he said to Esther, then they headed in that direction.

"What's good sis?" he smiled, then he looked at the man that sat at the table with her, he was brown-skinned and tall with waves. CMoney didn't know him, but the man oozed confidence, money, power, and respect.

"Hey y'all," Chante said hugging CMoney, then Esther." Ant, this my brother CMoney and his girlfriend Esther," she added introducing everybody.

"What's good, brah?" CMoney asked sitting his bags down before shaking Ant's hand.

"I can't call it," Ant said while they shook hands, first he took in Esther's beauty, then he looked CMoney over. He could tell he was young, but he seemed to be well off into getting money." Where you get yo teeth done at?" he continued.

"Atlanta, from this dude named..." CMoney said as Ant joined in.

"Frankie," the two men spoke in unison.

"Hell yeah," CMoney said nonchalantly with a smile.

"Oh yeah, he did my shit a while ago, he the best in Atlanta, and he good peoples too," Ant said, his grill was shining hard too, but he had paid a little more for his than CMoney had.

"Bae, we might as well eat here, what do you want?" Esther asked.

"Taco Bell, and get me a Cinnabon too, thank you baby," CMoney replied before Esther sat the bags down, she already knew that he liked nacho cheese soft shell tacos.

Chante whispered something in Ant's ear before walking off with Esther.

"Have a seat my man," Ant said. Soon as he sat down, his phone started ringing.

"Excuse me brah, I gotta take this," CMoney said before answering his phone. He gave Al the instructions on what he was to do after he listened to what he had to say.

Ant wasn't a nosey nigga by any means, but he couldn't help but overhear the conversation, and being from the

streets, he knew CMoney was at the head of the table in his own circle.

"I don't mean to be in yo bizzness, but how old are you?" Ant inquired after CMoney hung the phone up.

"Seventeen, but my birthday comin' up real soon," CMoney retorted and Ant nodded his head. CMoney reminded him a lot of himself at that age because Ant could see that he was a young boss nigga on the rise.

The two chopped it up like old friends about Lebron finally winning his first ring, the Trayvon Martin case, and a few other things as the ladies sat at the table engaged in their own conversation. Ant liked CMoney, he felt that he had a lot of flavor, poise, and desire to accomplish some things. Chante had told Ant about CMoney's kush problem, which Ant could help him with, and if CMoney played his cards right, Ant could make him a very rich man. Meanwhile, CMoney was oblivious that he was sitting in front of

Legacy's connect, the man that was responsible for supplying the work that

he was pushing in the streets, and helping him to live comfortably, but he'd soon find out in a big way.

∞

"Are you prepared to proceed, Mr. Montana?" the judge asked.

"Yes, your honor. This is another case…There was an article in the paper this morning about how crime is down, homicides were down, at least last year, they're back up again this year in this area, but those are just statistics. Here we're dealing with, on this particular day, two individuals basically. Martin Combs, the victim, was a young man whose life is over, and his family has to come to court and try to deal with this. Then we have Mr. Paul, who was, I believe, 22 years of age at the time this offense happened, and his family and loved ones are here as well. It's just so, so stupid, so meaningless, so counterproductive, obviously, in any way you look at it. But you sit back again with the benefit of hindsight, and you look at Mr. Paul's record, and he's no angel, but he's certainly not the devil incarnated based on his prior record," D.A. Montana said and went on in a further attempt to get the judge to give Boss basketball score numbers, so that Boss was unable to get back.

Boss sat back in his seat dressed in an orange prison jumpsuit. He couldn't believe that he'd gotten himself into this situation where these racist azz white people could determine his fate. He also couldn't help but to notice how feminine the male judge acted. How he poked his pinkie finger out while drinking from his coffee mug and the way he leaned on his desk while twirling his pen. Boss came to the conclusion that the judge definitely had some sugar in his tank and he bet his counterparts had no idea.

Boss knew he made a crucial mistake in trusting some of the people around him, he was a firm believer in death before dishonor, but obviously his views were far different from some of the people he fucked with, and he couldn't help but to wonder that if he had killed them, would he still be sitting in that courtroom today.

He shook his head at the thought of Rio's rat azz, he had been one of Boss's closet niggas, a nigga that he would ride for.

But that all changed when Rio got locked up on an unrelated charge and gave a statement against Boss to free his own azz. He didn't give a fuck that Boss was the reason he was doing so good on the streets, made it to where he could put food on his table, and the reason niggas stayed off his azz. He did not care about none of that obviously because he repaid Boss for all his generosities by showing up to court and testifying against him.

'With his bitch azz,' Boss thought. Then he smiled when he thought about that one Trick Daddy song as he tried to remember the words in his head. 'Muthafuck the po-pos, fuck the D.A. s, the P.Os, fuck the judge and the C.Os, witness of the victim's family, them snitching' azz hoes.' He smiled knowing the song went something like that.

The victim's auntie and sister spoke in a further attempt to get the judge to bring the hammer down on Boss, so he couldn't see the light of day again.

Boss's mother spoke on his behalf trying to lighten the mood, Legacy didn't speak because she thought it would hinder him since she was initially locked up with him until they let her go.

Legacy tried to suppress her tears, but she couldn't, deep down she knew the inevitable.

Chante was strong as ever and tried to console Legacy, but found tears falling down her own face. Chante knew that she had to get herself together because all the stress that she was under dealing with Legacy hurt her as well, and she didn't wanna have any complications with her pregnancy, so she went to the bathroom to get herself together.

Wayne and Train sat in the last row of the courtroom in silence, but they also knew what was about to come.

After Mr. Hastings made his final plea for leniency on Boss, the judge then said what he had to say.

"The bottom line is a human being, who was a member of our community, has lost his life. So, with that explanation, the total length…" the judge said while flipping through some papers…

"The total length of the sentence for count one is one of thirty years with twenty years of initial confinement and ten years of extended supervision…," the judge added but was cut off by Legacy letting out a hurling scream as Chante and Boss's mother tried to calm her down.

"I am giving the defendant his 211 days of credit, Mr. Paul, you have the right to seek post-conviction relief, and if you can't afford an attorney, one will be appointed to you," the judge said but Boss didn't hear any of that shit. He was somewhere else after getting sentenced to thirty years. 'Ain't this a bitch,' he thought as they lead him out of the courtroom.

∞

"20, 15, 10, 5, touchdown Falcons," Al yelled. Him and Dell were sitting in the spot playing NFL Madden 2012 and he saw Matt Ryan throw a 60-yard touchdown to Julio Jones. He always picked the Atlanta Falcons every time he played mainly because he loved the aerial attack that they had with Julio Jones, Roddy White, and Tony Gonzalez, with of course Matt Ryan at quarterback.

"Damn," Dell said knowing he should have left the safety back there, but it was a third down play with one yard to get a first down, so he brought the safety down to help with a run play, but he got fooled with the play action. His team was now down 10 points, but he knew the New England Patriots were not out of it yet. Tom Terriffic had already thrown for over 350 yards and it was only the third quarter, so he felt good about his chances to come back.

"Well see nigga, Brady finna march the field using Wes Welker and Gronk, that's gon' put me right back in the game," Dell said, then he caught something out of his

peripheral vision on the monitor that patrolled the lot. "You see this shit?" he added.

"What?" Al said putting the game on pause before looking at the monitor.

"All hell naw," he continued then rose to his feet and put his Berretta on his hip as Dell put his .357 on his hip, then they walked out of the house to confront the dude they saw on the camera roll into the parking lot and go in one of the hype's houses, they knew the dude had to be serving on their territory and that was not tolerated.

Al grabbed one of the little boys in the neighborhood's bikes and laid it in the middle of the horseshoe-shaped parking lot because the way the dude's car was facing, he knew that it was more than likely that dude would drive this way to leave the parking lot and he was right on point as the dude hopped in his car, rounded the back of the parking lot until he had to stop in front of the bike

"Damn who the fuck?" the dude said looking around, but there was nobody in the vicinity, so he hit the horn a few times and still nobody came. "Ain't this a

bitch," the dude added as he put his car in park, hopped out, picked the bike up and threw it out of the way. When he turned around, Al was standing there.

"Now why did you just throw my bike over there like that?" Al asked with his face scrunched up and head tilted to the side. The man retuned Al's stare and was about

400

to give him a piece of his mind but before he spoke, Al pulled out his Beretta and kept it at his side. The man's entire demeanor changed instantly when he saw the chunky pistol in Al's hand and Al sensed that, so he went on him.

"Now go pick it up," Al said menacingly.

"Ay lil' homie, I…" the man spoke but was cut off.

"Fool azz nigga we ain't homies now go pick up my muthafucking bike and put it on the kick stand before they have to pick yo azz up," Al spat while pointing the gun at the man as Dell walked up.

Seeing that this was no joking matter, against his will the man walked over, picked the bike up and put it on the kick stand.

"You happy now?" the man said getting slick because he had been punked out by some teenagers.

"You getting slick nigga?" Al said taking a step towards the man. "Hell, now I ain't happy and who the fuck said you can serve over here?" he added and with the

401

speed of a rabbit Al punched the man in the mouth and as he stumbled backwards Dell reached out and ripped the man's entire front pocked off his jeans. A wad of money fell out along with some change, a sack of dope and a condom. Dell checked his car and Al continued. He was not about to let the dude hop in his car as he had a pistol in there.

"I betta not see yo weak azz over here again because if I do you can cancel Christmas," Al added.

Dell came back with a cellphone and a 9mm Taurus pistol that he found under the driver's seat.

"Good lookin on all yo shit, now get yo bitch azz from over here, we the only ones getting money over here," Dell stated as the man ran to his car like Red in the movie 'Friday' while holding his jaw and smashed out.

Al picked up the money which looked to be about 2gees and the gees sack of dope as the boy who's bike he had used came to get it. Al peeled off $200 and told him to go buy himself a new bike. The boy thanked him then Al and Dell went back into the house to finish their video game like nothing had ever happened.

CHAPTER EIGHTEEN

Legacy sat in front of the computer screen at Chante's house. She had been staying there every day since Boss's trial initially started. She told herself that she was staying there because it was closer to the courtroom but the tiral had been over for a while. Truthfully told she needed to be around her sister for moral support because when that judge sentenced Boss to 30 years, he also sentenced her because she would be in prison too, not physically but definitely emotionally. Legacy thought that if she went home by herself, she might slip into a deep depression and that would complicate things even more. Needless to say, it had been a long week for her and she just didn't feel like herself.

Legacy had just hung up the phone with Boss. He had let her know that they had moved him from the Milwaukee Secure Deltantion Facility (M.S.D.F) to Dodge Correctional Institiution and the visiting form was already in the mail. It had been a long nine months since they had actually touched each other and Legacy couldn't wait to see him. She actually yearned to feel his

soft lips against hers and his firm hands grip her plump derrier as he always did.

The reason Legacy was on the computer was because Boss had stressed to her that he needed her to find him a good private investigstor. He told her that he had explained in more detail about what he was trying to do in the letter that he sent her along with the visiting form.

Legacy was still as loyal as ever so she hopped right on the computer, Googled private investigators in Wisconsin and found one by the name of Andrew Jones. As soon as she got Boss's letter she would go pay Mr. Jones a visit at his downtown office. Printing out the information that she needed, she folded the paper and left it on the computer desk just as Chante entered the house.

"Hey Tay." Legacy said as she sat on the courch and grabbed the remote.

"Hey," Chante said as she sat on the couch as well. She was skeptical about what she had to say to Legacy due to the fact that she had been keeping a secret from her, actually a couple of secrets. Legacy was her best friend

as well as her sister so it was time for Chante to come clean. "Leggy I need you to come with me to my doctors appointmenr," she added after reasoning with herself.

"Whats wrong with you?" Legacy asked while flipping through the channels.

"I'm pregnant," Chante stated after a brief pause.

Legacy almost got whiplash because she turned her head so fast and looked at Chante with her mouth open, she was shocked by the bomb that Chante had just dropped on her.

"How, who I mean...?" Legacy said trying to find the words to say.

"I'm pregnant by Ant and we've been secretly talking for months now, one thing led to another. And well you know how the rest happened," Chante tried to sum it all up as best she could.

"On what?" Legacy retorted even more shocked than before, she didn't even know they were sleeping together and now she was pregnant. Legacy couldn't think of a

reason why Chante hadn't told her about Ant. "Yeah I'm going with you but on the way you gon' have to spill some tea," Legacy added. Although she was glad that she would soon be an aunt, she needed to have some girl time with her sister on the way to the hospital.

∞

"You bogas as hell for taking me over that ugly azz girl house," Wayne said frustrated that Train had taken him over some chick's house that looked like Denis Rodman. So Wayne didn't even say shit to her which was crazy because he would just about fuck any chick that crossed his path but this girl was too ugly for him to even consider fucking with.

"You gotta take one for the team my nigga. Her cousin wanted me to bring one of my guys so I brought you, yeah she was ugly but she had a phat ass though so you was supposed to gon' head and take her down," Train explained. "Besides you need to get out and mingle you been in the house all day with Ebony's thick ass, cakin and shit," Train added.

Wayne hadn't been doing nuthin' but hustlin' and fucking Ebony during the day and at night he had been hunting for the nigga Rio who testified against Boss. Wayne felt like he owed Boss even though he would've did it on G.P but when Wayne was out of town his sister Sheree got raped by a nigga named Martin so that's why Boss ordered the hit on him and that was also the reason why Boss had just gotten convicted and sent upstate with all that time. Wayne couldn't wait until he ran into Rio, and as luck would have it, he wouldn't have to wait long.

"Fuck that shit nigga. I thought the bitch was a man at first." He and Train bust into laughter. "Never in my life have I encountered a bitch that ugly. If she was strapped we should have switched and you took one for the team," Wayne continued through laughter.

"You sill as hell," Train laughed as they pulled up to the lights on Fond de Lac and Hope Street, right in front of Playmakers.

"What the... I know that aint..." He continued while watching the blue RX 350 Lexus SUV up ahead make a left turn into McDonald's.

"Dawg I thin that's that nigga Rios truck right up there," he added.

"Where?" Wayne stared looking around clitching the .45 with the extended clip in his palm.

"Right there," Train pointed then he looked at Wayne and noticed that his eyes had turned dark which let him know that wayne meant business.

Train pulled off when the lights changed. As they rode past McDonald's, Train squinted his eyes as the dude opened his door to dump the tobacco of of the middle of his blunt. The dome light inside the truck gave Train a good enough view and, as far as he could tell, that was Rio.

"That's the bitch azz nigga," Train spat.

"Pull up in beauty island and cut the lights off," Wayne instruacted then pulled the hack back on his gun. Train

pulled in to the beauty supply store and cut the light off as he was directed.

"Let me see you heat," Wayne continued as Train passed him his Walther 9mm and Wayne pulled the hack back on that as well.

"Make sure the car facing out that exit by the time I get back so we can get to the side street," Wayne added while stuffing both guns in the front pocket of his hoodie before he pulled the hood on his head and slid out of the car.

Train had heard stories about how Wayne got down but he had yet to see it for himself. To keep it one hunnid, Train was a little nervous and excited all at the same time because Rio was about to get what he had coming. Train grabbed the screwdriver out of the glove compartment and slid out of the car to quickly remove his plates.

Wayne observed everythnig going on as he crossed the street. Rio's truck was at the first window paying for food and trapped in between two cars. 'Perfect' Wayne thought as he got closer. Wayne grew even madder when

he heard Straight Outta Poverty's hit 'For the Family' bumping in Rio's truck after the hoe azz shit he has just done to Boss. 'Nigga is somethin else' Wayne thought.

The dude in the Lexus truck sat behind the wheel puffing his blunt with his left hand, his right hand was on the chick named Tawanda's thigh who occupied the passenger seat. She was just how he liked his women: petite, light-skinned and a boss freak. He couldn't wait to get her home and get up inside of that. But unbeknowingly to him he wasn't going home with her at least not to a house.

He was so caught up in groping Tawanda that he didn't even recognize the immidiate danger he was in from the man who was dressed in all black and only a couple of steps away from the truck with two pistols in his hand.

"Ahhhh!!" Tawanda screamed when Wayne appeared standing next to the truck but Wayne didn't say anything he just raised the pistols and let them ride the inside of the truck as glass flew everywhere. Boc Boc Boc Boc Boc. Wayne hit the dude everywhere but up under his

feet then he sent three slugs crashing throught Tawanda's head as blood splattered in his face and on the windshield he shot her birds of a feather flocked together. The chick who worked at the drive through window started screaming and Wayne hit her in the chest with a couple of bullets. The car that was infront of the dude's truck pulled off, so Wayne, acting on instinct, pointed both pistols toward the car and pulled the triggers simulaneously. Boc Boc Boc Boc, Wayne shot at the cat making the back window explode and taking a tailight out as it sped away. The car behind the truck tried to back away and Wayne turned and fired. Boc Boc Boc Boc Boc. He sent five slugs through the windshield, taking the driver's life. He was on a rampage and leaving no witnesses to point the finger at him. One of the guns ran out of bullets but he was in a zone and kept squeezing the trigger. Then Wayne turned and fired a few more bullets into the dude's body.

"I bet you won't tell shit else," he spat as if the dude could hear him then he tucked the pistols in his hoodie

pocket and ran to the car, hopped in and Train sped away.

The two rode in silence, after what Train had just seen, he knew what he had heard about Wayne was true: he was a stone-cold killer and his heart was as stone-cold as a block of ice.

Wayne used his sleeve to wipe the blood from his face, he knew what had to be done to send a message in the streets that if you fucked somebody over in his circle, enough blood would be shed to paint the streets of Milwaukee. This was only a piece of what needed to be done. The next thing he planned to do was to go see the nigga CMoney and shit was gonna get real ugly.

∞

"Dawg I heard that nigga Boss got thirty years," Ken said knowing it was over for his azz.

"I know but fuck that nigga," CMoney spat. He had totally disregarded the whole Big Ball situation with Boss away doing all that time and it didn't seem that his

cousin was on shit. CMoney told himself that if somebody was the reason for one of his family members losing their life, he would surely pay them a visit, but he also knew that most niggas were hoes and didn't want any of those types of problems.

"On er' thang," Al co-signed.

They were all at one of the spots, CMoney had come out there to serve a few niggas some weight, but Dre told him to stay there until he got there, so he was sitting back with the guys watching a bootleg DVD of the movie 'The Bourne Legacy' while sipping a bottle of Patron. CMoney had been drinking a lot lately.

"Y'all seen that shit on the news that happened at McDonald's on Fond du Lac last night?" Dell asked after exhaling the weed smoke from his mouth.

"I seen that shit, whoever that was went ape shit," Ken said.

"One er'thang, they, weren't fucking around, five people got shot with three dying," Dell said, he was all about

blowing a nigga shit back, so the gruesome crime had him geeked up.

"Where the fuck is this nigga Dre at?" CMoney said to nobody in particular before he pulled his phone out and called him.

"What's good g-ball?" Dre answered.

"Shit, waitin' on yo slow azz, I got some things to do today too my nigga," CMoney stated.

"I'm on my way," Dre said.

"Aight love," CMoney retorted.

"Love," Dre responded and then ended the call. He made a left on 35th and Townsend, he had to piss bad as hell. Although that plagued him, he was felling pretty good about getting 'THE SHIT BAG' taken off two days ago, it was early, but the doctor said that he had progressed well and would be fine, which was great news for Dre. When he got to the corner of 37th Street, he looked to his left and saw Chante's orange Camaro out there, and he decided to go over her house to use the bathroom. Dre

pulled directly in the back of Chante's place, put his pistol in his Pelle pocket, and hopped out hitting his alarm.

Soon as he was about to press the doorbell, Chante opened the door.

"Hey Dre, what you doin' over here?" Chante asked happy to see him, he was like a little brother to her. Him and CMoney used to spend many nights over her house when they were younger.

"Sis, I gotta use yo bathroom bad as a muthafucka," Dre replied while holding his crotch.

"Go right ahead, I gotta go, so lock the door when you leave," Chante said, she was in a rush to meet up with Ant.

"Aight, who here?" he asked.

"Legacy's asleep in the back room, so don't make no noise, she stressed the fuck out," she responded.

"Aight," Dre said as he went into the house and closed and locked the door behind himself.

 Dre was on his way down the hall to the bathroom and he noticed all the room doors were open, but one of them was cracked, so he figured that was the room where Legacy was sleeping at, and he wanted to see her. He had always wished that he could have her one day. Legacy was a hell of a real chick that knew how to get that money. She was everything that Dre wanted in a woman, he just always felt like she was out of his league and that he was too young for her, so he never exposed his feelings towards her, at least not verbally, but if she could read his mind, she would have been on to him when he was a kid.

Dre opened the door a little more and peeked in, his eyes grew big at what he saw. Legacy was laid across the bed with the cover at her feet wearing a pair of lace peek cheek panties that exposed her butt cheeks and a matching bra.

"That ass look soft as a muthafucka," Dre said louder than intended as his member started to stiffen up. Dre thought about going in there to see if it felt as soft as it looked but he quickly pushed the perverted thought from his head. As he pulled the door back up and made his way to the bathroom, he thought about all the things he would do to Legacy if he ever got the chance to.

Dre raised the seat and with all the freaky thoughts running through his head he was fully erect so when he started to piss it hit everywhere but where he was aiming.

"Damn," Dre said to himself as he redirected his aim and drained his bladder. He was shaking his piece off when he heard a noise and looked towards the door to see Legacy standing there with her hands over her mouth looking at his dick. Then Dre watched her walk away and with every step she took her ass shook.

Dre quickly wiped the seat and floor with some tissue, flushed, and washed his hands before running out of the bathroom holding his pants up. When he walked into the

room where Legacy was originally sleeping, so he thought she was sitting on the bed looking sexy as hell.

"My bad for waking you up," Dre said thinking to himself that she was so bad.

"It's cool, I wasn't asleep, I heard you looking in on me, so I wanted to see how it would feel if I did it too you," she said but she had yet to make eye contact with him, so he followed her stare and realized that she was looking at the bulge in his pants.

Legacy would be lying if she said she didn't enjoy the view. Now Legacy wasn't a hoe by any means, a dream girl to most, but it has been 10 plus months since she had had some real dick. Watching pornos and fucking herself with a dildo was only doing so much, after a while she needed to feel the real thing, does that mean she was giving up on Boss? Certainly not, she would hold him down like a real woman should while her man is away. She would surely be there for him but right now she had needs the needed to be fulfilled and after seeing what Dre

was working with she was going to see if he knew how to use that thing.

"My fault," Dre said starting to buckle his pants.

"Don't trip," Legacy smiled, she knew he wanted her by the way he looked at her but was scared to approach her, so she gave him a little boost.

"So, you wana touch it huh?" she added

"Huh?" Dre asked dumbfounded.

"I heard you say my ass looks soft, so you wanna touch it?" she asked, Dre was completely taken aback by this. The woman he had been wanting since forever was now giving him the opportunity to do what he had been longing to do since he was a kid.

"Hell yeah," Dre said while walking round towards her as she stood up and turned around. Dre reached his hand out and palmed her 41 inches of ass, he smiled because it was indeed as soft as it looked

"You been wanting to touch this ass obviously so don't hold back now," she said, and Dre responded by gripping both cheeks, then he smacked it and watched it wiggle. "That's better," she added while turning around, then she put her hand on Dre's hard dick and massaged it through his jeans.

Getting the hint, Dre stepped towards her and kissed her while unfastening her bra, then he palmed her ass again.

Legacy stepped back and freed her 36DDs from her bra.

"Damn," Dre said to himself while looking at her big jugs with the freckles around the areolas. Legacy then laid back on the bed as Dre removed his coat, laid on top of her and sucked her titties.

"You got a condom?" Legacy asked.

"Yeah," Dre responded, like hell he had a condom, he was the magnum man.

Dre stood to his feet and helped Legacy out of her panties, then he undressed himself and put the condom on.

Dre couldn't believe this was happening, he was about to fuck one of the baddest chicks that he'd ever laid eyes on, and he was about to tear that pussy up. Looking over her voluptuous figure in amazement, her pubic hairs were cut low and lined up nicely, and Dre liked that. Getting between her thick thighs he was about to enter her, but she stopped him.

"On no honey, you gotta get a girl wet first," Legacy said pushing the top of his head and guiding him in between her legs. Dre definitely had to taste the appetizer before he dived into her entrée, he was not her man.

Dre had no complaints with that, shit, he wanted to taste her anyway, so he dove in and ate her pussy like it was a three-course meal. Dre dipped his index finger in and out and round and round while he sucked hard on her clit.

Legacy had to admit that Dre had a hell of a tongue, and she hoped his dickgame was just as proper.

Legacy was taken back by the next thing he did: Dre pushed her legs up towards her head and sucked from her clit, through her pussy hole, and all around her ass

before he put his tongue in, took it out, and blew around her booty hole. He sucked and licked her from the roota to the toota and that drove Legacy crazy as an orgasm seeped out onto Dre's awaiting tongue. Satisfied with that, he scooted up and slid into Legacy.

Dre almost nutted on impact because she was so tight and wet, but he held his composure and started stroking her. He knew by far that she had the best pussy he had ever been in

"Aggh," Legacy moaned as Dre dicked her down with aiming to please on his mind, then he turned her over and hit it from the back.

"Mmm shit," Dre said watching her ass jiggle like Jell-0. Dre put a hand on each cheek and grinded into her in a circular motion at a medium speed while looking at the ceiling. If he kept looking at that ass move like that, he was gonna bust and he wasn't ready for that just yet, so

he thought about everything he had to do today in effort to suppress his nut. Unbeknowingly to them both, Chante was in so much of a rush to go and spend some

time with Ant, that she had forgotten her cellphone on the charger, so as she went in the house, she heard moaning and skin clapping coming from the back room. Now, she saw Dre's car outside but didn't think much of it because he was there when she left, and he was always welcomed in her home, but Chante had to go and see what was going on. She hoped it wasn't Legacy pleasing herself again.

Chante tiptoed towards the back room and peeked around the corner and saw Dre's bare ass, he was in the room fucking Legacy from the back and she was moaning like crazy.

'This bitch snapped,' Chante thought with a smile. She didn't judge her sister, she probably needed some dick to get back on track and overcome what she was going through. Chante tiptoed to the room, grabbed her phone,

and left back out without them ever knowing she was there.

"Ummm," Legacy moaned and got to throwing it back on him because she was near her climax which made Dre pick up the pace until he couldn't take it anymore.

"Arrrrhh," he grunted as he ejaculated, and she came as well.

After Legacy climaxed, she heard Dre grunt, so she hopped off his shaft and looked back to see if his condom was still intact. Seeing everything was straight, a sigh of relief left her body because she surely couldn't afford to get pregnant by anybody who she didn't see having a future with. Legacy was still optimistic that Boss would come from under the situation he was in because that's who she wanted to be with.

Legacy sat up smiling, she was surprised by Dre, he ate a mean coochie, and he could slang some wood. Dre was satisfied as well, Legacy had a super wet shot, she was fine and moving them things, so he hoped that this would

turn into something more with Boss away doing 30 years.

Legacy put on her big T-shirt and grabbed some things to use in the shower. Dre thought she was going to ask him to join her, but he was more surprised by what she did next. Legacy walked over to him and kissed him on his chest.

"Thank you, baby, you don't know how much I needed that, now lock the door on your way out," she said turning to leave. "And nobody has to know about what we just did either," she added and went to get in the shower.

Dre stood there dumfounded but what could he say. Just because they fucked doesn't mean he is her man, but he hoped that the would keep having their rendezvous at the least.

Dre put his clothes on, flushed the condom down the toilet and left the house with a big azz smile plastered across his face as his phone rang. It was CMoney.

"Damn," he said while running to his car.

CHAPTER NINETEEN

A week later, CMoney stumbled into the house drunk as hell. Him, Ant, Dre, Ken, and a couple of Ant's guys had been at the Club 30 Lounge on Clark and Tevtonia for buck naked Wednesdays and CMoney had been drinking Moet Rose all night.

Esther had called him about an hour ago and told him to come home earlier than usual because she had a surprise for him. CMoney looked at his watch and it read 11:39 pm. He activated the home security system before making his way up the stairs and opening their bedroom door. Stepping into the room, the vanilla aroma permeated his nostrils from the thirty lit candles that were throughout the room. Then Esther appeared out of nowhere wearing a red silk robe that barely covered her ass cheeks, and a pair of matching heels.

"Hey boo," she said wrapping her arms around his neck and kissing him passionately. When Esther put her arms around him, CMoney looked in the mirror that was behind her and noticed that her whole ass was out, so while they kissed, he palmed it with both hands.

"Take your clothes off and get comfortable, I'll be right back," she said breaking their embrace.

CMoney immediately took off all of his clothes and got into the bed as Esther reappeared with a breakfast in bed tray. Setting the tray on the nightstand, she straddled him, and tongued him down before she used the remote to press play on the radio. 'Bedroom Music' by Bri Bandzz crooned through the speakers as she grabbed the bottle of chocolate syrup off the tray, poured it on his chest, and licked it all off. She then put that back, grabbed the melted caramel, poured it on his stomach, and repeated the same process. Lastly, she picked up the can of whipped cream, sprayed it around his pelvic area, in between his thighs, and on his balls. Esther licked it off, put his balls in her mouth and hummed on them while flicking her tongue back and forth over them. The pleasure that she was giving him drove him crazy.

CMoney wanted Esther to badly put his member in her mouth. She knew this, so she teased him by purposely avoiding his shaft, after licking up the small spots that

she missed she kissed her way back up towards his stomach, and as she was passing his dick, he made it jump and hit her on the chin in effort to get her to notice it and suck on it. She smiled knowing what he was on, but she still didn't touch it.

"Come with me baby," she said getting up, grabbing his hand and leading him out of the room. Once they got to the bathroom, he noticed that the candles were lit there as well. There was a hot bubble bath waiting on them. Esther told him to get in, then she washed all the sticky substances from his body. After that, she stood to her feet, removed her heels, and robe.

CMoney smiled because she was wearing his favorite outfit, and that was absolutely nothing.

"You like this?" Esther asked showing, him that her pubic hair had the letter C trimmed in it, but her lower lips were clearly shaven. CMoney smiled because Esther was always so spontaneous, and he loved that. Holding his hand out, he helped her into the tub, then she slipped down on his shaft and rode him sensually, making her

titties juggle with every bounce. She rode him back and forth causing waves of water to spill out of the tub on to the floor, and when she went up and down and round and round water splashed everywhere.

"Ummm, this yo pussy, and you can have it anytime you want it Okay?" she said putting an arch in her back as she kept riding him.

"Fo sho," he replied in pleasure. CMoney was in a sexual trance but he still knew that what she just told him was meant from the bottom of her heart which made his dick get even harder and he gripped her ass and matched her thrust for thrust until they both exploded.

Getting out of the tub, they dried off, and made their way to the bedroom to finish what they started. Soon as they got in the room, the sounds on 'Detonate' by Kaylee Crossfire was coming through the speakers as they got in the bed and Esther gave him what he wanted so badly as she took his shaft in her mouth and began licking the head in a circular motion like a snow cone in 100-degree weather.

"Ahh," he groaned just as she started sucking strenuously on the top of his head. Esther then positioned one hand on each side of his waist and bobbed her head at a rapid pace producing a whole lot of spit just like he liked it. Then she made steady eye contact with him while she deep throated as much as she could take. She then switched into the 69 position and continued her assault on his dick. She knew how to please her man and she did it very well.

CMoney sucked on her clit like a baby to its mother's nipple while fingering her with two fingers until her juices coated her lips. Esther lay in the missionary position and spread her legs as CMoney got in between them and gripped his dick and slipped it up and down her labium lips before he slid into her.

"Ahh, ummm baby," she moaned in delight as he stroked her intently with the passion of love that he had for her, then he sped his pace up and went deeper.

"Oww I can feel it in my stomach," she screamed as he dicked her down while sucking on her titties until he filled her insides with his white-hot creamy cum.

"I love you," CMoney said as soon as he came. He didn't want Esther to go nowhere because it seemed like every time he fucked her it got better than the last time and he loved being inside of her, more importantly he loved her.

Still in his drunken faze, his dick was still standing to attention as he grabbed her by the ankles, flipped her over and positioned her into doggystyle and slid back into her.

"Who's pussy is this?" he said aggressively while pumping in to her from side to side

"Oh, baby it's yours foreva," she replied while backing her ass into him. Pleased with her response, he put the pound game on her while ripping that ass. Every time his

pelvic area met with hers, the forceful impact made her ass create the wave like the water at the lake front and that only excited him more as he kept at it until he came. The two fucked and sucked each other until early in the morning. CMoney busted so many nuts that he knew he had to be a headcase by now. He looked at the clock and it was 4:12 am. He smiled because it was October 31st and he was now officially 18 years old. After what he had just shared with Esther, he couldn't wait until he was 19 years old he thought as he blew out all the candles and got back into bed and dozed off to Young Major's 'Ms. Prefect' with Esther sleeping on his chest.

∞

About 10.30 am the same day, CMoney squirmed in his sleep, the sex session he had last night with Esther was off the chain, so much so that it felt like they were still going at it because he could have sworn that he just felt the sensation of busting a nut. He opened his eyes to see Esther between his legs milking his dick with her mouth

for every drop of cum, then she noticed he had awakened.

"Happy birthday," she smiled after swallowing some of his babies.

"Thank you baby, how was breakfast?" he smiled reffering to the oral sex she had just given him.

"Good, you know it's the most important meal of the day," she said sarcastically as they shared a laugh. Truth be told, Esther wasn't really into swallowing but CMoney liked it so from time to time she would surprise him with it and keep him happy knowing what one woman wouldn't do another would.

"I got a muthafucking headache," he said placing his hands on his forehead.

"I figured you would, you was drunk as hell last night," she retored while getting out of bed. "Take this," she added, giving him two Tylenol and a glass of water that was on the nightstand.

"You always on time aint you," he smiled before putting the pills in his mouth with a sip of water.

"For you I'm ahead of time because I love you," she said.

Cmoney knew that to be true because her actions showed it. As he stared in to her honey-brown eyes, he wanted to grab her head and tongue her down but seeing as how she just had his joy stick and pleasure juice in her mouth, he couldn't bring himself to do that. He didn't give a damn that was his and it was out of the question. But the feelings he had for her were mutual.

"I love you too," he said seriously.

"Get some rest before tonight, I'm going to meet Nina at the hair salon and get my hair done," Esther said before kissing him on the cheek then she headed to the bathroom to brush her teeth before she left. CMoney smiled because she was everything a man could ever want in a woman then he turned on his side and fell back to sleep.

∞

CMoney pulled up in front of the house, tucked his pistol in his waistband, and got out of his Riviera with his drink in his hand. He had Dre pick him up so that he could go get the car out of storage before the party tonight.

Opening the door to the apartment, he stepped into the living room and was met by a woman that he had never seen before. "Hi, you must be Chris, I'm Nina, a friend of Esther's," the 5'5 32B-24-39 beautiful Puerto Rican and black woman with long dark hair said extending her hand. Once she said her name, CMoney knew she was the friend that Esther went to school with and had been telling him about. He remembered Esther telling him that Nina's family owned a Car lot.

"Yeah but everyone calls me CMoney nice to meet you," he said shaking her hand.

Nina was just as bad as Esther but CMoney would never flirt with or pursue any of Esther's friends or family members no matter what that was something that he couldn't do to any chick that he messed with who held the title of 'Wifey' while or after or during their

relationship. Since him and Esther had become an item, he hadn't had any sexual contact with any other woman.

"Likewise, oh, and happy birthday," Nina smiled.

"Thanks," he said before he ran upstairs, when he opened the door to their bedroom, he saw Esther standing up with one foot on the bed in only a black lace thong, oiling her skin down.

"Hey baby, did you meet Nina?" she asked smoothing her hands over her thick thighs.

"Yeah," he smiled while closing the door and licking his lips at all that ass she had coming behind her.

CMoney walked up behind her and tried to persuade her into giving him a birthday quickie before they left, but she wasn't having that, she had spent two hours in the hair salon and was not about to let him mess it up before the party. CMoney kept trying though. He asked for five minutes. From the back, she said no, he asked to just put the head in she said no. He asked for some head and she thought about it but still said no.

CMoney knew from his sister and his mother how important a woman's hair was, and she was still sore from all of last night's activities, but she promised that when they got home he could get some and that was good enough for him.

"What you drinkin?" she said hopping up and down trying to get her black leather pants, made by Cavalli, on over her derriere. Before putting a black tube top shirt on by Cavalli, she slid her freshly pedicured feet into a pair of black leather 4-inch platform pumps that were also made by Roberto Cavalli. Grabbing her red Cavalli blazer that stopped in the middle of her ass, she put it on.

"Some shit Dre gave me called purple drink, it's a concoction of codeine and antihistamine promethazine mixed with Sprite and Jolly ranchers, this shit tastes good too," he said then took a sip.

"You better be careful that shit is addictive," she said seriously before applying her lip gloss.

Esther noticed that CMoney had been drinking a lot lately and she was going to have to do something about it after the party. The only reason she didn't do it before the party was because she didn't want things to take a turn for the worst and the party didn't turn out right, but he was definitely going to hear about it later on she thought.

"Go get ready so we can leave, I'll put your clothes out for you," she added before he left the room to shower.

Esther bought CMoney's birthday outfit and he hadn't seen it yet, but if he didn't like it, he already told her that he was going right into his closet to find another outfit. Sure, Esther had style and great taste in her clothes, but he ain't too sure how she was at picking out men's clothes because he was not with that New Boyz skinny jeans bullshit epidemic that most of the world was on right now. He wasn't hatin though, that just wasn't his style by any means.

After showering, CMoney dried off, wrapped the towel around his waist and made his way back to the bedroom

where he put on his boxers, beater, and socks. He looked over the clothes on the bed and smiled. Esther had definitely captured his style. He put on the pair of triple black jeans by Robin Jeans, a red Robin's jeans T-shirt and a pair of red suede Bally shoes, which he had never heard of, he checked the receipt for the shoes because he was curious to know how much they cost, and they were $725.00; pricey was indeed his style. Opening the small box next to his clothes, he put the gold and diamond Rolex wrist watch on his wrist. The watch complemented his ensemble well.

CMoney put his chain on, brushed his waves and ran the jewelry rag over his teeth. Stuffing 8 gees in his pocket, he grabbed both phones, and put his pinkie ring on just as his phone rang.

"Hello."

"Happy birthday right my dude," Shawn said.

"Nice looking, you coming to my party, right?" he asked.

"Definitely, I'm bringing a couple of female friends with me if that's aight?"

"Absolutely, just no niggas," CMoney said, making Shawn laugh "it's on 117 and Burleigh, right?" Shawn asked.

"Yeah, it's on your left when you coming up."

"See you in a minute," Shawn said and then ended the call.

Esther had rented half of the bowling alley to celebrate CMoney's birthday with only family and friends. She was big on family and really not into the club scene like that, so she thought bowling would be a nice touch, and so did CMoney.

He read the text from Lou Lou, she told him Happy Birthday and she'd see him at the bowling alley, he replied, grabbed his gun, black leather Pelle Pelle coat, downed the rest of his purple drink and left the bedroom ready to go to the party. He had talked to Jeff earlier and

he wished him a happy birthday and Ant had called with the same thing.

CMoney couldn't believe that he was the weight man because he was cool as a bitch and still a player even though he was eating like that.

441

"You ready baby?" Esther asked as he came down the stairs, almost tripping, but he played it off, the drink was starting to take its effect on him.

"Yeah, you look good as hell," he smiled while kissing her then looked her over. The tube top that she wore had her braless breasts standing at attention and the leather pants looked printed on, she had ass everywhere.

"So, do you," she smiled.

"Y'all look cute together, all matching and everything," Nina stated while getting off the couch.   "Don't we," Esther boasted while looking him in the eyes as she put her three-quarter length black mink coat on and grabbed her red Birkin clutch.

"What up fool," CMoney said answering his ringing phone.

"Fam, shit drying up and its popping hard as a bitch," Al said.

CMoney knew that meant the spot was doing numbers but the product was low, so he had to do what was needed to keep his operation running fluently.

"Where Dre at?" he asked.

"Right here but he dry too."

"Where's Ken?"

"He left to go and get dressed."

"Tell Dre to wait there for me and I'll be there in thirty minutes," he said before hanging up.

Esther caught the azz end of the conversation and immediately became upset.

"Let me holla at you in the kitchen," he said to her. Once they were in the kitchen, CMoney explained

the predicament at hand and hoped that she would understand his position. Esther was definitely upset and feeling strange about the whole ordeal.

"Can't it wait until tomorrow? You are having a birthday tonight; besides I don't feel right about this with you being drunk and all," she voiced her concern.

"Don't worry baby, you go to the party with your friends and I'll be there twenty minutes after you," he said, wrapping his arms around her on the inside of her coat and kissing her.

"You promise?" she asked, still not content with the situation. He was her man the captain of their ship and she had to trust his decision. She hoped he would stop hustling now they were landlords. They owned three homes and were close to closing at the banks on 4 and 5, not to mention that she would soon be a doctor.

"I promise," he said looking into her eyes. "Thanks for the fit and the watch, you got me all swagged out," he said as they shared a laugh.

"You are welcome," she smiled. "You just better do as you say, or you won't be getting none tonight," she laughed.

"That's a lie," he joined in on the laughter.

Esther left the house as CMoney ran upstairs to do something. Esther's paranoia had him feeling kinda leary, coming back downstairs while buttoning the last button on his shirt he activated the home security system and left the house.

Esther let her window down and reminded him of his twenty minute promise before her and Nina pulled off in Nina's BMW.

CMoney hit the remote and watched the door raise up as he walked to the car. Hopping in he started it and turned the volume up to 'In Love with the Streets' by Diego and pulled off. Althought it was only a little after 7 pm, it was already dark. CMoney let his window down a little, just enough to feel the late October breeze because the lean was really starting to get to him as he drove to 77th and Hampton where his apartment was to get the drugs.

∞

"I thought you said you knew where this nigga be at?" Wayne asked with his face scrunched up.

"I know they be in the Medows, I just don't know what lot," Train said making a right out of the last parking lot on 95th Street. He made another right and drove until they came to the stop lights across the street from the YMCA.

"Where the fuck is this nigga at?" Wayne said angrily.

"I was thinking the same sh..." Train stated but was cut off as they both looked to the right at the headlights of a car coming down the narrow path with the bass vibrating hard as hell. They watched as the car made a left into one of the lots when they saw the glare from the big rims from the street lights. They knew there was a big possiblity that the had found who they were looking for.

"Go that way, that gotta be that nigga," Wayne said gripping the tech 9mm that was on his lap. He was preparing to finally avenge Big Balls's death.

Train made a right, drove down and turned into the second parking lot. Driving in a horse-shoe style, he rounded the back of the lot until his car's passenger side was in the back of CMoneys car. Wayne opened the door and hopped out before the car made a complete stop.

∞

Dell sat inside the spot smoking a blunt while talking on his cellphone to a chick he met at Quick Pantry earlier that day. Needless to say he was trying to get her to come over and jump on him as he spit some of his best game at her.

Dell heard CMoney pull up and saw him on the TV monitor from the cameras that they had patrolling the lot. He had been waiting on him to drop the work off to him so he was waiting on him to pull up. As CMoney stepped out of the car, Dell noticed a car zooming through the parking lot with the lights out and stopping right behind CMoney's car. Being from the street, the first thing that came to Dell's mind was 'Jack Move' meaning that

whoever was in the car wanted to rob them. "Fuck!" Dell shouted and grabbed his 10mm just as shots rang out.

∞

CMoney pulled up to the lights on 91st and Brown Deer. He knew that he should have put more work in the spots to avoid running back and forth but he wanted to see how Al and Dell were with maintaining the money and so far so good. He was only putting 128 grams at a time in each spot along with three pounds of kush to be sold in all $10 and $20 bags because CMoney and Dre handled the weight sales.

Money had been coming in hand over fist for CMoney and he was now buying 15 bricks at a time but 5 were for Dre. However he would be sure to get 20 on his next trip. This time CMoney brought a brick and 5 pounds of kush for each spot.

The lights changed and he pulled off. The purrple drink had him feeling woozy as hell. He was trying to shake it off but he was fucked up.

CMoney hit the turn signal and made a left into the parking lot and parked. After going in to the stash spot, he grabbed the bag with the drugs and got out of the car. Normally he would have been alert to a car racing through the parking lot but the effects of the drink had him tripping in a major way.

He took a step but was abruptly stopped by someone calling his name.

"CMoney," Wayne said, but only loud enough for him to hear. Wayne's finger was on the trigger of the tech with it aimed at CMoney.

CMoney turned around and immediately recognized the danger he was in, so he tried to reach for his weapon, but it   was too late.

"Trick or treat muthafucka," Wayne said menacingly as he pulled the trigger, Boc Boc Boc Boc Boc. CMoney was struck in the chest five times and the high caliber bullets caused him to fly off his feet as Dell came running out of the house. Boc Boc Boc, three shots rang

out from Dell's gun just before Wayne aimed the tech on him and fired.

∞

Dre had been in the bathroom for a while, the Gyro that he ate earlier was not agreeing with his stomach. However, he was happy that he didn't have to shit in a bag anymore. As he was wiping his ass, he heard two shots that were too close for comfort, so he had to go see what was going down.

Hopping off the toilet, Dre pulled his pants up and began running out of the bathroom and cleared the entire flight of stairs in a few steps.

Dre looked at the monitor to see what was going on and reached under the couch for the AR-15 Bushmaster with the 60 round clip and cocked a round into the chamber before running outside.

Dre looked at the man standing over his friend hitting his gun in the palm of his other hand because it had apparently jammed. Dre then pulled the trigger on the

assault weapon and watched the man flee from the barrage of bullets. Meanwhile, Al was coming through the gangway and saw what was going on, pulled his baretta out, and let it ride in the same direction that Dre was shooting.

Train started shooting out of the window to give Wayne some cover but his .45 was no match for the Bushmaster. Dre hit Wayne in the shoulder and in the leg before he hopped in the car as Dre filled the fleeing car with so many holes that it looked like Swiss cheese.

The AR-15 was capable of firing 45 rounds per minute and Dre took full advantage of that. At one point, the smoke got so thick that he choked on it, but he kept right on shooting. The car dipped up out of the parking lot as Al gave chase on foot while still shooting. After the back window shattered, his gun clicked signaling that it was out of bullets.

"Bitch azz nigga!" Al spat. He didn't know how that car made it out of there, but to call it a miracle was an understatement. Al ran over to where Dell laid on the

pavement in a puddle of blood and he instantly knew Dell was dead. Dell had taken a bullet to the neck and died while holding his neck in efforts to keep the blood from gushing out. Al kneeled beside him, put his hand over Dells eyelids, and closed them while shedding a tear.

"Al, he's gone my nigga, I need you over here," Dre said as Al ran   towards him. "Take these guns and that work to the crib down the hill before them people come. I'mma call you later, I gotta try to get fam some help, and kill that camera too," Dre added as Al scooped up everything. Then he picked up Dell's gun the and shot the camera down until it came smashing to the street.

"Fuck!!" Dre screamed, he couldn't let his friend die like this, not on the streets. He had to do something, or at least try. He quickly ran into the house, grabbed his keys and the video tape and the sack of money, locked the door and pulled his car up, all in under one minute. Dre then put CMoney in the backseat, hopped in and pulled off as the police sirens were nearing.

∞

Ken had just pulled up to the bowling alley with his truck beating 'Gone Make It' by Trub 6 Block featuring Bando. He was feeling good, his pockets were fat, his whip was nice, and he had a bad bitch on the passenger side and he was fitted to death in Louis Vuitton.

Ken had been kicking it with Tori tough and he had been hitting that regularly along with Keisha, this chick named Mya that he met, and his soon to be baby mama. Needless to say, Ken's sex problems were far behind him. He parked and hopped out with Tori who was looking good as hell in a tight skirt and heels with a red coat on.

They entered the bowling alley to hear 'Time of my life' by P Roc blasting out of the speakers as they found the bowling stations where everyone was. Ken greeted everyone and introduced them to Tori.

It seemed like everybody was there. Legacy, Chante, Esther, Lou Lou, Shanaya, his mother, his aunt Claire, who was CMoney's mother and several other people. He knew some and some he didn't. However, there was no

sign of CMoney and he wondered where he and Dre could be just as his phone rang.

"Hello?" he answered while stuffing his finger in his other ear to hear better.

"Slow down, what you sayin cuz?" he asked puzzled.

"I said come to the tip, somebody popped Money and Dell and shit ain't looking good," Al said in a frantic state of mind.

"What! I am on my way," Ken said ending the call.

∞

Esther was entertaining guests and enjoying herself, but she had been there for almost an hour and CMoney hadn't arrived yet. She was pissed about that to say the least, but her womanly intuition told her something was wrong, she tried calling him on both phones several times to no answer. Her madness suddenly turned into worries, so she walked over to where Legacy and Chante sat to see if they had heard from him and they hadn't.

Esther picked up the phone and was about to call him again when Ken came over to tell her something that crushed her to the core.

454

"Oh no," she barely got the words out before she went weak at the knees and almost fell, but Ken reached out and grabbed her. After regaining her composure, she grabbed her coat and purse as Ken told Legacy and Chante about what he had just heard.

Esther opened her Birkin bag and made sure her .40 caliber pistol in a .380 frame was locked and loaded with one up top. She had gotten her CCW license two months ago and had learned how to shoot.

Chante agreed to stay to keep suspicion down from CMoney's mother as Legacy went to holla at Shawn. After everybody talked to the people they came with, they all agreed to wait for them to get back, then Legacy, Chante, Ken and Shawn left the building, hopped in to Ken's truck and headed for the Meadows. They hoped for the best.

To be continued...

CPSIA information can be obtained
at www.ICGtesting.com
Printed in the USA
LVHW082250100421
684124LV00027B/587